SATAN! OH MASTER! I AM READY!

Within a matter of weeks he, Cleveland Winston Silvestter, would perform the Grand Rite to invoke Satan. With the Vibratory Q-Pickup Units he would actually be able to see the Emperor of Hell! He would be able to converse with the Emperor of Hell.

But first he had some things to take care of. With Satan's help, his plan to trap and destroy the Death Merchant would go simply and efficiently. Which would make it a mere bagatelle to get rid of the U. S. President and the Russian Premier at their Australian meeting. Which in turn. . . .

He chuckled. "In eight more days," the billionaire announced happily, "we will fly to New Eden. There we will remain *to await the end of the world!*"

D0826756

The Death Merchant Series

DEATH MERCHANT
Billionaire Mission

by
Joseph Rosenberger

PINNACLE BOOKS • NEW YORK CITY

DEATH MERCHANT: BILLIONAIRE MISSION

Copyright © 1974 by Pinnacle Books, Inc.

All rights reserved, including the right to reproduce
this book or portions thereof in any form.

An original Pinnacle Books edition, published for the
first time anywhere.

ISBN: 0-523-00339-0

First printing, May 1974

Printed in the United States of America

PINNACLE BOOKS, INC.
275 Madison Avenue
New York, N.Y. 10016

To Leroy and Dot Mezo.
Thirty-eight years is a long time.

CHAPTER ONE

There are those people who understand Death for the first time when He puts His icy hands upon someone they love, while others gain insight into the subtle ways of the Silent Reaper by experience, such as witnessing a fatal accident. Finally there are those rare individuals who, because they have lived with constant danger, have a kind of preternatural affinity for Death, a rapport that enables them, almost intuitively, to detect his "deadly" presence, sometimes even hours before He gathers the victim into His bony arms.

Richard Joseph Camellion was such an individual, a man whose experience would have permitted him to smell the rotten stink of Death in the middle of a perfume factory! He was mentally sniffing his presence now, this hot middle-of-June afternoon.

And it's not because I'm in a marble orchard either! Camellion thought grimly. Then his mind turned to Gordon Brothers!

"I have a list of 'tires' for you, Mr. Cortinn," Brothers had whispered, phoning the Death Merchant at his hotel and using Camellion's cover name. "Meet me in Greenwood Cemetery, here in Brooklyn. I'll be in the southeast end, where the graveyard comes to a kind of wedge. It's where Fort Hamilton Parkway intersects Macdonald Avenue. Get there as soon as you can. The list of . . . 'tires' won't keep for long!"

Brothers had phoned about 2:10, and since Camellion's hotel, close to the South Brooklyn piers, was not too far

1

from the cemetery, only a little more than an hour had passed between the time the Death Merchant had left his two-room apartment and the time he drove through the carved-iron gates of the boneyard. *Ahhh,* even as the Ford Pinto wound its way along the white gravel road, Camellion felt the insidious presence of his "Old Friend" . . . that Pale Priest of the Mute People whom he respected but did not fear.

An old pro who felt at home with all forms of violence, Camellion was used to that preternatural feeling that always came with detecting Death—how many times during the past eight years had he heard the furious fluttering of "Old Floorer's" wide wings? He had lost count!

The Death Merchant scouted the dumping ground for the dead as he drove along, thinking of the information that Gordon Brothers had for him. For the undercover CIA agent to have set up an unscheduled meeting could mean only one thing: He had finally, after all these weeks, obtained a list of the New Dawn members in Brooklyn—or was it something else? *I'll know in a very short while, won't I!!!!*

Camellion's cold blue eyes swept the area around him. Everything seemed normal in the city of the dead. Playing tag with the trees, the sun was sending shafts of bright light through the elms and maples, columns of heat that warmed the marble and granite tombstones and were welcomed by the flowers growing on well-kept graves, those well-tended symbols signifying the oldest battle in the universe—the eternal struggle between Life and Death, between the urge to continue, to procreate, and the forever blackness of the Final End.

Nothing unusual in the area. A young couple with children, standing silently by a grave . . . sentiment having driven them to return to where they had buried baby brother or sister. Men and women . . . singly or in couples . . . tears, the ultimate protest, flowing down their cheeks. An elderly couple visiting the grave of their "children," who had died as adults . . . cut down in the prime of life.

A damned ridiculous custom! The thought came to Camellion. *Putting people in the ground and sticking head-*

stones over them! "Dust thou art and to dust thou shalt re-
turn!" Then why spend four grand for a casket and a vault
to make damn sure "thou" can't return to dust? Because
parasitic funeral directors would rather plant bodies than
work for a living, that's why!

Close now to the southeastern section of the worm-and-maggot yard, Richard saw an elderly man walking slowly along the side of the road, an old-age pensioner with the vacant look of a man who's discovered that very often the green pastures of retirement are also graveyards—of idleness and boredom! The poor old duffer was probably going to visit—or was returning from—the grave of his wife. . .

Yes, everything appeared to be normal. Nothing unusual? Not quite! Camellion could still sense the presence of his old buddy. Death was there, lurking . . . waiting patiently. This was very abnormal, for in spite of what the average person might think, Death never loafs around a cemetery! He doesn't have to. The corpses under the neatly clipped grass are already His, have already succumbed to His final caress. No! When the Great God Death glides around a cemetery, He seeks only the living—and that is what bothered the Death Merchant . . .

The road curved, and Camellion could see that it ended a hundred or so feet in front of him, by the chain-link fence facing Fort Hamilton Parkway. Through the fence he could see traffic moving on the busy highway. He parked behind a Plymouth Duster whose driver was reading a newspaper and, leaning back, checked his weapons: two 9-mm Brownings in shoulder holsters—each pistol held thirteen cartridges—and two .25 Colt automatics in ankle holsters.

Once more Camellion looked over the area. He spotted Gordon Brothers. The CIA undercover agent was standing in front of a large marble monument, his back to Richard, a couple hundred feet to the left of the Death Merchant and, in keeping with his pose as a crane operator at the South Brooklyn piers, was dressed in a brown workingman's uniform. A couple hundred feet to the left of Brothers a burial service was in progress.

3

All very normal . . . There was the green canvas canopy, under which sat the weeping relatives and friends of the deceased and the family, doing their best to look solemn. The guest of honor was also present . . . the corpse in its casket, next to the open grave, ready to be lowered into the vault as soon as the priest finished his mumbo-jumbo and completed his throwing of water that was holy!

Since Greenwood was a public boneyard, where even an atheist like Camellion could be planted, Richard wondered why this corpse—and evidently its owner had been a Catholic—wasn't being dumped in ground that was "consecrated!" Not that it really mattered. The Death Merchant was concerned with reality, not tribal totems and superstitions that were rapidly dying, that could no longer survive in a world that preferred fact to fancy.

Camellion glanced in Gordon Brothers' direction. Seventy-five feet behind the agent two men were pulling small weeds from a grave mound; otherwise the area was empty. The Death Merchant got out of the car and walked over to the undercover man—a well-muscled man with a high forehead who continued to look at the tombstone in front of him as Richard moved alongside.

"What's so important?" Camellion asked. "Don't you know this is risky, meeting this way!" He noticed that the name on the tombstone was Jerome Libinski. Born Oct. 7, 1913 . . . Died Jan. 26, 1974.

I knew it! Richard saw it, to one side of a large mausoleum, fifty feet in front and to the right—the sun glinting on a gun barrel!

"I've got the list, the complete Brooklyn membership of the New Dawn," Brothers said in a low voice. "But I don't have it with —"

"Down!" hissed Camellion, who moved with incredible speed, his left hand a blur of motion as he yanked out a Browning pistol, his right reaching out and pulling Brothers down with him. They fell to the left, but even as they were crashing to the grass, they heard the roar of two pistols— .38 Colt automatics—the two slugs tearing over the area where they had stood only seconds before.

Before he hit the ground the Death Merchant snapped

off a shot at one of the two men who had fired—and what Camellion aimed at he always hit! He didn't miss this time. His slug slammed into the man's chest and knocked him sideways against his partner, who triggered off another shot, which brought a cry of pain from Gordon Brothers. Slow in falling, he had caught the slug in his right shoulder.

Camellion had been in such setups before, and he knew instinctively that the two gunmen were not alone—*We're probably surrounded! They waited until Brothers and I made the meet! Right now they're probably closing in around us!*

The Death Merchant had dived to the security of a tall headstone to the left of the one he and Brothers had been standing near. Behind this row of monuments was another, the grave-mounds facing in opposite directions, the stones about four feet apart.

"Get between the tombstones!" shouted Camellion. "It's our only chance—and our chances there are slim!"

Wriggling like an eel, he worked himself between two large stones, trying to pull Brothers with him; yet he knew he didn't dare pause to help the wounded man—*Or we'll both get cowboyed into eternity!*

He had crawled between the stones in the nick of time. No sooner had he snuggled down than all hell broke loose. A volley of shots came at them not only from the right, from the men who had initiated the shooting, but also from the left, as well as from behind them, from the direction of the road! A triangular cross-fire!

Four of the slugs bored into Gordon Brothers—one into his left temple, the other three into his side. He was dead before his face hit the grass . . .

Well . . . at least I don't have to worry about Brothers! He doesn't have to worry either—about anything!

Camellion realized he was in a very tough spot. Hunched down, he analyzed his predicament. He had aced out one of the clowns to the right; yet *two* men had just fired from that angle of the trap, which meant that originally there had been three men behind the mausoleum.

Quickly he slammed off a shot to the left, firing over the stone, then peered around the bottom edge of the monu-

5

ment, the one facing the north. Instantly two shots came in reply, the slugs hitting the face of the tombstone and digging pits into the brown granite!

Richard had gotten a mini-glance at the men to the left . . . *two* of them, one wearing sunglasses and a sharp goatee, the other slob a flat-faced ugly bastard whose mug looked as if it had collided with a Mack truck!

Richard inched around and, looking past one side of the stone to his rear, snapped off two shots at the hoods behind him. They immediately fired back, their slugs chipping the red granite stone protecting Camellion's rear. "Burnt fudge!" Camellion said aloud. "It's the two men who were pulling weeds from a grave! Well, now, one of them looks like 'Freddie the Frog!' "

On the other hand, reasoned the Death Merchant, he had one thing going for him: The six slobs were amateurs, or they would have whacked him out right away. Unprofessional as they were, they had underestimated the target and overestimated their own ability.

Their big mistake had been to assume that the two men who had fired first would get the job done. When those two had botched the hit, the other goofs had hesitated, their unprofessional pause giving Camellion a chance to dive for cover. *Now, they've either got to give me up as a lost cause or else try to get in closer to get me in a cross-fire! Yeah, a surefire cross-fire!*

As well as he could, the Death Merchant looked around him. The loud gunfire had achieved one thing: the big bad bangs of the .38s and the higher, shaper cracks of the 9-mm Hi-Power Browning were clearing the boneyard of live stiffs! A couple hundred feet to the left, the mourners at the funeral that had been in progress were running like frightened rabbits, the priest and his two server boys way out in front, leading the pack . . . all of which proved that while they were fond of singing *I Want To Go Where Jesus Is!* they weren't about to take any chances of getting there today!

Chuckling over the truism that live sinners were better off than dead saints—and probably much happier—Camellion decided that in spite of his precarious position it didn't made much sense to go mountain climbing over mole hills! Removing obstacles was his trade. *So remove all six of the slobs!*

Suddenly Camellion felt very annoyed. He didn't mind people trying to knock him off; that was par for the course of his life, part of the game. But just look at his suit! He had shelled out three bills for it only two days ago! And now the elbows and knees were already grass-stained! Somebody was going to have to pay, and far more than the cost!

Quickly, the two Brownings in his hands, he triggered off five shots, one to the left, two to the right, and three at the two slobs to his rear. He got a half-dozen big ones in return, from all three directions, the Super .38 slugs chipping the two stones between which Camellion was crouching, chips of brown and red granite flying in all directions. The corpses underneath the monuments must have turned over in their graves at the damage being done to their remaining links with the world of the living. Again Camellion fired back from around each end of the red granite stone in front of him, and to the left side of the brown granite monument to his rear. More shots in return!

With the disgusting thought that the police would have to arrive sooner or later, Camellion decided to use an old ruse. If it didn't work, he wouldn't be any worse off than he was now; he'd still be in the middle of a sinkhole!

After removing the .25 Colts from their ankle holsters, he sent off three more shots in three directions, using the 9-mm Brownings!

Another flurry of shots from the six would-be assassins —they were either members of the New Dawn or they had been hired by Silvestter's infamous occult organization! More red and brown granite chips were knocked from the two headstones protecting the Death Merchant.

Camellion did not return the fire. Instead, this time he uttered a false cry of pain and, throwing up his arms where they could be clearly seen by the enemy, let the two Brownings fall to the grass. Down between the tombstones he waited, listening, a .25 Colt in each hand.

"I Think We've Hit The Son of a Bitch!" The snarling voice, full of hate and excitement, came from fifty feet in

front and to the left of the Death Merchant—one of the men hidden behind a large monument shaped like a tower, with a large figure of Christ on top, His hands outstretched to the world.

No reply from the two slobs to the right of Camellion, the two slobs hidden behind the mausoleum that had the name BREMER carved in large stone letters over the narrow door. However, they did toss a couple more .38 slugs in Camellion's general direction. He did not return the fire. He waited, remaining very still, all the while very much aware of the risk to which he was submitting himself. If he had miscalculated, he too would end up beneath the soil, the daisies and the daffodils growing over his chest, the dandelions over his feet—*I'd be bored to death!*

Slowly he counted to ten, then looked around the right end of the brown granite tombstone. As he had hoped for and expected, the two halfwits to the right had made a fatal error in judgment. They had left the safety of the Bremer mausoleum behind which they had been hiding and were only ten feet from Camellion!

For the barest fraction of a second—or one 86,400th part of a mean solar day—the two men, skidding to a halt, gaped in astonishment at the Death Merchant. They had thought he was dead, or at least half-smoked-out of action. But there he was, very much alive, his hands full of blue-black pistols.

"He's Alive! He's—" the stupid-looking slob began shouting. The Death Merchant's slug cut him off and shut him up forever.

Four times the Colt .25s cracked, all four slugs going where Camellion wanted them to go!

His first slug caught Mr. Stupid in the mouth and zipped out the back of his neck, taking pieces of flesh and vertebrae with it. The slug finally pinged against one of the sylphlike angels decorating the top of an eight-foot-tall monument.

A second slug gave the dummy another navel, an inch above the one he'd been born with. He didn't mind the second shot tickling his intestines; the first one had already

8

sent him to hell! He fell backward over a grave, as dead as the body rotting six feet below!

Camellion's second and third slugs finished off the other boob, who looked so dishonest that Camellion got the idea he could have slept in comfort on a corkscrew—one slug hit him above the bridge of his nose, the other trotted into his throat at a side angle. A terrible I-don't-believe-it look dropped across his face—then he dropped, with all the speed of a sack of wet cement . . . his brains blown apart, his left common carotid artery belching blood!

Without bothering to look behind him, Camellion jerked around to the left, to face the opposite direction; at the same time he flattened himself against the red granite tombstone of the grave facing north—a quicker-than-lightning move that saved his life.

Not more than eight feet away the two men—who had come in from the left—fired, the loud roar of their .38s mingling with the higher, more piercing cracks of the Colt .25s. The .38 Specials came damn close! The Death Merchant felt his suit coat jump as a big one cut through the silk material on the left and burned a crease along his rib cage—and his right trouser leg jerked as the second steel-coated slug ruined the bottom half of the suit!

That does it! The whole goddamn suit can now be used for a dust rag!

Angrily Camellion slammed two more slugs into the boobs, although his first two shots had half done the job—half because the flat-faced ugly son of slut was still trying to get off another blast at him. He was having a hard time lifting the iron in his hand, the DM's first slug having made a neat little hole in his flowered sportshirt. Nor had it done his left lung any good! Camellion's second slug into the bleeding slob completed the job, stopping his heart. But reflex caused the man's finger to compress the trigger and the .38 pistol boomed, the slug zipping by Camellion. The only damage it did was to amputate the wing of a stone angel on top of a tombstone behind him. From now on the cherub would have to fly low, on one wing and a prayer!

The other crumb, the idiot with the sunglasses and goatee, had been blown away with one of the Death Merchant's first shots, the slug having drilled through his sunglasses and smashed into one of his baby blues. As dead as a wholesale district on Sunday, he was doing a spin to the grass, his head tilted up to the sky, blood flowing down his cheek from the blown-out eye.

This goof's a bird watcher! Camellion's second slug caught him in the side, and "blood beard" fell forward toward Camellion, the .38 iron sliding from his stiffening fingers.

Scooping up the .38, Camellion spun and in a flash saw he'd been right! The two men who had been by the road, pretending to pull weeds, were a lot closer now, dodging from monument to monument in an effort to get closer to the Death Merchant, who triggered off four fast shots. They had jumped behind stones but, nevertheless, one of the slugs gave one man more than just a crease; it ripped a long bloody ditch, almost a fifth of an inch deep, across his shoulder. Crying out in agony, the goof practically fell on his face, snuggling down behind a large monument.

These last two hit men used common sense. They had seen the Death Merchant knock off their four partners, and now that hurricane of destruction was zeroing in on them! They had had enough! On their hands and knees they backed away, keeping the large tombstone between them and the Death Merchant. Edging around another large stone, the two hoods, keeping low, raced in retreat, headed for the road.

Camellion didn't waste ammo in a futile effort to shoot through granite. He picked up his two Brownings, his eyes on the two men who by now had reached the road and were getting into the Plymouth Duster parked in front of his own car. The engine roared and the car shot down the road! It made a wide turn toward the end of the fence and, tires squealing on the gravel, headed for the outside entrance.

The Death Merchant returned the 9-mms to their shoulder holsters, dumped the Colt .25s into his coat pockets, and raced to his own car. Soon he was roaring in pursuit, determined to finish the job.

No candidate for the Indianapolis Speedway, the driver

of the Plymouth wouldn't have won any prizes as he hurled the car down the winding, twisting road. Halfway out of the marble orchard, careening around a curve, the boob almost lost control. One side of the car slammed up against a tall monument close to the road, the crash toppling the cross at the peak of the stone and crumbling the right rear fender. With the Death Merchant coming up close behind him, the driver somehow managed to get the Plymouth back on the road and aim it toward the entrance. He came very close to sideswiping another vehicle as he roared through the gates, momentarily slowed down, and whipped the car to the left on Fifth Avenue. The Death Merchant was right behind him, practically riding his rear bumper, close enough to aim at the Plymouth's left rear tire.

Steering with his right hand and firing with his left, Camellion triggered off two shots, the Browning jumping in his hand.

Two loud bangs from the 9-mm and the left rear tire of the Plymouth went flat! The car began wobbling all over the road, the driver desperately fighting the wheel, the oncoming traffic shying away from the Plymouth. The driver did the only thing he could do: He swung sharply to the left and headed southwest on Thirty-seventh St., which paralleled Greenwood Cemetery, skidding to a stop a few hundred yards down the street.

For the three men in the Plymouth, it was Panicsville with a capital P! Knowing they couldn't continue with a flat tire flumping all over the place, they decided to leave the car and run across the road to the BMT tracks and yards that lay directly across the road. A good plan, only one flaw: forgetting that the man pursuing them was the terrible Death Merchant.

The three candidates for the morgue had left the Plymouth and almost made it to the railroad yards when Camellion slammed on his brakes, jumped out of the car, and cut loose with his two Brownings. Dodging and weaving, he raced after them, his long legs pumping over the hot concrete.

His first bullet caught the driver squarely between the shoulders, helping him to reach the tracks a few seconds

11

sooner than he had expected. The 9-mm not only chopped his heart in two, but knocked him flat on his face. He lay there like a big rag doll, his blood flowing into the grass and weeds.

The Death Merchant's second and third slugs missed because "Freddie the Frog" and the man he had previously wounded had dropped down the exact moment he fired. Jerking out their own pieces, they let fly four shots at Camellion, who had reached the other side of the road and was charging into the railroad yard after them. All four slugs, while coming very close, missed. Zipping across the road and through the chainlink fence of the cemetery, they finally ricocheted off a tombstone.

Completely unnerved by the sheer guts of the man the world associated with violent death, the two terrified men ran for their lives. So did the half-dozen workers repairing a section of track. Hearing the gunshots and seeing what was going on—they thought it was a Mafia gun battle—the workers ran for the roundhouse, not even taking time to look back.

Nothing is more dangerous than a trapped animal or a coward. Two trapped cowards are twice as dangerous, which is why the two men turned, crouched down and began firing at the twisting and weaving Death Merchant. One slug ripped along his right side! Another almost clipped his left earlobe. A third cut through his legs—three inches higher and he would have received a free transsexual operation!

So fast was Camellion moving that he didn't even have time to spot aim as he returned the fire . . . All his slugs missed except one, which slid into one man's gut! With a long "Uhhhhhh," he put his hands over his blasted belly, sat down between the rails of the track and began the only-once-in-a-lifetime experience of dying!

As nervous as a prostitute in the vice-squad room of a police station, "Freddie the Frog" jerked around and looked behind him when he heard the warning whistle of the diesel engine fifty feet down the track behind him.

Undecided what to do, he swung back to face the Death Merchant.

Too late! Camellion was on him, twisting the .38 iron from his hand! Suddenly the world went a deep shade of gray for "Frog-Face" as Richard clipped him across the chin with the side of the Browning, the pain only half as great as his fear. Dazed, he didn't even scream when the Death Merchant lifted him high in an arm and under-the-crotch hold and pitched him to the opposite track—right in front of the slowly moving diesel!

A short high-pitched scream and "Frog-Face" died so fast his mind had no opportunity to register pain; the wheels of the engine ground him into bloody hash. Like a half-inflated basketball, his head bounced along the wooden ties . . . mouth open . . . eyes staring . . . long hair flying . . . blood spraying over one steel track.

The Death Merchant had not witnessed the last croak of "Frog-Face!" He had turned and was running back toward his car, listening to the police sirens getting closer and closer. Reaching the Ford Pinto, he roared away and was soon lost in the traffic on Fort Hamilton Parkway.

He was thankful that he always carried a change of clothing in the car. He certainly couldn't go back to his hotel looking like *this!* The Edison was a dump, but the clerk still had eyes. One glance and he would know that Camellion had been in a little war.

There was no problem. *I'll pull into a service station and change in the restroom . . .*

Two and a half hours later Camellion was back in his tiny apartment in the Edison Hotel. He lay on the bed in his undershorts, a glass of iced tomato juice in his hand, a very dirty suspicion, growing like a melanoma, in his mind.

How had the New Dawn known about his meeting with Gordon Brothers?

The answer was inescapable: In the parlance of the intelligence community—there was a "leak in the dike . . ." A bastard in the the bulrushes—and his name wasn't Moses!

Listening to the haunting strains of Tchaikovsky's *Francesca da Rimini* on a small tape recorder, Camellion began to sort the various possibilities. A leak in the CIA structure

13

itself? Possible, but not too probable! Brothers had told someone else that he had set up a meet with Camellion in the cemetery? This, too, was possible, but only half-probable. Assuming he had—

The telephone on the night table rang.

Camellion picked up the receiver—"Cortinn here"—surprised to hear that the voice on the other end of the line was that of Nathaniel Wiseloggle, the CIA agent responsible for coordinating the operation code-named "The Billionaire Mission."

"Mr. Cortinn, this is Harry Black," Wiseloggle said, using his own cover name. "Meet me tonight at eight thirty in Greenwich Village. You will be there?"

"Yes."

Wiseloggle hung up, and Camellion returned the receiver to its cradle, a thoughtful look on his lean face. "Greenwich Village" was actually the code name for one of the main CIA stations in New York, an apartment in the Martin Luther King, Jr. Towers, just north of Central Park in Manhattan.

For a meeting to be set up there on such short notice, something had to be very wrong! The Death Merchant wondered: Had the CIA developed more information about New Dawn's scheme to assassinate the President of the United States?

CHAPTER TWO

"You are absolutely certain there has not been a mistake?" Cleveland Winston Silvestter asked. Leaning over, he carefully placed the 150-pound barbell on the floor. "The Death Merchant killed all eight agents?"

"There has been no mistake, sir," Steele replied. "They

managed to kill Brothers, but failed completely with Camellion. He killed every last one of them. According to police reports—and they've been verified by our agents at police headquarters—he even followed the last three out of the cemetery and finished them off in a railroad yard. I'm sorry, sir . . ."

Silvestter stood erect, the trickle of a smile curling around his lips. He looked almost amused.

"There's no need for you to feel sorry, Jerry," he said mildly. "The failure was not your fault. There will be another time for Camellion, and he will die. He has only God on his side. We had truth on ours! We have Right and Justice! We have Lucifer and cannot fail!"

Steele did not reply, nor did Scott McKillip, who was also present in the large gymnasium. As part of the penthouse on the ninety-third floor of the Silvestter Building in mid-town Manhattan, the gym was every bit as unique as the man who owned it: Its three outside walls and the ceiling were made of very thick, two-way security glass, which appeared to be a mirror from the outside, but ordinary transparent window glass from the inside. The total effect was weird, as though one were sitting on top of the world, surrounded by emptiness, yet somehow protected from the elements. It was as if one could walk right off into nothingness! However, the view was also magnificent, especially at this hour of the night, with the city of New York spreading out in a vast panorama of colored light that glowed and flickered, as if in competition with the stars that could be seen through the roof of the gym. Looking toward the east, one could see United Nation headquarters perched on the bank of the East River, the Assembly Hall and other buildings blazing with light. Rockefeller Center to the north! The Empire State Building to the south. The west side, since it was a part of another room, was an ordinary wall.

The ninety-three story Silvestter Building itself was the heart and nerve center of the worldwide Silvestter financial empire. And the tall, slim-waisted man in the gym, removing his sweatshirt, was the absolute head of that empire.

Appearance can be an illusion. Cleveland Silvestter did not look like a man reputed to be the richest human being

15

on the face of the earth, a man whose wealth was said to be in the neighborhood of five billion dollars—and since there was not one stockholder in any of his various companies and corporations, every single penny was his! The fact was that Silvestter did not appear to be a lot of things he actually was!

A slim, rather handsome man with all his own teeth, Silvestter looked ten years young than his fifty-nine years, mainly because he was without an ounce of fat and had not a single strand of gray in his chestnut hair, which was brushed up and curled back from a high forehead. What one first noticed were the large brown eyes and finely chiseled nose, both contributing an air of sensitivity and intelligence to the healthy tanned face.

A high school athletic coach! That's what Cleveland Winston looked like! But what he appeared to be, or could have been, had no bearing on his success. If looks alone could bring riches, poor people would be as rare as teats on a bull!

Born into money, Silvestter had gotten his start from his father, who died in 1938, and left his only son a successful ball-bearing factory in Massachusetts. Silvestter's own genius had done the rest . . . his fantastic aptitude for business, his ability for knowing the world stockmarket, when to buy and when to sell. These qualities had helped him become an atomic-age Midas, qualities that had made him the sole owner of steel mills, shipyards, factories and oilfields. He owned three fleets of merchant ships, not to mention tin, iron, and tungsten mines, along with large chunks of various other combines throughout the world. The largest sheep ranch in Australia was owned by Silvestter. However, he owed none of his success to sheer luck, because the man who attracts luck always carries with him the magnet of preparation. Silvestter was always prepared . . .

In spite of his fantastic wealth Silvestter was a very narrow man, a twisted man with a blight on his soul, a rot that had been there since birth. A misogynist, he had never married; he had never as much as held a woman in his arms. Also a misanthrope, he considered people nothing more than two legged vermin. Still, he was not a man untouched by the dominating passion of love. To the contrary, his loves literally possessed him!

Constantly growing stronger, day by day, were his twin loves: a desire for power and a mania for physical perfection, both of which occupied most of his waking hours, to the extent that he not only worked out in a gym two hours each day, but also took weekly lesson in karate and Kung Fu; his instructors were world-renowned experts in the Oriental martial arts.

Silvestter was also a man who knew human nature, and although he used neither tobacco nor alcohol, he never castigated nor chided his associates and underlings for such physically harmful and financially wasteful habits; he realized that a man's ability to do his job can be seriously impaired if he is deprived of his favorite stimulant—and Silvestter wanted peak efficiency at all times.

Oddly enough there was one thing the billionaire could not stand and would not tolerate—a roll of toilet paper from which one had to draw the paper over the roll instead of under it. Consequently at all times there was a standing order at all his plants, factories, and mines, as well as his various homes throughout the world: Always make sure the roll is placed in such a manner that the paper can only be drawn from the *bottom* of the roll and never from the *top*. Even Silvestter's three fleets of merchant-marine vessels had to follow this rule.

Silvestter had a third love—*Satanism!* The kind that came straight out of the Middle Ages, genuine worship of the Devil, identical in emotional intent with the Christian worship of God! Only Cleveland Winston Silvestter's "god" was the Devil, or Satan, or Lucifer—or any of the various names used to identify the Crown Prince of All Evil.

An extremely intelligent man with a constantly inquiring mind, Silvestter had become interested in spiritualism at the age of twenty-five. He discovered very quickly that one could not acquire knowledge of the occult by walking the wide path that led to professional spiritualists whose only talent lay in sleight-of-hand conjuring. Silvestter began to study on his own, devouring first the holy books of the world's major religions—the Bible, the Koran, the Rig Veda . . . He purchased a rare copy of the *Zend Avesta,* the sacred scriptures of the ancient Persian Zoroastrians, in which he read, in the *Zartusht Namah* section, how Ahura Mazda was met and opposed by an evil spirit—the spirit in later times called Shaitin or Satan!

As the years passed and Silvestter's obsession with the occult grew, he applied himself toward the more practical aspects of the unseen and the unknown—Extrasensory Perception and all its various departments, to the extent that he became a recognized authority!

Other famous tycoons wrote articles on business or "how to succeed," but Silvestter, in national magazines, published pieces on the various aspects and intricacies of *cognition, precognition, and clairvoyance;* on *telepathy* and *teleportation,* or *vibrational empathy,* the ability to heal, read another person's aura, and perceive others' spiritual guides. Now and then one of the Sunday supplements carried one of his articles dealing with *psychometry,* or, the ability to know the past of a person or object through touching; or *mind-control,* which includes both the projection of thoughts into another person's mind—as in Voodoo—and the rare psychokinetic power to bend or alter metals and to make objects dematerialize and rematerialize.

What else was left? It was in 1961 that Silvestter began the study of Magic and Sorcery, both of the White and the Black varieties, starting with the two books of the *Kabbalah* (or *Cabala* and *Qabalah),* the *Sepher Yetzirah,* or Book of Formation, and the *Zohar,* the Book of Splendor, and, working his way up through such Kabbalists as Simon Magus, John Dee, Nostradamus, Paracelsus and Agrippa. He studied other Adepts, including Eliphaz Levi, and the great nineteenth-century spiritualists, such as Blavatsky, Swedenborg, and Gurdjieff. Finally he graduated to the infamous "black books," or *Grimoires,* those imparters of diabolical wisdom and unholy power, books that gave specific instructions as to how the sorcerer could actually converse with the demons of Hell, including Satan Himself, as well as His two chief lieutenants, Astoroth and Beelzabub.

When Silvestter finished studying these fantastic books,

he was a changed man, convinced that at long last he had discovered Truth—that which genuine Satanists had known all along—the real power of this world was not God but Satan! It was Satan, not God, who controlled the destiny of the human race—and rightfully so! For Silvestter had discovered another great truth—all the religious books of the world contained nothing but lies and twisted half-truths; and he became convinced (again like the true Satanists) that the true god of the universe was Satan, who had been usurped from His rightful position by a spirit that was actually evil, a spirit who confused men's minds, a spirit men worshipped and called God. This explained why there was so much misery and evil in the world: because the spirit men called God willed it, because he delighted in seeing men suffer!

Insane philosophies are often founded on "truths" compounded of fantastic absurdities! And so it was around the "truth" of Satan's being the true god of the universe that Silvestter devised his credo. His paranoia had progressed to the point where it was a simple matter for him to believe that it was *he* who was the Chosen Disciple of Satan, the instrument by which Satan would regain his rightful throne in heaven, His former position in the universe. Christ might have been a resurrected god. And Muhammad the Prophet of Allah. But he—Cleveland Winston Silvestter—was the high priest of the genuine God. He—Cleveland Winston Silvestter—was the Chosen of Satan!

Unlike other Satanists throughout the world, especially in Rome and Paris, who were content to worship Satan through the Black Mass and other obscene rites, Silvestter needed much more. His own unique insanity demanded that as the instrument of Satan he, and he alone, bring about the restoration of Satan to his throne, an event which could only come about with the complete destruction of twentieth-century civilization, with the destruction of the entire human race! Then and only then, after the influence of God was erased, would it be possible for Satan to come into His rightful inheritance. Humanity, which was evil, would be destroyed! There would be a new dawn, a new beginning, and the world would begin afresh, peopled with those children of Satan who would survive the holocaust, the end of the world.

Coupled with Silvestter's misanthropy, his religious paranoia progressed toward the next stage: that of bringing about the physicial destruction of world civilization. First, Silvestter had to find the right kind of associates, other than Scott McKillip, who had been his personal secretary and majordomo for over twenty years. But Silvestter needed another man, a man with organizational ability. The task was not too difficult, considering Silvestter's strange talent for always choosing the right man for the right job. He found what he required in Jerry Joseph Steele, an ex-CIA agent who would have slaughtered his own mother merely to gain the gold in her teeth.

Together, Silvestter and Steele organized the worldwide New Dawn, a secret society "dedicated to world peace and brotherhood among all men," a task that required the better part of three years, and a title that was as deceptive as the "god" to which the organization was dedicated. The purpose of New Dawn was not "peace" or "brotherhood," but death and violence, and, ultimately, the annihilation of the entire human race, which could very easily come about if the world were plunged into a full-scale hydrogen war!

All that was needed was the spark! New Dawn would furnish that spark by assassinating various world leaders and blaming their murders on enemy nations. Eventually the world would be plunged into World War III! With Silvestter and Steele doing the planning, the members of New Dawn finally struck!

May, 1973! Topiel Grossrosen, the Premier of Israel, was blown to bits in his home by a bomb, in spite of the security surrounding him. The blame placed on the Egyptians. Evidence, carefully worked out by Silvestter and Steel, indicated that Premier Grossrosen had been killed by the E. I. S., the Egyptian Intelligence Service.

Grossrosen's death had the desired result. Peace talks between the Jews and Arabs were canceled . . . .

August, 1973! Andre Pelabon, the Premier of France, was murdered by rifle fire as he rode down the Avenue des Champs Elysees. Instantly all of France began screaming about the "vicious Jew assassins." A wave of anti-Semitism swept the nation! One could not really blame the French. Practically irrefutable, the evidence pointed to the Shin Bet, the intelligence arm of the Israeli security forces.

January, 1974! An attempt was made on the life of Fidel Castro—an attempt that failed! The bullets severely wounded the Cuban dictator, and for days he lingered between life and death before starting to reclimb the ladder back toward health. The attempt to place the blame on the American CIA did not fail!

March, 1974! A rocket exploded close to the royal palace at Riyadh, Arabia! Fortunately Prince Fidahi was only slightly wounded; yet the attempted assassination served Silvestter's intended purpose. Since parts of the rocket were found to be of Russian manufacture, the Arab League accused the USSR of trying to kill the ruler of Arabia!

April, 1974! The world was astonished when the People's Republic of China began accusing the Soviet Union of trying to poison not only Mao Tse-tung, but Chou En-lai as well! The USSR's delegate to the UN countercharged the Red Chinese with "fostering the biggest lie in history, in an attempt to stir the fires of international dissension!"

The delegate from the People's Republic of China then produced evidence that the GRU, the Soviet espionage apparatus, had indeed tried to poison Mao Tse-tung and Chou En-lai. And although the evidence was circumstantial, it was more than sufficient to make the world wonder and hold its breath in anticipation that the two giants of Asia would attack each other—the greatest fear throughout the world being that the USSR would employ a preemptive nuclear strike against the Red Chinese. The Soviets almost did . . .

Only two assassinations remained on New Dawn's schedule: the murders of both the American President and the Russian Premier! Their deaths would be the last two strokes against the world of *God-the-Evil!* Yes, Silvestter was convinced, World War III would blossom like a deadly flower over the planet. Humanity would be destroyed—except for the High Priest of Satan and his followers. The reign of *Satan-the-Good* would begin and last for all eternity!

Toward this day of victory, when all humanity would vanish from the radioactivity emitted by hundreds of mushroom clouds, the billionaire had constructed an underground city on his 850,000-acre sheep ranch in Queensland, the continental state located in northeast Australia. There, in the New Eden, Silvestter and his people would await the end of all evil, the end of the world, and the beginning of Satan's gentle rule.

Once more there would be a Garden of Eden on earth, and Silvestter would be its new Adam!

Silvestter had removed his sweatshirt and slipped on a silken robe held out by Jerry Steele.

"Come along," the billionaire said. "We'll go into the library and discuss what must be done about the Death Merchant."

Turning, he strode from the gymnasium. Steele and Scott McKillip sauntered after him into a wide and spacious room with steel doors at each end. Silvestter went to the center of the room, turned on a tall lamp, and dropped into a black armchair. Steele and McKillip settled themselves in armchairs across from him, Steele, as he sat down, asking, "Do you have any intuitive feelings about Camellion, sir?"

"Not at this moment—no!" Silvestter replied easily, crossing his legs. "Camellion is dangerous to us, yet he doesn't present an insurmountable obstacle to our final goal!"

He paused slightly, gazing rather intently between the two men, at a spot behind them—another of his eccentricities! Silvestter could talk to a man for hours and not look at him one time; then again, he might stare at him the full length of the entire conversation! All this was normal to Jerry Joseph Steele and Scott McKillip, who considered Silvestter almost a god! Had not Silvestter discovered the *truth* that for untold thousands of years had been withheld from humanity? Was Silvestter not the Chosen One of Satan? Yes, he was! Steele and McKillip knew that he was, with all the same certainty that the Pope of Rome knew that Christ had been born of a virgin named Mary! And since Silvestter was the Chosen One, Satan himself had to be guiding him! With such a dynamic combination carrying its flag, how could New Dawn lose?

"Tell me, Jerry," Silvestter said, "why do you ask about my intuitive feelings. Surely, you of all people aren't frightened of this Death Merchant. For almost six months he has been prying into the activities of New Dawn, and we have always been several steps ahead of him. There aren't any moves he can make, there's nothing he can do without our knowing about it, eventually."

"You're absolutely right, C. W.," Scott McKillip mused. He put his elbows on the chair arms, placed his hands together, and began to turn one thumb slowly around the other. "For example, his meeting tonight with Wiseloggle and Cleever. By tomorrow afternoon we'll know every second of the minutes of the meeting!"

Steele was somewhat taken back by Silvestter's inference that he might actually be afraid of the terrible Death Merchant. He wasn't, as long as he was in the Silvestter Building!

Unlike other New York City office buildings, the Silvestter structure did not contain the offices of any other company, the entire building being used exclusively for the operation of the net that covered the world—the Silvestter enterprises.

Security in the building was as great as in the Pentagon!

Every employee, upon entering the building, had to place his palms on a pedestal containing a closed-circuit TV camera and speak his name into a microphone. The computer in the Security Control System instantly identified the employee by his palm and voice prints and then permitted him to enter through a special-type seven-foot turnstile, special in that it had a top barrier guard that prevented anyone from climbing through. A ceiling plate prevented climbing up, over and down the rotor, while foot guards prevented crawling under the rotor.

All glass in the building was double-strength burglar resistant. The locks were even more special. All the main locks were coded and could be activated only by pushing the proper combinations of buttons. The doors to special offices were secured by coded locks activated by cards and pushbuttons, although they could be used in conjunction with keys.

The employees didn't know it, but every office floor contained cleverly hidden TV monitors (even the washrooms). There were other precautions. During the day one hundred security guards patrolled the giant building, their number increased to one hundred and fifty after 6:00 P.M. Along with these well-trained men, the complex D-System went into effect during the night hours . . . devices that could detect an intruder by motion, sound or vibration, by the breaking of an electrical circuit, or by the interruption of an invisible light beam.

It was not a figure of speech to say that a fly could not get into the building without the warning light flashing on one of the electronic consoles in the Main Security Office on the fifteenth floor.

Steele felt he had to reassure Silvestter of his bravery, and he said, "I respect the Death Merchant for his various abilities, C. W. But I'm not afraid of him . . . physically or otherwise."

Silvestter's reply was surprising!

"Perhaps it would be better if you were," the billionaire said slowly, "if we all were . . ."

Quite unexpectedly he sat up very straight, closed his eyes, and put his hands to the side of his head, as though he were trying to suppress a headache!

"*I feel it!* I am positive of the thought!" he said loudly. "Satan Himself must be whispering to my soul!"

Steele and McKillip, leaning forward, tensed and stared at Silvestter, convinced he was being obsessed and possessed by the Master. Almost holding their breath, they waited, an expression of awe on their features.

"The Death Merchant is a greater threat than we earlier believed!" Silvestter said, his voice still loud, but hoarse. "I know intuitively that he is the one man, the only man in the world, who can wreck our plans. However, he will not, and we are safe from his interference!"

Opening his eyes, Silvestter lowered his hands from his head, leaned back in the deep chair, and sighed in contentment. The voices in his mind, when they came, induced in him a mood of exhilaration, a kind of don't-give-a-damn lightheartedness. He was now ready to seize and hold one dream amid many dreams. Once more his gaze, ignoring the two men, traveled past them to the far wall, which was covered with bookcases containing volumes on black magic, sorcery, witchcraft and demonology, each volume bound in red leather and monogramed with a gold "C.W." Here were all the infamous books of the black arts, whose mere possession, during medieval times, was sufficient to warrant burning at the stake—and the Church burnt thousands. There, behind glass, were the *Grimorium Verum*, the *Great Grimoire* and the *Grimoire of Hondrius the III*, along with the *Lemegeton*, the *Greater Key of Solomon*, and the *Testament of Solomon*. There were other books, including the *Arbatel of Magic*, and the famed *Book of the Sacred Magic of Abra-Melin the Mage*; next to it rested Aleister Crowley's classic, *Magick in Theory and Practice*. The bookcases also contained hundreds of less well-known works on the forbidden arts.

Steele and McKillip appeared to be confused, their foreheads furrowed in concentration. What C. W. had just said was a paradox.

"C. W., I don't understand!" Scott McKillip said, pursuing the matter. "You say Camellion is a danger! But you also say we are safe!"

"He means that we are secure only as long as we keep track of what the Death Merchant is doing," Steele explained gently. "Am I not correct, sir? Whether I am or not, I think we should concentrate on killing Camellion as quickly as possible. When I was in the CIA, our prime rule was that a dead enemy cannot be a dangerous enemy!"

"A very sensible rule," grunted McKillip, recrossing his legs.

Silvestter interposed with unusual sharpness. "But not in this specific case—not yet!" he said without moving his head from its uptilted position. "In the past six months, while we have been apprised of Camellion's movements, he has still managed to elude our every trap. The cost to us has been high! He has killed at least—how many now? Twenty, with these last eight! He has killed twenty of our best agents, the best we had in the greater New York area! Do you know why—do you?"

Neither Steele nor McKillip spoke, realizing Silvestter's question was purely rhetorical.

"The reason is self-evident!" the billionaire said, his voice rising with passion. "The reason is that Camellion has the swine God of the Christians protecting him! That hidiously evil Christian spirit of war and misery is protecting Camellion, which is proof enough for me that Camellion is our main enemy! I know it! I feel it! I can almost hear Satan whispering in my brain!"

His face took on such an intense look of hate that the two men across from him turned their heads away, Steele looking down at the thick black rug, McKillip's gaze traveling slowly around the room. The blood-red glass of the lamp cast a bright but ghastly light, reflecting grotesquely on patterns of swords, pistols and muskets on the far wall. In back of Silvestter, beside a white marble mantelpiece, a stuffed Bengal tiger loomed up on its hindlegs, its forepaws reaching out, its eyes—two large rubies!

Like the CIA, McKillip also had a rule: Never question anything C. W. did. Nonetheless, he often wondered about the motive behind C. W.'s. having had rubies placed in the eyesockets of the tiger. For years he had wondered; yet he had never asked Silvestter for the reason. He never would; he never intruded upon the Boss' eccentricities. In this respect his personality was as odd as his looks. McKillip wasn't a man any woman would look at twice—even the first time!

A short, stocky man with a nervous manner, McKillip was in his middle fifties. He didn't look like the man he really was: not only a first rate personal secretary, but a tax expert who had forgotten more about capital gains than IRS would ever know. At first glance his face appeared to be perfectly round. This was because of his shiny black hair (dyed) and long, curving sideburns, which, although they did not completely encircle his face, came within an

26

inch or more of doing so. Out of this face peered small, dark, always-suspicious eyes behind large, turquoise-frame glasses, beneath which was a long nose and a wide mouth.

McKillip's attention turned to Steele, who had spread out his arms and was saying, "C. W., if Camellion has the protection of God, which is proof that he is our most dangerous enemy, isn't that all the more reason we should make every effort to kill him as soon as possible? I could have Boyd send agents from New Dawn's Death Squad to the Death Merchant's hotel and—"

"No!" Silvestter interrupted. He leaned far back in the large, stuffed chair, so that his eyes stared almost straight up at the high ceiling. It, too, was painted a dull black. "Camellion will die at the proper time. That time will be when Satan brings it about . . . a time that will work itself into the natural order and flow of our continued success. For us to try to hurry the process would achieve only to anger the Master of Hell. For now we will wait and see what develops at the meeting Camellion is attending tonight."

Feeling that the Devil helps those who help themselves, Steele did not make any comment. What good would it have done? Once C. W. had made up his mind, he was as immovable as the Rock of Gibraltar. Very well, they would wait. So be it . . .

"Scott, give me the report on the Aura Sensitizer tests that were made today!" Silvestter said, the change of subject indicating that he considered the discussion of Camellion closed.

McKillip reached into a leather folder and took out a notebook, which he opened. For a few moments he consulted the report he had written in his own special brand of shorthand, while he thought about the device inspired by Silvestter and perfected in secret by the electronic geniuses of Silvestter Dynamics, Inc.

The principle was based on the premise that every human body is encased in its own individual electromagnetic field, the Odic Force, or Aura, radiating outward from the organism, one and one-half to three and one-fourth inches in breadth at different places.

27

Winston Silvestter was not the first man to experiment with the human aura. For centuries clairvoyants had claimed to have seen the human aura, but it wasn't until 1911 that W. R. Kilner devised ways of showing it experimentally. He did this by two methods: first, by looking at the human body through a dilute solution of a dye called *dicyanin;* and second, by looking at a very bright light through a strong alcoholic solution. Later H. Boddington discovered a type of glass manufactured in Czechoslovakia that dispensed with the use of solutions. Kilner also used carmine and since his time a number of other dyes had been found to be more or less satisfactory.

However, Silvestter was the first man to devise a practical way of identifying the aura of any individual by *listening* to its electrical impulses. Just as no two persons have identical fingerprints, neither do they have identical auras, each pattern of impulses being the only one of its kind.

The Aura Sensitizer captured the auric vibratory pattern of an individual and stored it in a memory bank, to be used for later identification, the entire process functioning somewhat in the manner of a voice-print ID machine, only instead of audible sound, the A-S device picked up electromagnetic waves between 15 kHz and 14,000 GHz.

"The California tests were highly successful," McKillip said. "They were conducted on twenty-seven different subjects, at three ten Pacific Time, and in each case the Sensitizer was able to record the individual emanations of each subject and transcribe the impulse patterns to the memory cells, which in turn transferred them to the identification disks. The disks were then inserted in the Cor-Cell Units of the Sensitizer, and the test subjects, twenty-seven in number, mixed in with a group composed of one hundred and seventy-eight other people. In each case, the Cor-Cell units correctly identified each subject, all twenty-seven, up to a distance of one hundred and sixty-seven-three tenths feet. Beyond one hundred and sixty-seven-three tenths feet, the Cor-Cell units will not function effectively."

McKillip closed the notebook. "There is a final notation, C. W., from our production chief," he said. "He mentions that the lab can begin production of Vibratory Q-Pickup

Units and the Cor-Cells immediately, as soon as you give the authorization."

"Has the trouble been corrected with the magnetic core storage?" Silvestter asked. "As I recall, our people couldn't get the core magnetized to represent a binary of seven or four."

McKillip opened the notebook and again consulted its pages.

"Yes, there is a note here," he said. "I quote: 'In regard to the previous problem of core storage: binary correction completed by adjusting the linear motion of the waveform.' The report also mentions the previous problem with the magnetic Variable-Reluctance Transducer. Note three says —and I quote: 'A change has been made in the parameter by giving a greater capacitance to the variable-frequency oscillator.' "

Closing the notebook, McKillip glanced up. "Should I give them your authorization to begin production, C. W.?"

Silvestter did not reply. He continued to stare up at the ceiling as though hypnotized, his hands folded over his chest, his mind lost in the reality of what the very near future would bring—contact with Satan Himself!

Yes! Within a matter of weeks, he—Cleveland Winston Silvestter—would perform the Grand Rite and invoke *Lucifuge Rofocale,* the name given to Satan in *Grimorium Verum.*

He would actually be able to see the Emperor of Hell!
He would be able to converse with the Emperor of Hell!

All was in readiness at the Temple of Conjuration in New Eden. The wand of hazel had been cut at sunrise, during the lonely hour of Mercury. The Grand Kabbalistic Circle—twenty feet in diameter—had been prepared!

Only fourteen more days!
SATAN! OH MASTER! I AM READY!

Jerry Steele, rubbing his hands slowly together, tilted his shaggy head toward McKillip, his expression as grave as his low voice.

"Tell me, Scott, how small are the Vibratory Q-Pickup Units and the Cor-Cells?" he asked. He reached into the

29

left-hand pocket of his sports jacket and took out his cigarettes.

McKillip directed a private smile at the chief of the New Dawn, and returned the notebook to the leather case.

"If you're asking if the units can be carried in one's pocket, the answer is no," he said, waiting to see the disappointment on Steele's face before adding, "but each unit will fit into an attaché case!"

A reflective glimmer glowed in Steele's light gray eyes, cruel eyes set in a lean, sharp-chinned face topped by a high forehead and heavy dark brown hair that always looked as if it needed combing. The body matched the face in toughness—240 pounds of solid muscle on a six-foot large-boned frame.

Silvestter awakened from his dreams of glory and self-aggrandizement. He said, "Scott, have Communications contact our people in California immediately. I want half a dozen of the units manufactured and flown here as quickly as possible!"

"I'll attend to it at once, C. W.," McKillip murmured, looking up. He cleared his throat. "Our people at Dynamics will probably be curious about the rush. Shouldn't I give them some special reason?" he asked, the question prompted more by his own curiosity than by anything else.

"No, you shouldn't," Silvestter said, the tone indicating he was annoyed. "I don't employ the lab people to ask questions!"

Moving himself, he sat up straight in the chair and for the first time looked at McKillip and Steele, a direct eyeball-to-eyeball stare, his large brown eyes reflecting red from the shaded lamp next to him.

His voice was still filled with irritation. "You will, however, emphasize that I want the units as soon as it is possible to produce them—and as far as you two are concerned, I don't mind telling you that two of those units are going to help us kill the Death Merchant. As I said previously, the time for his death will fall into the natural sequence of things, into the natural order of our successes. I tell you this: The Aura Sensitizer will be the weapon that helps

us to put the Death Merchant in a trap, one from which he will not escape!"

With a low chuckle McKillip tucked the leather case under one arm and rose to go to the elevator that would take him to the Communication Center on the seventieth floor, where, day and night, personnel were always on duty at the teleprinters and four shortwave radios.

"I would like to be there when Camellion dies," he said thoughtfully, pushing against his glasses. "I hope he dies hard!"

"He will, but you will not be there to witness his demise!" Silvestter said, slowly turning his head, his eyes following McKillip, who had taken a few steps, then stopped to listen. "In eight more days, we will fly to New Eden. There we will remain until the End of the World!"

The billionaire had expected a startled reaction, and he got one from both of his aides, McKillip turning sharply, Steele's hand, holding a cigarette lighter, pausing in midair, the flame flickering.

"Eight more days!" Steele exclaimed, his quick intake of air almost a hiss. "Then we'll be in Australia when the President and the Russian Premier are killed!"

He frowned, hard lines forming around his mouth. He snapped off the cigarette lighter and removed the cigarette from his mouth, all the while conscious of Silvestter's constant stare.

"But C. W.," he finally said, "the CIA is aware that an attempt is to be made on the President's life! We have yet to work out a new plan for killing him! Have you forgotten?"

"The original plan will work!" Silvestter said. "We decided on that weeks ago, did we not?"

Steele hesitiated, a curious expression on his face.

"Well . . . yes, the original plan will work," he stammered in confusion. "The only flaw is that the agents carrying the explosive will also die with the President. With the Secret Service expecting an assassination, it's almost a—"

"Our agents will die for a good cause!" intoned Silvestter portentously and in a cultured voice. "They will die for Satan."

Steele's voice was almost a whisper. "We will use Plan A then?"

"Yes. You can begin implementing it tomorrow."

Motioning with one hand, Silvestter indicated to McKillip that he should go to the Communications Center. McKillip left the room.

Steele slowly nodded, his mind turning over the rich soil of memories. He thought of the years he had worked for the billionaire, at a salary of $300,000 per year. At first he had considered Silvestter merely an eccentric but extremely dangerous crackpot. Gradually, however, he had come to believe that the billionaire was the Chosen One of Satan! Now he was absolutely convinced of it, more than ever. Yet a very sharp thorn of dark fear kept digging at the foundation of his conviction, constantly poking at his confidence. . .

Richard Camellion!

Steele didn't like the persistence of the thought that refused to remain silent . . . that whispering in his brain. . . insisting that in any conflict between the Death Merchant and the Devil—

God help Satan!

CHAPTER THREE

"Mr. & Mrs. Raymond L. Koosgoodie" read the name on the nameplate of Apartment 806 in the Martin Luther King, Jr. Towers, situated on the corner of Fifth Avenue and West 116th Street, northwest of Central Park in upper Manhattan.

There were five people in the six-room apartment: Mr. and Mrs. Koosgoodie in the living room and three men in a back room that under ordinary circumstances would have been a bedroom but was being used as a storage room.

32

On the floor of the storage room was a blue-patterned carpet that had seen better days, so old its original colors remained dubious. A highly polished walnut table, much burned at the edges, stood on one side of the room; white corrugated cartons were stacked against the opposite wall, some cartons containing *Two-Way Loud Scream Burglar Alarms,* others filled with colored ballpoint pens in ten-gross lots, which along with the burglar alarms Enco Enterprises advertised in the mail-order sections of national magazines, giving its address as a Post Office drawer in Grand Central Station.

Ostensibly the owners of Enco, Mr. and Mrs. Koosgoodie operated the business, fulfilling orders promptly and immediately refunding money to dissatisfied customers. The last thing they wanted was anyone complaining to the Postal Inspection Service, not because they were doing anything illegal, but because any PI investigation would bring to light some very strange facts about the couple known as "Raymond and Elaine Koosgoodie." The inquisitive PI boys might wonder how the Koosgoodies managed to live on the meager returns of Enco Enterprises. Another probability was that the Postal Inspectors might discover that Raymond Koosgoodie was not a paraplegic who had to spend his waking hours confined to a motor-driven wheel-chair and that he had not been shot in the spine during the Vietnam conflict! Further postal inspection probing would then no doubt reveal that the true names of "Raymond and Elaine Koosgoodie" were actually Nelson S. Pines and Gloria Humphries.

If these facts were exposed, the New York office of the Central Intelligence Agency would have to step in and quietly inform the postal people that their snooping had uncovered a CIA "house"—Station Yc/2B, whose "front" was Enco Enterprises.

Should any of this happen, the damage would be irreparable. A new "house" and "front" would have to be set up in a different part of the city, and Station Yc/2B would cease to exist.

Why was Pines posing as a paralyzed veteran? So that

his never leaving the apartment would not seem unusual to the other tenants, who didn't know that he actually stayed home as a security measure, to make sure no enemy agent could slip into the apartment and bug the place. (On occasion Pines did venture out, but always late at night and always in disguise; Gloria was always there when he did.)

The three men at the walnut table in the storage room sat in serious discussion, their faces shadowed from the downward glow of the high-intensity lamp. The man at one end of the table was a one hundred and seventy-five-pound six-footer, with deep blue eyes set in a lean, ruggedly handsome face, a middle-thirties man who wore his hair in a short burr, a style that made it very easy for Richard Camellion to wear almost any kind of wig.

At the other end of the table, puffing furiously on a Kirsten pipe, the kind with the body made of aluminum, sat Nathaniel A. T. Wiseloggle—thin and fortyish, but tall and powerful, whose head of thick blond hair, combed straight back, harbored an oasis in reverse—a bald spot on the crown.

Nat Wiseloggle was the coordinator of The Billionaire Mission, which is to say it was his job to synchronize actions and forward reports to and orders from "The Hub," CIA headquarters in Langley, Virginia. In this sense Nat was the liaison connecting home base and the agents on each plate in the ballgame between the forces of good and the forces of evil.

The third man by the side of the table was a pokerfaced, lanky individual in his early sixties. An ex-Colonel in the US Marines, Charles "Red" Cleevis was the Assistant Director of the Central Intelligence Agency's Plans Division—and even the Director of the CIA didn't know why they called him "Red," since his hair was dark brown and streaked with broad fingers of gray. The reasons was simple enough: Cleevis' father had wanted a son with red hair. Not getting one, he had nevertheless, nicknamed the little boy "Red," and the name had stuck.

Over the years Red's job had given him an ulcer of the duodenum. Richard Camellion was not contributing to his recovery! For the past hour the Death Merchant had continued to disagree with Plan *Poaka*.

The word *poaka* meant "pork" to the Maoris in New Zealand; to the CIA men at the table, it meant something entirely different. Plan *Poaka* was the code cover of the strike to be made against Cleveland Winston Silvestter's underground city in Australia, the billionaire's New Eden!

The Death Merchant had made it very clear that in his opinion the attack plan smelled to high heaven! A further annoyance to Cleevis was the bitter awareness that he couldn't tell Camellion to keep his damned mouth shut and do as he was told. He couldn't because Camellion (whom Red privately considered an inexplicable enigma) was not a regular agent of the CIA, but a free-lancer, an expert with such a deadly talent that Washington couldn't afford not to employ him—at an astonishing $100,000 per mission! What's more, he was worth every damn dime of it: He always got the job done, one way or another . . .

Once again Camellion voiced what he thought of Plan *Poaka,* pointing out to the other two men that it was ridiculous to go to all the time and trouble of executing an attack on Silvestter's base in Australia when the world headquarters of Silvestter Industries was less than two miles away!

"With some planning it wouldn't be impossible for me to slip into the Silvestter Building and obtain a list of New Dawn's world membership," the Death Merchant said, sardonic-humorous lines deepening around his nose and mouth. "And don't give me that nonsense about the building's security setup being one of the best in the world. We all know there's no such thing as an unbeatable electronics protection system—and we do have five of our own people among Silvestter's employees! If I can get into the main conference room of the Kremlin and get out without being detected—and you both know I've done it!—I could get past all Silvestter's gadgets! But what you're suggesting, this Plan *Poaka!* You're saying we should go to the Bronx by way of Oregon!"

He leaned back on the plain wooden chair, tilting it so that it rested only on its two back legs, watching the two men, from the side sweep of his downward gaze, who sat

35

hunched over the table like two conspirators—which they were!

Red Cleevis was determined to be patient and not lose his temper. He was moistening his lips, getting ready to speak, when Wiseloggle beat him to the explanation of why the CIA considered an attack on Silvestter's Australian complex a practical venture.

"According to our reasoning," Nat said calmly, "Silvestter should be flying to Australia in a week or so. I suppose you want to know what our belief is based on. I'll tell—"

"I know why! The time is getting close to the President's scheduled assassination!" Camellion said lazily. "Unless Silvestter and his helpers have pushed up the schedule or have changed their plans to include a delay. Why don't you have the FBI or the Secret Service take Silvestter and Steele and all the other Satan slobs in for questioning?"

Camellion already knew the answer to that one, but he wanted to hear Nat's explanation. He didn't! He heard Red Cleevis'!

"Camellion, you know damn good and well the government doesn't have a single shred of evidence against Silvestter and his New Dawn!" Red said sullenly. He put both hands on top of the table and began tapping his fingers against the polished wood. "Why, if we arrested C. W. Silvestter, most likely the Justice Department would be accused of using 'SS' tactics and attempting to push 'fascism' on the American people! And since New Dawn puts out a lot of 'peace' and 'brotherly love' publications, you know what the fruitcake section of the country would say, don't you? That Uncle Sam's a warmonger and trying to railroad a man dedicated to peace—and you know the kind of legal talent Silvestter has! If we even questioned the man, we'd end up looking stupid!"

Wiseloggle said, "And with Watergate still fresh, if the government made accusations against Silvestter it couldn't prove . . . you know the result, Merchant . . . But forget any ideas you might have about a one-man attack on the Silvestter Building! That's out! Our agents who have managed to infiltrate personnel wouldn't be able to help you.

36

They all have jobs that keep them away from the Security Office . . . elevator boy, janitor, jobs like that . . ."

Wiseloggle folded his arms, put them on the table, and looked levelly at Camellion through blue clouds of pipe smoke, his eyes clearly saying, *Now tell me I'm wrong and don't know what I'm talking about!*

Camellion couldn't and he didn't, knowing that Wiseloggle was correct. Everything he had said was very logical. Richard was almost certain he also knew the reason that lay behind the CIA's wanting him to lead a force against Silvestter's sheep-ranch base in Queensland, Australia.

The big brains in The Hub want Silvestter and his men wasted—but not on American soil! That, too, was credible! *Yes indeedie . . . more than tenable. Disguise the whole operation, kill Silvestter, and keep the stink away from American soil! Not bad at all! But what do the Aussies think of the plan, or do they even know about it?*

Smiling cryptically, Camellion turned slightly and reached into the left pocket of his sports coat, which he had hung over the back of the chair, and withdrew a box of lemon drops. Wiseloggle and Cleevis watched him in the manner of two cats who had just been told by a mouse to go to hell! Damn it! That was the trouble in dealing with the Merchant of Death—you never knew what he'd do next! Camellion's mercurial bent was another thing that annoyed Red Cleevis; he disliked people whose opinions he couldn't predict. The only thing he could predict about Camellion with any accuracy was that the man was completely unpredictable!

"Very well, gentlemen," Camellion said, opening the box of lemon drops, "the CIA wants me to lead a force into Queensland, kill Silvestter and everyone else at the underground city as quickly and as efficiently as possible! What do the Aussies think of the plan?"

Wiseloggle and Cleevis hit each other with brief, startled glances. Cleevis cleared his throat in an effort to conceal his relief that Camellion had guessed the truth, while Nat Wiseloggle moved a finger along one side of his flattish nose, and his amiable fleshy mouth slowly formed a smile. He took the pipe from his mouth, holding it by the bowl.

37

"We have the full cooperation of the Aussies," he explained, as friendly as the neighborhood Good Humor man, putting the pipe against the side of an ashtray. "So you don't have to worry about this being a 'slip-in' deal. The fact is the Australians are more than anxious to get rid of Silvestter and his damned base out in the wilds of Queensland! Isn't that right, Red?"

"Prime Minister Herthington and his cabinet haven't done anything about Silvestter because of his vast investments in the country," Cleevis said quickly, seeing the questioning look on Camellion's face, "but after we explained how that crackpot Satanist and his New Dawn bastards were responsible for all the assassinations and attempted assassinations, he and his security people saw the wisdom in our scheme to remove Silvestter from this earthly scene. That's your job, Camellion, sending the son of a bitch to hell!"

"You're telling me that Herthington doesn't mind that we're going to whack out Silvestter on precious Australian soil!" Camellion said, moving a lemon drop around in his mouth. "Hmmmmmmmm."

His voice suddenly became razor sharp. "Don't get CIA-clever with me! And don't hold anything back, or you can get yourselves another boy to do the job. Now, what's the real story?"

Camellion's momentary consternation had made Cleevis nervous, but not Wiseloggle, who tilted his head at an angle and, leaning back, locked his hands behind his neck.

"We're not giving you a con, Camellion," he said earnestly. "I said the Austirialians were anxious to get rid of Silvestter, and that's the full truth. They're even going to furnish a man from their AIS to help us! Now, isn't that nice of them!"

Camellion remained skeptical. "Just like that?"

"No, not 'just like that!' " Wiseloggle continued in the same easy manner. "At first the Aussies wouldn't have a thing to do with the scheme, although they wanted to get rid of Silvestter . . . that is, they wouldn't until our diplomatic boys reminded them that their land of kangaroos

38

might get a hell of a bad name if something happened to our President and to the Russian big guy and the world found out that the Australians had continued to harbor the people responsible, even after they had been warned. We even intimated that the Soviets might think the Herthington government had entered into some kind of conspiracy!"

"The old blackmail angle . . ." Camellion said.

"Exactly!" Nat said in a hard voice. "You might say our threat sort of set their 'billies' to overboiling and didn't exactly set them to singing 'Waltzing Matilda'!"

Cleevis said, "What's important is that they finally agreed to let us have a free hand. Of course, they're sending their man along for their own purposes—you know that!"

"To keep an eye on us and get a true picture of what happens after we get to the underground city," Nat Wiseloggle finished.

Camellion's eyebrows raised. "We?"

"*We!*" repeated Nat. "I'm going along." He smiled. "To keep an eye on you and report back to The Hub. But seriously, there are other reasons why I'll be there."

Cleevis shrugged as he took a pack of cigarettes from his inside coat pocket and prepared to light one.

"Satisfied now?" he asked. "Or what else do you want to know before we get down to some tough planning?"

He touched the flame of a small silver lighter to the tip of the cigarette.

"Oh . . . I have a few," Richard said with a wry-mouthed smile. "Such as What do we do if Silvestter doesn't go to Austrialia? And don't tell me The Hub hasn't considered that distinct possibility?"

"Sure we have," Cleevis said at once, a twin stream of smoke blowing from his nose. "If the son of a bitch remains in the States—"

"You're just dying to blow hell out of the Silvestter Building, aren't you?" Nat said, shaking his head! He picked up his pipe and began knocking the bowl against his palm.

"And you'll get the chance if Silvestter doesn't go to Australia," Cleevis said. "But we don't feel he'll want to be around when his New Dawn boys make the attempt against the President—not that it will do them any good. The President is so well protected it would take an H-bomb to blow him way!"

An amused expression flowed over Wiseloggle's broad face as he said fiercely, "Yeah, not even Silvestter's mythical devil could devise a way to get within a hundred feet of the President—no matter what New Dawn tries or when they try it!"

He paused unexpectedly and banged the table with his fist. "I've often tried to reason out how a man as brilliant as Silvestter could be so completely nutty in one department. I'm speaking of his Satanism. It's true that most people have relegated a belief in the devil to the realm of mythology, where such a belief rightly belongs. But even if Satan did exist, how could any sane man believe that the devil was really a 'good guy'? To me the whole idea of Satanism is too fantastic to even be possible! How can anything evil be 'good'?"

"You're right, yet you're wrong," Camellion said very seriously.

"You've got to keep one thing in mind: The people who worship the devil do not regard him as evil. To the genuine Satanist, like Silvestter, the devil is a just and merciful god. The catch is that the word 'just' or 'merciful,' applied to the Devil and his followers, does not carry its conventional Christian meaning, since the Satanists believe that what we call good is really evil, and vice versa. To commit what we call evil is really virtuous to the demon lover, who believes that God is evil, the result being a complete denial of the whole Judaeo-Christian moral code and the rules based on it. The followers of Lucifer, Satan, or the 'little god' admire pride, lust and force; they are entirely preoccupied with sensual pleasure and worldly achievement. They are in all their glory with violence, cruelty and passionate sensations. They abhor Christianity, with its virtues of humility, self-denial and cleanliness of mind."

Camellion popped another lemon drop into his mouth and noticed the thoughtful expressions on the faces of both CIA agents, who reminded the Death Merchant of men trying to figure out how to pull their feet out of the mud.

"You used the term 'little god,' " Cleevis said, pushing out his head and peering at the Death Merchant. "Is that another name for the devil?"

"The word 'devil' means little god," Camellion explained. " 'Devil' is a diminutive from the root *div*, from which is also derived the word 'divine.' In a sense that explains the close connection between 'God' and the 'devil' and gives evidence that both are derived from the same source—from man's own fertile imagination. One is dependent on the other!"

Camellion laughed, a low laugh of irony. "After all, you have to have *Evil* in order to have a conception of *Good*. Let's face it! If the world didn't have a devil, how would the foolish Christians explain all the evil in the world? After all, their god is perfect! Hell, evil couldn't possibly come from a good-guy god, which is why the poor dumb devil always gets the blame. Actually, when the Old Testament was first turned into Greek, the 'Satan' was translated into *Diabolos*, meaning an 'accuser,' with the implication of a false accuser, a slanderer, and this is the word from which the English 'devil' is derived."

"But you have to admit that Christianity is much better than Satanism!" Wiseloggle thrust out. "That's a self-evident fact!"

"It's not self-evident and it's not a fact," Camellion retorted. "Whether it's Satanism or Christianity, each form of belief is based on the acceptance of sheer myth as concluded fact. Each is a narrow form of belief, and both are childish."

Red Cleevis had been reared as a Baptist, and he resented what he considered blasphemy. He shifted uncomfortably in his chair, trying to keep his anger a secret. Why should he be upset? he asked himself. Camellion's agnosticism was well known. What did any agnostic or atheist know about the True Living God? But Red had to know. He had to find out. Camellion's intelligence was also well known . . .

"I assume, Camellion, that you don't believe in the Bible!" he said condescendingly. "I suppose you think it's all one big fairy tale!"

Another religious boob!—but Camellion replied, "The Bible is nothing more than an anthology of Hebrew and late Greek literature. What happened was that the entire mess was dumped together and edited by a group of Roman Catholic bishops who were under the impression they couldn't make any errors. Before this editing job, the Bible didn't exist. The *Septuagint* was around—the Hebrew Scriptures and their translation into Greek; and there were numerous codices, or Greek manuscripts, of various parts of the New Testament, such as the four Gospels. Of course, there were other writings floating around on the ancient seas of superstition, including the Epistles of Saint Paul and Saint John, and such documents as the *Acts of Saint John,* the *Apostolic Constitutions*, and the *Didache.* There were also the Epistles of masochistic morons, such as Ignatius, Clement and Polycarp.

"Future misery began to be fashioned when the Bible was translated by ignorant, superstitious men and fell into the hands of the masses who were just as ignorant and uneducated . . . although I must admit to the psychological paradox of component duality with which many people are burdened . . . people who are able to rationalize any kind of belief, no matter how ridiculous that belief may be. Such people can be supercritical and one hundred percent logical in matters of science, but as credulous as cretins in matters concerning any kind of eternal social security in some distant-in-time never-never land. But . . . people don't understand death! In order to conquer the idea of nothingness, humanity has had to evolve a system of existence in some kind of peaceful land after death—plus a 'Hell' for those who disagree with them!

"The world would have been spared a lot of pain and suffering if Christianity had evolved into a religion of tolerance as, say, Taoism or Buddhism. Instead the religion of the Bible is as intolerant and militaristic as any Hitler . . . a religion that has to go out and conquer the world—and God help those who disagree with it, if you'll pardon the pun! Why do you think such hymns as 'Mine Eyes Have

42

Seen the Glory,' and 'Onward, Christian Soldiers' are so popular?

"The great tragedy is that none of it, not a damned bit of it, has anything to do with the real creator of this universe! The 'god' of Christianity is nothing more than a mental idol, a god of the man fashioned in the likeness of the great monarchs of Chaldea, Persia and Egypt!"

Cleevis snapped, "You are saying that Christianity is not a religion of peace? Is that what you mean, Death Merchant?"

"I deal only in facts!" Camellion shot back. "And I have refused to let myself be influenced by a religion that is more interested in money than in men! Behind the Biblical idea of 'Jehovah' stands a political pattern of tyranny, of rule by violence, of mental and moral slavery. And so is everyone else who happens to be familiar with the Bible— and I'm speaking of religious tyranny! Remember that!"

"I happen to be familiar with the Bible," Cleevis growled, "and I don't feel Christianity is intolerant. I just think you're prejudiced."

Pursing his lips, Camellion leaned back and yawned, thinking that to be ignorant of one's ignorance is truly the malady of ignorance!

"Since you're familiar with the Bible," he said slowly, looking at Cleevis, "perhaps you can tell me when Jesus Christ was actually born—assuming he ever lived in the first place!

"Luke says Christ was born when Cyrenius was governor! But Cyrenius was not appointed governor until after the death of Herod, and the taxing could not have taken place until after ten years *after* the birth of Christ. Luke may have been 'inspired,' but he still made a ten-year mistake!

"Matthew says nothing about the date of the birth, except that Christ was born when Herod was king. It has been proved that Herod had been dead ten years before the taxing under Cyrenius. Therefore, if Luke is telling the truth, Joseph, being warned by an angel, fled from the hatred of Herod ten years after Herod was dead! If Matthew and Luke are both right, Christ was taken to Egypt ten years *before* He was born, and Herod killed all the babies *after* he—and I mean Herod—was dead! How about it, Red? Can you clear up the confusion for me?"

With an angry motion, his face clouded with confusion, Cleevis stubbed out his cigarette, but before he could speak, the Death Merchant hit him with another barrage of Biblical inconsistencies.

"Matthew and Luke both try to show that Mr. Christ was of the blood of David and that he was a descendant of that whore-mongering King!

"Well now, since both of those boys were 'inspired' by the so-called Holy Spirit, they ought to agree with each other—but they don't!

"According to Matthew there were between David and Jesus twenty-seven generations and he gives all the names.

"According to Luke there were between David and Jesus forty-two generations and he gives all the names!

"In these genealogies there is a difference between David and Jesus of some fourteen or fifteen generations!

"How about that, Red? Can you explain how such two 'inspired' writers could make such a mistake?"

Cleevis made a snorting noise, his nostrils flaring, and angrily took another cigarette from the pack.

Wiseloggle had pushed his chair back slightly from the table and sat watching the Death Merchant and Cleevis, his eyes mere slits. Cleevis was a fool! He should have known better than to lock intellectual horns with Camellion. Time to pull Red out before he lost his temper!

"I suggest we get back to the business at hand," Wiseloggle said loudly. He shifted from Cleevis and turned to the Death Merchant, hoping Red would take the hint.

Relieved at being rescued, Cleevis nodded heavily and lighted his cigarette, snapping shut the lighter with an exaggerated flourish.

"Camellion, you'll leave for Europe just as soon as C.W. Silvestter heads for Australia," he said in a businesslike voice, thinking that as soon as he could get to a Bible, he would check the genealogy of Jesus Christ! That damned Camellion! He was like a computer that had been programmed with the Encyclopedia Britannica! All right!

44

Now he could ask why he had to go to Europe to make a strike against the Silvestter base in Australia!

The Death Merchant toyed with the box of lemon drops. He had placed the box flat on the table and was tapping each end with his fingers.

"The 'hole in the dike'! What have you done about it?" Camellion asked in a gentle voice, his head lowered as he continued to play with the box. "We all know there's a double somewhere along the line, but everyone wants to pretend he doesn't exist!"

He raised his head, his almost savage stare first slamming into a surprised Wiseloggle, then moving to a startled Cleevis.

"You can hardly say the last deal was nothing but my paranoid imaginings, unless you're ready to explain how eight New Dawn dimwits were waiting for me and Brothers in the cemetery! Or when my car was rigged with a dozen sticks of dynamite! How do you explain that? I'd have been blown all the way to Gowanus Bay if I hadn't set up my own particular precautions against such a cute little whack-out trap!"

Very slowly Cleevis rubbed his chin with his cupped hand.

"There can't be a leak," he said gruffly, "not in the sense that anyone in our apparatus is a double agent. What you're suggesting simply isn't so. Therefore, there has to be another explanation for the traps laid for you. There has to be! Hell, you've made a lot of enemies over the years! Take the Mafia for example. Every major 'family' in the country would like to see six feet of dirt pushing you down in the ground!"

"Steele used to be in the CIA," Nat Wiseloggle pointed out. "He knows our methods and has built up a first-rate private intelligence system for Silvestter. That's your spy and informer—New Dawn's intelligence apparatus! It's definitely not a leak in the CIA!"

Returning the box of lemon drops to his pocket, Camellion didn't pursue the matter. He had survived all these years and was confident he'd be around quite a few more. *Let the CIA live in an idiot's world of rosy myopia and re-*

45

fuse to believe that Silvestter could buy one of its "incorruptible" agents—I know better! I'll find the double in my own way, and I'll give him my own brand of justice!

"You won't have any trouble in Rome; I'm sure of that," Cleevis said solemnly and reached into his inside coat pocket, giving Camellion short curious glances and wondering why he hadn't mentioned Europe. "You'll be in charge of Plan *Poaka*, but only the Director knows the agents who will be working under you. With the exception of Nat here, they'll all be foreign agents—Russian, British, French, and Australian! How does that grab you?"

Camellion's scraggy face, shadowed as it was in the light of the high-intensity lamp, looked sinister—and remained blank.

Cleevis pulled a long white envelope from his coat pocket and placed it on the table in front of Camellion, who didn't offer to pick it up, his apparent indifference another annoyance to Cleevis. He ground his teeth in irritation, tapping ash from his cigarette.

Nat Wiseloggle took over the briefing. "Open the envelope, Camellion. Our orders are that you open the envelope in front of us."

The Death Merchant removed a sheet of paper—folded like a letter—from the envelope, unfolded it and placed it flat on the table. He looked at the drawing on the paper.

"Do you know what that is?" Wiseloggle asked.

"A Necker cube. The term, used in psychology, indicates an ambiguous figure consisting of a cube whose edges fluctuate in perspective. I assume that somewhere in the lines is a micro-dot!"

"You don't have a magnifier at your hotel?" asked Cleevis, who then answered his own question. "No, I don't suppose you do. It doesn't make any difference because our orders include seeing to it that you magnify your instruction dot here at Station Yc/2B. You are to do it alone, in a closed room, with no one else present. Do you understand?"

"Only you and the Director will know those instructions, where and how you're to meet the other agents in Rome," said Wiseloggle. "There is no possible way that New Dawn

46

can learn the contents of the micro-dot, which you will read and memorize, then burn."

"Unless you talk in your sleep or the 'Old Man's' working for C.W. Silvestter!" said Ceevis, with a high forced laugh. At the moment, he gave Camellion the impression of a man motivated by secondary elaboration, the tendency for one to reassure himself by making light of a serious matter.

"The other agents are also unknown to each other," Wiseloggle went on, moving his hands over his blond hair. "They will meet for the first time when you and they assemble in Rome."

The Death Merchant looked at Wiseloggle. "You said that you're included in Plan *Poaka*. You will be going to Rome with me?"

"No, not with you," Wiseloggle answered, glancing toward Cleevis, who had pushed back his chair and was rising.

"I'm going to the john," Red said and left the room.

Resumed Wiseloggle, "We have men watching the Silvestter Building and Silvestter's mansion on Long Island. Once we conclude that he's left the country and is on his way to Australia, you and I will have a final meeting here at Station Yc/2B, after which you'll leave for Italy. All I know at this point is that I'll meet you in Rome. I won't get my final orders until after you've departed for Europe. The Hub figures such precautionary measures should insure top security!"

Folding the sheet of paper, Camellion returned it to the envelope, which he put in his right coat pocket.

Wiseloggle folded his hands on the table, smiled and said pleasantly, "I can't feature your having any trouble in Rome—or maybe I should say 'we,' since I'll probably be flying in right behind you. But if something should go wrong, you'll be able to handle it! I'm still amazed when I think of the way you extricated yourself from the trap in the cemetery! You were damn lucky, Camellion! And so were a lot of bystanders. My God! If the people attending that funeral had been closer to the shooting—what the New York papers would have made of that!"

The Death Merchant remained silent, his mouth twisted in a crooked kind of smile. Wiseloggle glanced at his wristwatch, picked up his pipe and knocked the ashes from the bowl into the ashtray. He stood up, stretching slightly.

"Let's have some coffee or a drink; then you can get to work on the micro-dot," he suggested, turning and moving toward the door.

Camellion picked up his coat from the back of the chair and followed Wiseloggle down a short hallway into the living room, which was decorated in a Chinese motif, the wall panels of black lacquer thinly patterned in red-and-gold dragons, glistening under the light of two lamps with fringed silk shades. The lamps stood on small teakwood tables, each table at the end of a long couch, on which sat Nelson S. Pines and Gloria Humphries, the two of them watching the ten o'clock news on television. In front of them, on another low teakwood table, was a stainless-steel coffeemaker, resting on a silver tray; next to it, on another tray, were cups, spoons, a cream pitcher and a sugar bowl.

Nelson Pines waved his hand hospitably toward the coffeemaker as Gloria Humphries got up and turned off the television set.

The Death Merchant considered Plan *Poaka* something right out of Weirdsville! *I wonder what bright boy thought that one up!* He didn't like the idea of going into Rome "blind." He particularly disliked having all his moves monitored and reported back to Silvestter and Steele.

Minutes later—after Red Cleevis had returned from the bathroom and the five of them were drinking coffee and making smalltalk—the Death Merchant had decided what he would have to do. *I'll play the game their way and still beat them. It will be extremely dangerous, but isn't living itself?*

"Nelson, we need an E-S Magnifier and screen," Cleevis said to Pines. "Camellion has some period work to do."

"There's one in our bedroom he can use," Pines said, looking toward the Death Merchant. "I'll get it out for you when you're ready, Mr. Camellion."

He was a fair-haired, fair-complexioned young man in

48

his late twenties. His eyes were sharply intelligent, but set too far apart.

Camellion agreed with a nod of his head, pretending not to notice that Gloria Humphries was trying hard to conceal her obvious embarrassment over Nelson's having referred to the bedroom as theirs. Gloria was aware that the other men in the room knew that she and Nelson weren't married, and he had to open his big mouth and let them know that he and she were sleeping together.

Gloria was a short, thick-bodied rather than fat woman of about thirty, and not unattractive, her mouth small but full-lipped. The first thing you noticed about her was the long black hair, hanging down around her neck and shoulders, then her eyes: long, heavy-lidded, of an India-ink blackness . . .

On one side of the living room was a large red-and-green macaw, standing on a tall wooden perch, held to the rounded horizontal stick by a small gold chain around one leg, its wicked eyes glaring at Camellion, Cleevis and Wiseloggle, all of whom the bird considered intruders. The bird fluttered its feathers, scraped its claws on the perch like a bull getting ready to charge, and threw back its beak to utter an inhuman screech of disapproval.

"Damn it, Oswald! Shut Up!" Gloria yelled back.

Again Oswald set up an unholy scream!

"If he's not yelling at us, she's yelling at him!" Nelson explained with a grin. "He belongs to her and hates my guts!"

The Death Merchant put his coffee cup on the teakwood table in front of the couch, stood up, and turned to Nelson.

"I'd appreciate your showing me the magnifier," he said.

"Sure thing. Follow me," Nelson said agreeably. He stood up, indicating that Camellion should accompany him.

Red Cleevis waited until Pines and the Death Merchant had left the room; he then lit a cigarette and smiled at Gloria.

"Do you have a Bible handy?" he asked. "There's something in the New Testament I'd like to check . . ."

CHAPTER FOUR

In his seventies, dressed in a suit that had been out of style even before the era of Mussolini, the man, hunched over, walked slowly along the Via di S. Gregorio, moving in a direction that would eventually take him to the *Colosseo,* or, as the English history books call it, the Colosseum.

The old man had a face as timeless as the wind, leathery and age-blown . . . his eyes deep-set and concealed behind dark glasses . . . his pale and bloodless-looking lips almost hidden by a thick handlebar mustache, each end drooping down over his wrinkled cheeks, almost to the length of his stubby gray-white beard.

No one paid any attention to the man as he shuffled along, leaning now and then on a plain wooden cane. Rome was full of septuagenarians trapped in a limbo of existence . . . useless in life but unable to die . . .

Those few who did give the old man a quick glance as they passed him might have thought there was something wrong with his white hair, which, as thick as it was, seemed to have prevented him from pulling his hat down firmly on his head. His coat, of some thin brown material, was almost thread bare and certainly far too long; at times the old boy had to push it completely aside before dipping into the pocket of rather baggy trousers and fishing out a lemon drop.

Richard Camellion couldn't have cared less how he looked. Appearing to be what he was not had been his stock-in-trade for years and had saved his life on more than a dozen occasions. Anyhow the coat more than adequately concealed the twin bulges of the powerful .357 Magnum revolvers snuggled in shoulder holsters.

A pessimist who was forever suspicious of sunny skies, Camellion didn't believe for a moment that his luck wouldn't turn twice as sour as vinegar. It had to! It always did! Reluctantly, however, he had to admit that so far the mission had progressed smoothly. The last four days had been as tranquil as a summer picnic in Arkansas, his expert eyes and danger-conditioned mind had not detected anything the least bit suspicious.

He had taken a Pan Am flight from New York to Rome disguised as Father Vincent Scheuler (Sts. Peter and Paul Parish, St. Louis, Missouri), an elderly white-haired priest who, so he confided to other passengers, was fulfilling the dream of a lifetime: a visit to Rome, to the Eternal City. Glory to the Most High! He would actually get to stand in St. Peter's Basilica, after all these years of waiting and hoping! He would be able to visit the Catacombs, and pray at all the other holy places. Why, with any luck, he might even get a glimpse of His Holiness, the Pope himself!

Camellion changed disguises after arriving at the Leonardo da Vinci Airport and renting a room at the airport's hotel. Some three hours later he had taken a bus into Roma (thinking that prices had risen since his last visit; this time the bus fare for the twenty-two miles was 1600 lire, about $2.60 American) and had registered at the Americana di Roma, a motel-type hotel with two swimming pools, on the Via Aurelia. He was now Roderick K. Snell, a bald, nearsighted businessman from Gary, Indiana —red-faced, loud-talking, and with a weakness for alcohol . . .

According to the carefully worked-out schedule, he would have to remain "on ice," inactive for the next two days. He could either sit in his hotel room and say his prayers or loaf around the dirty city and gawk at all the "famous sights," which he had seen a couple dozen times before. Nevertheless, he chose to move about the city. If any New Dawn assassins were lurking about, why not make it easy for the slobs of Satan?

Nothing happened! He loafed about the city, spending some time on the east bank, where most of modern Rome and much of ancient Rome is located, the approximate center of this area, of the broad, converging avenues, being the Piazza Venezia.

Drinking Strega brandy or espresso, he visited the restaurants of the Via del Corso, the busiest thoroughfare of the city, which leads north from the Piazza Venezia, and to the east of which lies the most fashionable section of the Italian capital, the center of shops and business and modern hotels.

To break the monotony he joined a guided tour. With several dozen other rubbernecking tourists, he walked around the ruins of the Colosseum and the Forum, bored to distraction. He became even more restless as the guide conducted the party through the Pantheon and the Palazzo Venezia, a handsome Renaissance palace built about 1450 for a cardinal who, when he bacame Pope Paul II, used it as his residence, as did other popes after him. *That's right,* thought Camellion, *don't lay up worldly treasures! Instead give it all to the Church!*

Naturally the guided tour included St. Peter's Cathedral (more correctly called the Basilica of St. Peter), the largest church in the world, whose enormous interior was surprisingly bright, rich with marble mosaic, and religious memorials.

On the morning of his third day in Rome the Death Merchant changed into the disguise of an elderly Italian and, carrying a large suitcase, slipped cautiously from the Americana di Roma. By cab he went across the city to one of the inexpensive *pensioni,* or private lodging houses—this one the *Scalinata di Spagna*—and registered as Signor Vito Campanella.

In the afternoon he went to the office of the American Express company and inquired if he had any mail waiting there for him. There was a letter, which the clerk handed Camellion after the Death Merchant presented expertly forged credentials identifying him as "Vito Roberto Campanella."

Back in his room Camellion opened the brown envelope, which contained a smaller envelope. Inside the smaller envelope were two photographs—front and profile—of a man

52

and three sheets of coded instructions. *At last we'll get some action!*

The Death Merchant decoded the orders, memorized them, burned them, and flushed the ashes down the toilet bowl. But he kept the two photos.

Smiling, he stretched out on the bed. Fine! Tomorrow afternoon, at 3:30, at the Colosseum, he would make contact with the first agent—Lieutenant Colonel Pavel Telpuchovskii of the KGB/GRU, the Soviet Union's contribution to Plan *Poaka*.

Camellion stared at the ceiling, thinking . . . Nat Wiseloggle would also be arriving tomorrow and registering at the Americana di Roma. Only a week ago, back in New York, the two men had met in Camellion's tiny apartment at the Edison Hotel. Wiseloggle had arrived with a couple of suitcases and explained that he was taking a plane for "The Hub" that same day: "I'll see you in Rome . . ."

At ease in his disguise as Vito Campanella, the Death Merchant stared at the Colosseum, the gigantic weather-worn ellipse looming up sinisterly in the distance, the old stones mute testimony to the blood that had been spilled within the six acres they enclosed. And as the Death Merchant approached the amphitheater that had been the largest and most important in the Roman Empire, it seemed that he could hear 50,000 spectators roaring—pointing thumbs down—for the death of some unfortunate gladiator or pathetic Christian about to be martyred.

Originally the eighty entrances of the Colosseum had been arranged so that the entire building could be cleared in a very short while, but owing to structural weaknesses that had developed over the ages, many of the entrances were now closed off. However, there were still some twenty or thirty entrances through which tourists were coming and going.

"Vito Campanella" walked through one of the entrances with a group of tourists . . . hoping for Heaven, but knowing what he would do if he met Hell . . . He knew that finding Pavel Telpuchovskii would require some hard and tedious searching.

53

Although the inside area wasn't all that large, there were quite a few tourists moving around. Much of the ground level was a mish-mash of stones, some as large as six feet square. A couple of acres had been excavated, and they lay exposed, revealing a network of rooms and passageways that two-thousand years in the past had imprisoned the victims, both human and animal, to be tortured and slaughtered during the games. Wooden walks with railings led down into the dungeons, which appeared to be almost diabolical in the bright sunlight. Italian *Touristi* guards were stationed at various positions, not only in the underground areas, but also in other sections of the ancient Colosseum, along the high galleries and sections being repaired. Their job was to funnel the tourists along the proper routes and prevent them from going into areas that were unsafe.

The Death Merchant looked around him. Blue sky above, messed up with a lot of scattered clouds. Around him rose the old stone galleries, as if waiting to fall on him, as if they were his bitter enemy. For a second he had the absurd impression that he was standing in the bottom of a tremendous stone bowl whose rounded sides had been carved into thousands of seats, many of which were now wrecked, the stones removed.

This is one hell of a way to make a living! Camellion thought. *But it beats working for one's bread and beans!*

His eyes searched the knots and clusters of tourists, many of whom were laughing and taking snapshots of each other posed against the old stones; others were serious-faced, listening solemnly and attentively as guides explained the history of the *Colosseo* and gave a running commentary on the various sections and how they had been used.

Camellion moved about the ground level, his eyes constantly moving, searching for the man in the two photographs. Some fifteen minutes later he found Pavel Telpuchovskii . . . a tall, well-built man of about thirty-five, standing close to one of the catwalks leading down into the excavated sections and dressed as the plan sheets said he would be—light green slacks, Italian sports shoes, and a green and beige jacket. He was bareheaded.

The Death Merchant walked over to the KGB agent and spoke to him in Russian. "Good afternoon, Pavel Telpuchovskii. Are you prepared to eat *poaka* in the land of kaolas and numbats!"

Telpuchovskii didn't turn toward Camellion; he continued to look away from the Death Merchant, his eyes probing the galleries. Like Camellion, a professional, the Russian was also prepared for any eventuality.

His reply fitted into the second half of the contact code.

"They eat *poaka* only in New Zealand," he said in a low voice. "I would rather dine on *cotleta pojarskaya* in *Moskva.*"

Camellion completed the third and final part of the contact code.

"*Da,* chicken cutlets are very tasty. It is a specialty of the *Aragvi* restaurant in Moscow—I'm Richard Camellion."

To his left, high in the galleries, he noticed a couple looking down at him and the Russian intelligence agent.

Telpuchovskii's sharp, dispassionate features softened slightly. There was a dark shadow over his full, heavy face; evidently he was one of those men who had to shave twice a day.

"I guessed you were the Death Merchant," he said softly. "Your talent for disguises is well known . . . a talent that in the past has caused much concern on Arbat Square," he added, proving he wasn't without humor by referring to KGB headquarters at the *Arbatskaya Ploshchad,* on the opposite side of the Kremlin from Lubianka prison.

Camellion couldn't help but smile. "And no doubt at thirty-four Maurice Thorez Quay," Camellion said, which was the address of the main building of the Ministry of Defense, where the *Glavnoye Razvedyvatelnoye* had its headquarters—the GRU, the Soviet Union's worldwide intelligence/espionage apparatus.

The Death Merchant saw the man in the distance, 450 feet away, up in the fifth tier of seats, staring down at him and the Russian.

"Have you spotted him," he asked the Russian, moving his hands into his coat and unsnapping the straps over the trigger guards of the Magnums in his shoulder holsters, "and the couple to the left, up in the galleries?"

"There are two more behind us!" the Russian replied. "I spotted them five minutes ago." Suspicion covered his brow like a high fever. "There is no way they could have known my identity in advance. They had to have followed you! But how could they have known the disguise you would use, unless there is a leak in your main American *Otdel?*"

"There is!" Camellion admitted grimly, glancing at the Russian who was slowly turning around. "But we haven't time to—"

Along with the Russian, Camellion flung himself between two large stone blocks as the New Dawn assassins, springing the trap, opened fire. The Colosseum rang with the echoes of at least a half-dozen shots, two of them rifles!

Coming close to Camellion and Telpuchovskii, the slugs chipped stone, while the loud gunfire triggered instant panic among the tourists and guides. Men cried out in alarm! Women screamed in terror! And the rush to safety, away from the area, began, people shoving against each other in blind fear.

"There's at least seven of the *galvankiks!*" Telpuchovskii muttered, glancing at Camellion. "And they have us boxed in. Any suggestions, my American friend?"

"We've got to draw them out," Camellion said. He noticed that the Russian had pulled two 9-mm Stechkin Machine Pistols from shoulder holsters, but that he hadn't changed the pistols to full automatic firing. "We'll get them to return the fire—which won't be hard to do—and I'll pretend to catch a slug. If we're lucky, they'll toss away caution and expose themselves."

They rose up and snapped off two shots in the direction of the couple in the galleries, and at the man—now to their right—in the fifth tier.

Instantly a tornado of shots rang out in reply, not only from the three in front, but also from four or five other gunmen to the rear of the Death Merchant and the Russian agent—the slugs coming closer than the previous blast.

One bullet actually cut through the left sleeve of the

56

GRU man's coat, to the side of his wrist, while several other pieces of steel death came within inches of both sides of Camellion's neck. Still another tore through his old-fashioned hat, knocking it off his head, exposing his thick, white wig-mounted hair.

With a very loud cry of false pain, Camellion jerked back and, for only a fraction of a second, reared up before falling over to one side, in such a manner that around one edge of the back stone he could look up at the galleries to their rear.

Pavel Telpuchovskii dropped to the other end of the front stone, switching his stechkins to full automatic.

The murderous couple to the left stood up! In their elation over thinking they had hit Camellion, they had momentarily forgotten that Telpuchovskii was still in action. The man, young and hollow-faced, held a very short-barreled rifle, the kind that could be dismantled and carried in a small bag. The woman appeared to be holding some kind of revolver.

She dropped her weapon, screamed in agony, and fell backward when Telpuchovskii, firing from around the corner of the stone, slammed three 9-mm slugs into her white blouse, right between her pointed boobs! Just as quickly he let her partner have four quick rounds in the belly. The rifle slid from the man's hands as he fell forward and pitched down the steps, all the way to the gallery below.

Two other gunmen in the tiers had risen. Camellion was watching. Twenty feet apart but standing on the same gallery, they had poked up their heads and shoulders—not very much, not at such a distance! But it was enough for the Death Merchant! His twin .357s roared and one hood's head burst like a balloon as the big slug exploded his skull. He didn't yell. He had died too fast for the impulse of pain to have been transmitted to his steel-chopped brain!

The other man wasn't as lucky! Camellion's slug tore through his left earlobe, the shock of the bullet's passing through flesh knocking him around, spinning him like a top! Pain and fear did the rest. He reared up sideways. *You poor dumbell!* Camellion immediately put a slug

57

through his right hip, the round boring through his colon and smashing out his left hip. Whoever the slob was, he would never be constipated again! Both hips smashed, almost insane with agony, the New Dawn terrorist crumbled to the space in front of the seats. He'd be dead and in the basement of hell by the time the Italian *polizia* found him.

Two more New Dawn assassins in the galleries curving within Camellion's gaze had also half-exposed themselves, but since they were almost a hundred feet to the left of the two men the Death Merchant had just killed, they could only look down at an angle that prevented them from seeing the back corner of the stone from which Camellion had fired.

Nor could the Death Merchant see them, but he knew they were there, somewhere, having heard their earlier shots—and he had an excellent ear for distance.

More than a little terrified, because they knew they were up against experts who could fire with deadly accuracy, the two men made a quick decision: They would go to the highest gallery and take up a safer position, one that would enable them to look down between the two stones protecting Camellion and Telpuchovskii.

Cautiously, crouching far down, they began moving upward. That was their mistake. Camellion had inched around to the other end of the stone and, peering upward around the corner, saw the tops of their backs.

Like shooting turtles! Again the Magnums boomed! A blunt-nosed .357 slug bored into one man's back, making spinach of his spinal cord and tearing out his liver as it sped out his front. He fell flat on his face and, dead, lay there like a deflated paper bag, his blood running into the thick gray dust.

Camellion's second slug missed, barely grazing the other man's back, stinging his shoulder on its journey skyward. A battle-hardened professional would have instantly fallen flat and remained there. This joker didn't. Instead he did the worst possible thing. He lost his head and rose up, hoping to succeed in his dash to the last tier upward, only ten feet away. Then he lost his life as the Death Merchant put a slug between his shoulder blades. The man died faster than his legs could turn to rubber, a big, bloody hole, the size of a baby's fist, in the center of his chest, marking the exit of the bullet.

The remaining assassin on the opposite gallery, the man decked out in a cassock, had kept up a steady stream of fire at Pavel Telpuchovskii, who was at a distinct and dangerous disadvantage. For one thing, the phony priest was using his head—he was staying put! For another, he had zeroed in on the Russian, having steadied the short barrel of his PK-Carbine across the top of a stone, in contrast to Pavel who, snap-firing around the corner, didn't have time to aim.

Camellion noticed that low-profile ribs with accuracy tuners, devices that improved both aim and accuracy, had been fitted to the slides of the Russian's machine pistols.

"Listen," Camellion said, "I've got an idea. I'll get his attention by firing from the other corner. That should take his attention off you for a few seconds. Do you think you can pick him off with those super-pistols of yours in so short a time?"

Telpuchovskii considered the plan, his face as gloomy as a Ukrainian peasant's. "If that *sibujek's* really any good with that rifle, one of us could get killed—you know that! If you're right, that's exactly what could happen. Personally, my *Amerikanski* comrade, I'd rather be wrong and alive, than right and dead!"

He stuck a pistol around his side of the stone and snapped off a shot. He hardly had time to pull his hand back when the man with the rifle fired back.

Zingggggggg! The high-powered rifle slug stuck the stone and angled off!

"I prefer being right and remaining alive!" Camellion said as he reloaded his Magnums. "We can't move from here until we eliminate him. Take a look around. The tourists and guides have made like rabbits. What do you think will happen when the *Carabinieri* get here? I've had experience with those goofs! They fire on anything that moves when they go into action."

"*Da*. you are right!" Telpuchovskii said. "Open fire when you're ready!"

Camellion thrust his twin Magnums around the edge of the stone on his side and, judging the distance and angle from the previous rifle shot, pulled the triggers of the Magnums—twice on each revolver.

The four slugs didn't come close to the New Dawn assassin; they struck the stones of the tier above his head. However, Camellion's shots did cause him to turn his head slightly toward the end of the stone from which Camellion had fired.

That short pause was all Telpuchovskii needed. Surprising Camellion by rearing up, one hand steadying the wrist of the arm holding the machine pistol, he aimed and emptied the weapon at the tiny blob that was the man's head! Five slugs missed! Two didn't. The first entered the man's mouth and blew his throat and neck apart, the second hit him high on the forehead, taking off the top of his skull. He slumped, Death (the terminal illness we're all born with) taking over completely.

The Death Merchant studied the now-empty bowl like amphitheater, over which hung a sinister silence. Between the arches of each story were mammoth columns—some of the Doric order, others of the Ionic and Corinthian—which had been applied as decoration to the supporting tiers behind them, the nonstructural columns illustrating the use of structural devices for purely aesthetic purposes. Without these decorative accents, much of the imposing vigor of the arches following the long oval wall would have been lost in monotonous repetition.

But Camellion was not interested in the architecture of Ancient Rome. Escape from the giant pile of useless stones was what concerned him! And it was a long, long way to the nearest outside entrance! He disliked thinking about what would happen if he and Telpuchovskii, going out, met the *Carabinieri* coming in! There would be a lot of dead spaghetti, and Camellion didn't like to waste innocent people. He didn't intend to let those same innocent people shoot him down either!

"We've no choice. We'll have to run for it," he said, watching the Ivan who was reloading his machine pistols, "unless you have a better suggestion."

60

Telpuchovskii nodded toward the catwalk leading down to the network of excavated underground rooms and passageways. The catwalk was only twenty feet away.

"We can get to the outside by going through the catacombs," he said. I got here a few hours ahead of you and made a complete reconnaissance down there. One passage leads out underneath the sidewalk; it's blocked off on the inside and outside both, but we won't have any trouble squeezing by the barriers."

Camellion removed his dark glasses, his blue eyes two question marks. Was the Ivan actually serious?

Correctly deducing Camellion's thoughts, Telpuchovskii smiled fatalistically. He had eaten a lot of *blascokivik!* His teeth were very white and even.

"I agree," he said, his manner curt and direct. "If you or I had planned this ambush, we'd have more *Mokryye Dela* boys down there as backups. Any intelligent enemy would do the same thing."

His use of the term *Mokryye Dela* told the Death Merchant what he had wanted to know: Telpuchovskii was an expert in the KGB murder and kill-quick section, an agent of the Thirteenth Department, for only Soviet assassins used the phrase so loosely and familiarly—*Mokryye Dela,* which translated into English meant "wet affairs." In the connotation that Telpuchovskii had used it, it meant "blood-wet," such as in murder and violent death.

"If so," the Russian went on, "the odds are that there will be less of the enemy than of the Italian police, which we might meet if we took one of the ground-level exits. Agreed?"

Without waiting for Camellion to reply, Pavel's eyes swept around the Colosseum. He moved quickly then toward the catwalk leading downward, the two Stechkins hanging loosely in his hands. Camellion caught up to him very quickly. *This Ivan has nerve and knowhow! The GRU brains sent a good man—at least in the kill department . . .*

At a slow trot they ran down the ramp, across which, spaced every two feet, a small board took the place of what would ordinarily have been a step: And when they came to the end of the ramp, they were at least twenty feet below the ground level of the Colosseum.

Stretching out ahead of them was a thirty-foot passageway, two high walls of gray travertine stone on either side. The floor was also of stone. Blue sky above, stretching outward into infinity.

Richard and Pavel were halfway down the passage when what they feared might happen—did! Two men came at a slow trot around the right corner of the passage, one man carrying an attaché case, from which ran a twisted wire that ended in an earplug in the man's ear. In his other hand he carried an Italian .32-caliber Bernardelli pistol. The other joker—who also looked like a Sicilian—carried a 9-mm FNA submachine gun!

For a moment the two meatballs hesitated, alarm and surprise opening their mouths and widening their eyes. In a frenzy they raised their weapons and began firing, the man with the attaché case yelling in a loud voice, "They're down here!"

He triggered off two quick rounds at Telpuchovskii, who on his side of the passage was directly in front of him, but the Russian hadn't wasted time looking at the scenery. He fired as he dropped flat, his slug catching the wild-looking wop in his left shoulder. The man cried out in pain and staggered back from the mouth of the passage, half-falling to the left. The Russian's second slug smacked him in the calf of one leg. He dropped his pistol and sank to his knees . . .

The man with the submachine gun—he looked as if he had bumped into a case of walking leprosy—blew off a long blast of pure nine-millimeter death at the Merchant of Death, who dived sideways and down, firing both Magnums as he did so! The vicious lines of machine-gun slugs burned the air extremely close to Camellion, some of them boring through the side of his flapping coat—but close was not good enough.

His two slugs didn't miss! They slammed into the spaghetti elbow bender, slicing upward through his gut and banging into his breastbone with ten times the force of a pickax thrown by a homicidal maniac, both bullets knocking him six feet backward. Without as much as a *Mama mia!* the garlic snapper fell to his back, as broken as a thousand-piece jigsaw puzzle with half the pieces missing!

It was obvious to Camellion and Telpuchovskii that the man with the attaché case had yelled a warning to other troops in the labyrinth of rooms and passageways.

"Get that attaché case!" Camellion hissed at Pavel. For years he had played his hunches, like a dice nut, and he was usually right! Now his intuition was almost screaming that the case contained a clue as to how the New Dawn assassins had seen through his disguise as "Vito Campanella."

While Pavel rushed into a room to the left, intending to cut through the series of ancient doorways to reach the wounded man with the attaché case, the Death Merchant stuck the Magnums in his belt, scooped up the FNA submachine gun, and charged into a room to his right. The empty room contained two doorways, one leading off to a forward room, the other opening to another passageway. Camellion chose the corridor and, practically tiptoeing across the cell, stuck his head around the corner of the doorway. Down the passage, about twenty-five feet in front of him, three men were coming up in a slow creep, all three wearing dark glasses, dressed in sports clothes, and carrying pistols. *Well, now! They look like extras in an Italian Mafia movie!*

"Buona fortuna, stupidos!" said Camellion, and he jumped into the passage, his finger squeezing the trigger of the submachine gun at precisely the same instant as two more men came into the passageway from another room toward its right end.

The FNA jumped in his hands, the muzzle flashing flame and belching slugs! One man got a cut-up job across his middle as the slugs churned the macaroni and Chianti he had eaten and drunk for lunch.

And then the submachine gun jammed, becoming as useless as a one-legged man at an arse-kicking contest!

Camellion—a flurry of blurred motion—dived to the deck, jerking out the two Magnums and firing before his shoulder hit the uneven floor stones of the wide passageway.

The garlic gobblers didn't find it the least bit difficult to believe their good fortune. As members of the Roman branch of New Dawn, they attributed the jamming of Camellion's submachine gun to the interference of their Master—Satan.

If they had had time to think about it, two of the Satanists would have found that to expect a miracle from a mythical Satan was as ridiculous as limiting the power of a make-believe God—but *die* was the only thing they had time for!

One man gasped out a long, painful "AHhhhhhhh," as a .357 slug tore upward through his belly, bored out his back, and narrowly missed the crud behind him. Another Lucifer-lover got a .357 little joe in the throat, the slug sliding over his Adam's apple and right out the back of his head. A riot of red, the sap spun, gurgled, and fell sideways, a crimson stream spurting from his throat like the tail of a colored comet!

Meanwhile the third man snapped off three fast shots at the Death Merchant, who in the process of rolling over in the opposite direction was on his back. The Satanist's slugs tore up dust where the Death Merchant had been. At the same time the Death Merchant fired backward, sending off two rounds at the man he couldn't—at least for that tiny second—see. On his back, Camellion had to fire with the Magnums stretched out to the sides of his head! Blind firing that had better pay off. It didn't and it did! One slug missed; the other hit the man smack damn dab in the center of his low forehead, opening up his brain case as though it had a zipper! It was *Arrivederla* to Life and *Come sta* to Death for the meatball! He died on the spot, pieces of bone, blood, hair, and brains flying out into the muggy air.

The two remaining New Dawners decided not to rely on Satan for protection, but on down-to-earth common sense. The slug that had missed one joker had barely grazed the temple of one of the men still on his feet. That was enough for him! Before Camellion—by now he had rolled over and was on his belly—could snap off a shot, the goofy guinea had scrammed through the doorway of a room to his left. His companion had the same idea of escape. He jumped through a doorway to his right.

Fudge!—Camellion jumped to his feet and practically threw himself through the partially wrecked doorway of the room directly opposite him, to the right—and almost got his head blown off!

The man, who had ducked into the room up the passageway, was crouched in the doorway connecting the two cell-like rooms, the pistol in his hand still smoking from the exploded cartridge whose slug had just left the barrel. The slug came so close to Camellion's flesh that it ripped not only through his coat but through a belt loop on his right side, even grazing the leather of the belt as it passed by.

Unable to stop his momentum, Camellion swung his right arm around and fired as he fell. He fired again as he hit the stones.

"Awkkkkkkk!" The Death Merchant chopped the man in the chest, and he squawked louder than Oswald, Gloria Humphries' macaw! The second little joe knocked him sideways, the steel catching him in the hip—both slugs giving him less chance for life than a snowball's chance in Vesuvius! He fell with all the swiftness of spaghetti caught bagless in a cloud burst, in Hell so fast he surprised even the devils in the lower pits.

A couple more fast shots from across the passageway, from the room to which the other garlic snapper had fled!

The sharp crack of a wop *pistola!* The deeper whoommmm of an Ivan 9-mm Strechkin!

Camellion ran into the room in front of him, rushed to the doorway, and looked out across the corridor.

"Howdy, buddy!" Pavel Telpuchovskii said mildly. He stood over the other dead creep, looking toward the Death Merchant and smiling.

"Where's the attaché case?" asked Camellion. His hand dipped into his coat pocket. He brought out shells and began reloading the Magnums.

"I checked the man who has it," Pavel replied. "He's not going anywhere. I thought you might need some help and"

—he waved the 9-mm Stechkin toward the corpse at his feet—"apparently you did."

The Russian paused and cocked his head, listening.

Camellion also heard the shouts from up above on the ground level.

The *Carabinieri* were pouring into the Colosseum!

The two intelligence experts locked eyes for a brief moment, both men thinking the same thing: If the wop cops on the ground level got to the excavated area, they could walk along the top of the walls and cut them to pieces!

Still on guard, Camellion and Telpuchovskii cut through the various room until they came to the lateral passage, at one end of which, propped up against the wall, was the man Pavel had shot in the shoulder and in the leg.

In agony, too weak to move, he glared up in hate at Camellion and the Russian, snarling weakly as Camellion bent down, jerked the earplug from the man's ear, and picked up the attaché case.

The man's mouth moved and he said weakly, "We m-made a mistake, but Satan, the Master, will see that you get—"

One of Telpuchovskii's Stechkins roared, the slug giving the man a face lift, one that blew his nose right through the back of his head.

"Everybody's wrong sometimes," he said, shoved the weapon back into its shoulder holster, and motioned for Camellion to follow him.

"This way," he said. "The passage that leads up onto the outside street level is this way. If we can reach the Via di S. Gregorio, we'll be half-safe. I've got a car parked there."

They left the corpse, ran down the short passage, turned inward, and raced down the corridor that began from the end of the ramp on which they had first come down into the excavation from the ground level. The end of this passage terminated into another areaway intersecting it, and Telpuchovskii took this entryway, turning to the right, Camellion, carrying the attaché case (it felt very heavy), right behind him. They hurried down the corridor, some fifty feet, to where it left the open excavation and moved out underneath the street. At this point a network of one-by-ten-inch boards cross-crossed the mouth of the opening, to prevent any tourist from entering the passage that lay beyond. But Camellion and Telpuchovskii were conducting their own tour.

Hurriedly they pulled loose one end of a board, loosening the nails almost to the middle of the slat. Camellion held one end pulled away, preventing it from snapping back into place, and the Russian inched through. Once on the other side, Telpuchovskii held the board outward while the Death Merchant slipped in; then he let it snap back into place.

They moved down the dark, dank passage, the sunlight having vanished once they had entered the section leading out underneath the sidewalk, the low stone roof only a foot or so above their heads.

As fast as they could, they moved down the tunnel, which narrowed as it turned and slanted upward toward the Via dei Fori Imperiali, the broad avenue that stretched along one side of the Colosseum to the ruins of the Forum, which at one time had been the heart and center of the old Roman Empire.

Finally they saw a broad shaft of yellow light slanting downward between the wooden barrier blocking the very end of the passage on the street level. They rounded a sharp turn and ran smack into bright sunshine that hit their faces and for a moment made them squint. A flight of narrow stone steps, as ancient as man's hope for peace, led upward to the opening in the sidewalk, by the outside wall of the Colosseum. The barrier, a wooden grill made of two-by-fours laid flat over the opening, looked like a formidable opponent. Richard and Pavel sighed in relief when they found that since it was not fastened to the sidewalk, all they had to do was place their backs against it and rear up in order to push it from the opening.

The wooden grill fell sideways, and Camellion and Telpuchovskii climbed over the last step onto the sidewalk. To their dismay they found that they were surrounded by at least a couple dozen bystanders, who peered at them with a mixture of fear and curiosity.

Damn! Four of the rubberneckers, not five feet away,

were *Carabinieri,* their Latin faces intense and suspicious, their Beretta submachine guns pointed directly at Camellion and his Russian partner in crime.

Telpuchovskii glanced fearfully at the Death Merchant, a glance clearly asking: Well, what do we do now? Camellion showed him!

"They're right behind us!" Camellion screamed in mock terror. *"Arab terrorists with hand grenades. They're going to kill everyone in sight!"*

He might as well have screamed that The End of the World was only one minute away, his false warning a bombshell that exploded and scattered instant panic through the crowd of men, women, and some children. They ran in every direction possible but up and down, the *Carabinieri* looking like refugees from a comic opera in their gaudy uniforms, running faster than the others!

"I'd give praise to the Lord if I weren't a Communist!" Pavel snickered as he and Camellion ran around the vast Colosseum toward the Via di S. Gregorio. Out in the road reinforcements of *Carabinieri* raced by, sirens wailing. There were even two armored cars. *A waste of time!* mused Camellion. *Those jokers couldn't catch a mild cold in a flu factory!*

They reached the Via di S. Gregorio, turned, and went down half a block to where the Russian agent had parked his rented Fiat. Soon they were driving north, headed toward the Via del Corso, Pavel at the wheel, a cigarette dangling from one corner of his mouth.

"How do we contact the other agent?" he asked. He drove cautiously, at a moderate rate of speed, his eyes on the road.

"The pyramid method," Camellion replied. "I was to meet you. Tonight you and I will meet the MI Six agent. He in turn with contact the Frenchie."

"And then?"

"And then we go to Australia."

Telpuchovskii nodded slowly. It was apparent he had something on his mind.

"My orders are to destroy the Silvestter Australian base at all costs," he said. "I assume yours are the same?"

"You assume correctly," Camellion replied. "Wipe the base from the face of the earth, even if I have to get myself blown apart to do it—which I don't intend to do! Get myself killed that is!"

The Russian's laugh sounded almost evil. "It's a dirty business we're in, my *Amerikanski* friend," he said philosophically. "To our *Otdel* chiefs, we don't count . . . not a damn bit!"

"We never have," Camellion said, "since the day we were born . . ."

CHAPTER FIVE

Satan himself would have had to work overtime to suspect that the mansion of Count Giuseppe Benso di Giolitti was a CIA safe house and one of the most important stations in Europe for almost thirteen years. The American spy agency had acquired the house because the fortunes of the Count had been wiped out by World War II. A di Giolitti had never worked for a living, not more than five hundred years, and that was the fate that would have overtaken the proud Italian nobleman had not the Central Intelligence Agency, well aware of his desperate plight, offered him a solution to his dilemma: The CIA would supply him with money to maintain him and his *signora* in the pre-World War II style that had been his normal way of life. In return Count di Giolitti would permit the Americans to use a tiny part of his vast mansion as a CIA station. *But before you decide,* the CIA had told him grimly, *remember this—if you agree, there will be no backing out for you. Cross us, change your mind and inform the Italian authorities, and you and your wife will have a fatal accident —and that includes your children! Capire?*

Indeed, the Count did understand! To him Heaven was wherever men believed passionately enough, while Hell was being broke and without a single lira! Convinced that his prayers to the Virgin (and to dozens of saints) had been answered, Count di Giolitti readily agreed to what the CIA had proposed.

The CIA went to work with its usual efficiency, installing a complex of rooms underneath the large wine cellar, the entire job disguised as "remodeling." Powerful short-wave transmitters were smuggled into the mansion, along with coding and decoding devices. There were even cots for agents who for some reason or other might have to remain hidden for a period of time.

Over the years "Station Iceberg" had become one of the chief Mediterranean CIA centers, into which flowed reports from agents in Africa and the Near East. There was no difficulty. Why should there have been? The di Giolitti name was respected throughout all Italy. For anyone to suspect the family mansion contained a CIA station was as unlikely as their considering it possible that the Pope was the head of a Russian spy ring or that God smoked pot!

The mansion itself sat like a valuable relic (which it was) on the Via Veneto, one of the most elegant streets in Rome. Only two blocks southeast of the Villa Borghese Park, the mansion was of the Lombard style of Roman-esque, the façade a two-storied arcade with a low gabled roof, flanked on both sides by small square towers. To the rear of the mansion was an open-air rectangular court surrounded by tall aleppo pines.

The only things surrounding Richard Camellion and the four men with him were walls painted hospital green and a low ceiling to match, from which hung two fluorescent light fixtures, each reflector containing two bulbs. Filing cabinets, modified so that the drawers could be secured by lock bars, ranged the length of one wall. Shortwave radio equipment filled one end of the long, low room, the opposite end having a door, and a desk surrounded by decoding devices.

Camellion sat at a card table, his back to the filing cabinets; the other men, also sitting on steel folding chairs, gathered around him, Nathaniel A.T. Wiseloggle to his right, Pavel Telpuchovskii to the Death Merchant's left. J. Warren Kimber and Philippe de Gasquet studied Camellion from in front of the card table.

"Does everyone understand the plan for our departure? Any suggestions for its implementation?" Camellion asked.

He held the Magnum he was cleaning up to the light and looked through the muzzle end of the barrel. Lowering the revolver, he snapped the cylinder into place and began wiping the gun with an oily rag.

Wiseloggle sat bent over, one hand braced on his knee, his forearm across his other knee, his hand holding the Kirsten pipe.

"You're doing the planning, Richard," he said placidly. "When I stop to think of how you and Pavel were almost killed this afternoon, I think your idea of taking the long way around is a good one. But I'm worried!" He sighed deeply, straightened up, and looked thoughtfully at his aluminum pipe. "You were in disguise, and yet the New Dawn trigger boys knew who you were. It's an utterly impossible situation! There was simply no way they could have known!"

"Ah, monsieur, it was Napoleon who said, 'Impossible . . . is not good French,'" Phillippe de Gasquet commented drily. "The fact remains that Camellion and Telpuchovskii were attacked, and because they were, we are forced to make the conclusion that the Silvestter *cochons* knew who they were shooting at. *Mesamis,* there is a hook in the apparatus!"

Of medium height and weight, shock-headed, and at thirty-eight growing florid of face, the Frenchman was not a handsome man, though he did have large and curiously sensitive eyes. It was the pencil-thin mustache that detracted from his looks. It looked as if it had been painted on his upper lip, giving him the appearance of a man trying to be something he was not. However, the way he looked had nothing to do with his ability, and that was why he was sitting in one of the rooms of Station Iceberg: He was one of the best agents in the SDECE, the *Service de Documentation Extérieure et de Contre-espionage*—the Service of

71

Foreign Documentation and Counterespionage, or the French Intelligence Service, comparable to the CIA.

"What assurance do we have that the New Dawn chaps won't use the same mysterious technique—whatever it may be—to deduce our flight plans from Rome to Bombay and plan another ambush?" asked J. Warren Kimber, his eyes, as steady as his voice, fixed on the Death Merchant, who was running a cleaning rod back and forth through the barrel of his other Magnum. "I suggest we plug the leak and pull out the hook as a prerequisite to our flying to Bombay and then taking the yacht to Brisbane. As I see it, we're depending on sheer luck!"

Gasquet nodded very slowly and folded his arms. "I would agree with you, were it not for the time factor involved," he said reflectively.

"We fly out from Leonardo da Vinci Airport tomorrow," Camellion said. There was such finality in his voice that Kimber took it to be a dismissal, and the Englishman didn't like being dismissed, especially by a man he considered an impudent American, any more than he appreciated the idea of working with a Russian GRU agent.

Kimber was a lean, hard-as-nails man with good shoulders, the wide mouth of an orator, and a high forehead. At forty-seven he was an old veteran of SIS, the British Secret Intelligence Service, which had emanated from the former Special Intelligence and MI 6. branches. An odd-looking Welshman with an enormous Adam's apple, he had thinning red hair as wiry as the rest of him. He would have been a fairly nice-looking man, if he hadn't had almost as much hair on his upper lip as he had on his head—an enormous mustache which, from the looks of it, he never trimmed.

"And if we are ambushed?" Kimber persisted in a gruff voice, almost glaring at Camellion. "What would you then propose? We must also consider the possibility that the New Dawn uglies won't hesitate to put a time bomb on the plane! I'll tell you something else, laddie: The fact that we have our own private plane makes no difference to me!"

"Oui! We can expect a time bomb!" Gasquet echoed, his voice low, as if he might have been talking to himself.

72

The Death Merchant was holding the Magnum up to the light and peering through its grooved barrel.

"They can't put a bomb on a plane they can't identify," he said ironically in reply to Kimber, continuing to look through the barrel. "Your people in Malta have orders to guard the plane at all times once it is selected. There will be three SIS agents on board at all times. They will also remain in the plane after it lands at da Vinci tomorrow morning. The same security precautions will be taken with our CIA people in Bombay. There will be no chance for New Dawn agents to get on board the boat and plant T-bombs—and that includes limpets to the hull!!"

Stroking his thick mustache, Kimber did not make any kind of reply, his long nose quivering in frustration.

Pavel Telpuchovskii, leaning out over the card table, stubbed out his cigarette in an ashtray, his dark eyes glancing at the Death Merchant. He had already made up his mind about the Frenchman and the Limey—useless baggage. *Da . . . narodnyie mstiteli!* Pavel felt like laughing.

Instead he said, "Camellion, are you still convinced the device in the attaché case has something to do with how the enemy spotted you?"

He got up from the chair and walked over to one side of the room, to where an old-fashioned coffeepot sat on a two-burner hot plate on a table between a small stainless-steel sink and a portable refrigerator.

"Yes, I'm convinced," Camellion said firmly. He laid down the Magnum. "But the only thing I have to go on is a hunch. According to one of the radio men here at Iceberg, the gadget is some kind of listening device. Frazier dubbed it an 'audio amplifier,' which doesn't really tell us a thing!"

"That term's a—what's your English word for it?—a misnomer!" Pavel said, his back turned as he poured the coffee. "Because the device will only emit a beeping pattern when the small disk is inserted in the machine. What perplexes me is that sometimes, even when the disk is in place, the machine is silent, with no sound coming through the earplug."

The Russian turned from the coffeepot and began walking back to the card table. Camellion, who had been wiping the Magnum with an oily rag, paused and gave him a long, searching look.

"When did you discover that the device wouldn't make any sound at all through the earplug?" he asked.

Pavel put the coffee mug on the edge of the card table and sat down, his face clouding in thought over Camellion's question.

"This afternoon," he answered in a quiet voice. "You were at the airport meeting Wiseloggle. What is so important about the time?"

He looked curiously at the Death Merchant. Wiseloggle, Kimber and Gasquet frowned from the intensity of their own puzzlement.

"No special reason," Camellion said soberly, but his tone revealed that he was looking for a connection between —between what? He didn't know himself, and that was the source of his frustration! Still, there was something there, something he couldn't quite put his finger on. It was as disconcerting as groping in a dark cellar for a black cat—that had never been there in the first place!

"The device obviously does something!" Nat Wiseloggle observed, relighting his pipe. "You are going to send it back to Washington for analysis, I know—aren't you?"

"Eventually, yes," Camellion said. He picked up the Magnum, returned it to its shoulder holster and repressed an acid belch. The Fontina and Barolo wine he had had earlier was not agreeing with him. He belched, telling himself that he should have known better than to eat cheese that had the aroma of Alpine pastures.

"I say, Camellion, about leaving tomorrow . . . when we go from here to the airport," J. Warren Kimber said. "You haven't told us whether we will go as a group or leave individually." The British agent's voice was friendly, as though he and the Death Merchant were old friends. "I think it would appear highly suspicious if all of us left here as a group."

"Decidedly so," de Gasquet chimed in. He got up and walked to the refrigerator. He opened the door and looked inside.

Wiseloggle said, "I'll buy that."

"We have no choice but to assume that the *glavni vrag* —the main enemy—does not know of this station house," Pavel Telpuchovskii pointed out. "If they did, the Italian police would have raided us by now. We must assume that the enemy will be watching the airport, the bus stations and the railroads. We know that the New Dawn assassins know *you,* Camellion. It would be unwise for any of us to accompany you to the airport, although I personally think that four guns are better than two."

"That's good thinking," Nat Wiseloggle commented, his blond head bobbing in agreement. He laid down a screen of gray-blue pipe smoke in the Death Merchant's general direction. "How do we go to the airport, Richard?"

"The British plane is scheduled to arrive at Leonardo da Vinci airport tomorrow morning at ten o'clock," Camellion said. Leaning back in the chair, his hands reversed on the butts of the twin Magnums, he paused as Philippe de Gasquet returned and sat down, a glass of cold pineapple juice in his hand.

"We will go separately to the airport," Camellion said, "leaving here at fifteen-minute intervals, beginning with" —he turned to Wiseloggle—"you, Nat." He swung around. "Then you, Kimber. Then Gasquet. Telpuchovskii will follow. I'll leave last. Any questions?"

"We each leave by private car?" Pavel asked.

"I'll tell you that tomorrow morning." Camellion searched the faces of the other agents. "Anything else at this point?"

The other men remained silent. Camellion got up, went over to the refrigerator and poured himself a glass of pineapple juice. Somehow the taste couldn't synchronize with the aroma of Wiseloggle's Amphora tobacco.

"This is such a lovely old city, I almost hate to leave it," Wiseloggle said. "Of course, you have to be a racetrack driver to get anywhere by car."

"I won't mind leaving one bit," Pavel Telpuchovskii said bluntly. "All I've heard since I've been in Rome is church bells. Every day at noon the bells pound your ears. I find it all very boring."

"Those are the Angelus bells," explained Philippe de

75

Gasquet, who was a Roman Catholic, though he hadn't been to Mass in twenty years. "It is a form of Catholic devotion commemorating the incarnation."

The French agent placed his glass next to him on the floor.

Pavel smiled a smile that was half-sneer and half an expression of amusement.

"I think you'll find the true reason why the bells ring at noon lies in the past, in the Church's Dark Ages nonsense that storms were caused by devils who were bent on destroying 'God's' churches with lightning!" Pavel laughed out loud, a heavy kind of infectious laugh. "Which is only another example of Christian ignorance and stupidity, of an imperialistic and authoritarian overlord of a church bent on sociopolitical domination."

Gasquet's already-ruddy face turned an even deeper shade of crimson, in response to the Russian's charge against the Church.

"Monsieur, what you have said is sheer nonsense." He began quietly enough, then fury got the better of him, and he lashed out. "Lies! All lies! Nothing more than Communist propaganda to make the Church look bad!"

"In that case, my French comrade, Saint Thomas Aquinas must have been working for Karl Marx instead of God!" Pavel said in amusement, Gasquet's furious expression goading him on. "He said in his *Summa,* 'Rains and winds, and whatsoever occurs by local impulse alone, can be caused by demons.' This *gochnik* went on to say, 'It is a dogma of faith that the demons can produce wind, storms, and rain of fire from heaven and that the demons can be cast back into their foul Hell by the ring of blessed bells.' "

"I say," chuckled Kimber, biting off the end of a cigar, "I hope Silvestter doesn't have his devil blow up a typhoon while we're at sea!"

Gasquet stared open-mouthed at a smiling Pavel Telpuchovskii, who was saying, "As I recall, Saint Jerome also declared the air to be full of devils, and so did Saint Bonaventure, who was a 'seraphic doctor' of the Church!"

The Russian tilted his head back slightly and blew smoke rings into the air. "Ahhh, this wretched woman lies

76

under a tyranny of foolishness," he said, the volume of his voice cut in half. "Things are believed by Christians of such absurdity as to make one think that half the planet is peopled by idiots!"

Wiseloggle had picked up a deck of cards and was shuffling them indifferently. Kimber stroked his thick red mustache as lovingly as an old maid stroking the back of her favorite tomcat. Camellion sat down at the card table and placed the glass of pineapple juice in front of him. He had a deep suspicion that Pavel had deliberately baited the Frenchman. Why not? That was the Russian's weakness: At times he couldn't control his twisted streak of sadism— *And one of these days, it's going to blow him away into the land of the quiet and lonely dead . . .*

Philippe de Gasquet had the appearance of an animal that would have liked to spring, yet was not quite sure if such a move would be the right one.

"I don't believe a word you've said!" Gasquet practically shouted, his words falling like boulders into canyons of silence. "How could a man like you, raised and educated in a godless land like the Soviet Union, know anything about any saint." His eyes bombarded the Russian with visual karate chops. "It's all Communist propaganda!"

Pavel wasn't the least bit disturbed, his face as devilish as any mummer's mask.

"You're free to believe anything you want." His voice was lazy, sounding on the edge of sleep. "I've told you the truth. It's because I was educated in a godless land that I know the full truth about religion. Read the *Summa* yourself, then tell me that Mr. 'Saint' Aquinas didn't believe that storms were caused by lightning!"

The clever Pavel, knowing that Camellion was not only well-read in such subjects as comparative religion, but also had the gift of total recall, turned to the Death Merchant for confirmation.

"Have I not told the truth, Camellion?"

"The fathers of the early church did have some astonishing ideas," he said. "For instance, they had the theory that the earth was surrounded by hollow spheres, but they couldn't quite decide whether the spheres were made of

77

glass or ice. And they were certainly against research by experiment and observation, condemning science as an instrument of our old friend, the 'devil.' "

"I find that difficult to believe—how anyone could be so stupid!" Nat Wiseloggle said, taking out his tobacco pouch.

"I don't believe it at all!" Gasquet said in a subdued voice.

"I don't give a damn what you believe," Camellion retorted calmly. "The fact remains that in—yes, it was in 1243 that the Dominicans interdicted every member of their order from the study of medicine and natural philosophy; the Franciscans followed suit. In 1287 this interdiction was extended to physics and chemistry—and we're still paying for this monstrous stupidity. For more than two-hundred years all research stopped in Europe during the Dark Ages. No doubt we'd have had a cure for cancer and other diseases years ago, if Rome hadn't dominated the then civilized world. Instead of Rome I should have said the Church and its damned popes."

"But what about 'devils' causing storms?" insisted Pavel.

"You're correct," Camellion said brusquely. "It was believed that the ringing of bells scared hell out of demons who were responsible for storms in general and lightning striking church steeples in particular. Of course, it took American knowhow to achieve what bells and pious prayers and holy water couldn't do!"

Now, even the usually stolid Wiseloggle glanced at the Death Merchant in confoundment, and he, too, wondered how "American knowhow" could have achieved what the infallible popes—the good right hands of God—couldn't do!

Amused at the four faces of surprise turned and staring at him, Camellion finished, "An American named Ben Franklin. He invented the lightning rod . . ."

CHAPTER SIX

The day was as calm as the chapel of a convent, the Indian Ocean as peaceful as a sleeping baby, with only the intense heat from the boiling-brass sun marring the voyage that so far had been without incident of any kind.

Lonely Lady had been appropriately named. She *was* all alone in this area of the ocean, her gracefully curving prow cutting through the water. Only 233 miles due south of Java, she pushed toward the Timor Sea, riding the waves like a proud empress, in an area of the Indian Ocean that placed her north of the continental state of western Australia.

Referred to as a "yacht" by Jackson Jorah Harmsworth, who had bought the craft with money furnished by the CIA, *Lonely Lady* was a cruising sailboat, a seventy-five-foot brigantine that could be handled with ease by as little as a crew of four. A sleek white-hulled craft, she was a boat built to weather violent storms and to withstand the weight of crushing waves breaking over her decks. Instead of the tall masts of the racer, *Lonely Lady* had masts that were lower and much stronger. Her sail area was less, reducing strain on hull and rigging, although the canvas, rigging, and construction were heavier.

A cruising sailboat she was, but still different from the conventional type, in that she lacked an open cockpit in the stern. While the cockpit was there, it had been enclosed by a low cabin extending to midship, almost to the main mast, a low, flat-roofed cabin whose port and starboard sides could be removed for a length of nine feet, the stern to the width of the deck. Usually the cockpit remained open, unless storm clouds appeared on the horizon, in which case the sides and stern portion would be put into place, an operation that could be accomplished within the space of five minutes.

There was another difference that made *Lonely Lady* truly unique. She was also a motor sailer, not that this was unusual in itself. There are thousands of motor sailers that have an engine larger than an auxiliary, which is used primarily for getting in and out of the harbor; and that is what the *Lonely Lady* used to move from the harbor, or into it —her small auxiliary engine! But because there were those unusual times that she needed speed and a lot of it, she also carried a 1400-horsepower gasoline engine that could propel *Lonely Lady* through the water with a power that to any observer did not match her looks, as sleek as they were. That powerful engine was working now, all eight pistons working at only half-capacity, driving Lonely Lady forcefully through the Indian Ocean. Greater speed was not needed. The Death Merchant and his party were on schedule—right to the minute.

Alone, barefooted, Richard Camellion stood on the foredeck of the cabin housing, the hard polished deck boards torturing the callus on the ball of his right foot. Bareheaded, wearing only white ducks and large brown-tinted sunglasses, he was braced against the forerailing, studying the horizon—forward, port and starboard—through powerful binoculars, his keen blue eyes searching, his thoughts on what had been and what could be . . .

Camellion and the other intelligence agents had not had any trouble in going from Station Iceberg to Leonardo da Vinci Airport in Rome. The British aircraft from Malta— the plane had turned out to be a De Havilland jet, the larger executive type—had landed at the airport on schedule. And the Death Merchant and the others had boarded the jet and had flown to Bombay, India, on schedule.

That very same Monday, in the evening, the *Lonely Lady* pulled out of Bombay's foul and crowed Back Bar Harbor, Harmsworth and his three crewmen (who were posing as college students from America) making a great show of raising the jib and mainsail. Hours later, when *Lonely Lady* reached the open waters of the Arabian Sea, stretching along the west of the Indian peninsula, Harmsworth and his crew took down the sails and, on the Death Merchant's order, switched power to the gasoline engine.

With the bearded Harmsworth at the wheel, the boat headed southeast . . . on past the Amindivi Islands . . . through the Laccadive Sea and finally into the Indian Ocean. Then the boat turned east and, now north of Australia, pointed her bowsprit toward the Timor Sea.

The plan was to sail south of Djawa (Java) and the Sunda Islands . . . into the Timor Sea . . . onward into the Arafura Sea, south of New Guinea . . . continuing through the Torres Strait and then into the Coral Sea. Finally *Lonely Lady* would turn south and head for the wide Pacific, with Brisbane her final port of call.

Camellion saw nothing on the horizon, nothing but haze and emptiness. He took the binoculars from his eyes and let them dangle from the strap around his neck. Suspicious as usual, he took a look around the boat. Two of the "college boy" crew were forward, close to the bow; the third CIA crewman was portside.

Everything was in order. God was in His Heaven, Satan in His Hell, and *Lonely Lady* on schedule. Camellion headed for the stern, using the narrow stairway leading down from the roof into the interior of the cabin. He found the four other agents of the party gathered in the area of the open cockpit . . . Jackie Harmsworth at the wheel, Pavel Telpuchovskii and J. Warren Kimber, both shirtless and in naval shorts with webbed belts, discussing that phase of demonology in which the sorcerer attempts to conjure.

"Let me make sure I understand you, laddie," Kimber was saying as Camellion sat down in a canvas deck chair. "Unless I misunderstand what you've said, I must conclude that you believe it's possible for a so-called Magician to stand in a so-called Magic Circle and perform a 'magic ritual' which will force a demon to put in a nasty appearance!

His lips parted in a broad smile. "I say now, you have to be pulling my leg, old boy! Come now, old chap, admit that you are . . ."

"If you believed that, you'd have to believe in the Devil!" Nat Wiseloggle interjected, speaking both to Kimber and Telpuchovskii. He sat across from Kimber, his long, hairy legs stretched out in front of him.

"Which I do not!" admitted Kimber promptly, flicking his cigarette over the side of the boat.

Gasquet, next to him, seemed surprised, his eyes wide. "But Warren, you believe in God, do you not?" he asked, moving his intense gaze to the Englishman. "If you believe in God, you have to believe in the Devil. You have no choice!"

"What do you mean by 'God'?" responded Kimber. A man who did not like to be questioned about his intimate personal beliefs, he was annoyed that de Gasquet had asked such a question.

"If you are asking me if I believe in your version of God, a Biblical version that makes Him a kind of paranoid 'superman' with a long beard . . . a kind of cosmic Adolf Hitler who demands blind obedience from people who must exhibit blind faith—if you're asking me if I believe in this kind of 'human' god, the answer is *no!* To me that is fundamentalist foolishness!"

De Gasquet tried to formulate a reply but was hampered by the fact he was unable to refute the logic of Kimber's belief.

He was relieved when Jackson Harmsworth boomed in a loud, gravelly voice, "It's all a lot of goddamn crap, this nuttiness of calling up demons! I once read me a book on the subject. I was in jail at the time, in Singapore, serving thirty days for giving a couple of British sailors their lumps. Got me this book when the library cart was pushed through the cell block. It was a book on Black Magic . . . a lot of goddamn crap how you call up the Devil and how a bloke could make a pact with Old Nick . . . sign your name in blood and all that kind of goddamn crap. Understand, while old Nick would give you anything you wanted, at the end of twenty years you had to give him your soul to trot off to hell with. Trouble was, the book—I think the part about the pact was taken from something called a 'grimm-oree'—the book made the Devil out to be some kind of halfwit. I say that because this 'grimm-oree' gave all kinds of instructions to the magician how he could pull a double-X and slip out of the deal. Hell, yes, the way that grimm-oree made it out, poor old Beelzebub had to be an idiot, as if he couldn't read the same book and know what the sorcerer was up to. Like I said, it's all a lot of goddamn crap!"

Naked except for green shorts, Harmsworth was not an official agent of the Central Intelligence Agency but, like the Death Merchant, was a free-lance adventurer who lent his efforts solely for money; yet there was no danger that he would ever switch to the Other Side. Smuggler, gun runner, and even the owner of a whorehouse in Brisbane—all these things he was, but in spite of his carefree what-the-hell turpitude in certain directions, he was an American who loved the land of his birth, looking at treason the way hundred-percent men look at homosexuality—with horror!

A screwball who would rather be called a son of a bitch than ignored, Jackie was prone to tell all sorts of strange, conflicting stories about himself, including the ones about his origins. Either he was the bastard son of a famous American movie actress or a black-sheep member of an old British family—depending on which side of the Atlantic he preferred at the time. However, the CIA knew the full truth about him—born in New York City in 1928 . . . served in the US Navy, on a PT Boat in World War II . . . honorably discharged . . . became a seaman, jumping ship in Jakarta, Java, in 1964. Since then Jackie had been many things . . . bartender, guide, pimp, wrestler . . . anything he could do to make a buck. After he'd won a pile of money in a crap game, he had promptly bought a small sloop and gotten into the smuggling racket—cigarettes, opium, women . . .

Quite by accident he came to the attention of the CIA when, in 1969, he had gotten into a brawl in Hong Kong with five British sailors who had made insulting remarks about Uncle Sam.

"I'll flatten anyone who runs down the United States to me!" Jackie had growled in court. "And that includes you goddamn limeys sitting up there on the bench!"

His remark had earned him an extra thirty days in a

Hong Kong slammer and at the same time had brought him to the attention of the CIA. An agent happened to be among the spectators in the courtroom. Since then, off and on, Harmsworth had worked for the CIA.

A big-bodied, barrel-chested man, with one of those ordinary no-distinguishing-features-faces, Jackie was still an individual people looked at twice, not so much because of his huge body, which had been burnt chocolate by the Far Eastern sun, but because he wore a full, luxurious beard, as black as any Moor, and was as bald as the dome of Saint Peter's ! He made sure his cranium stayed that way carefully shaving his head every day.

Richard Camellion said, "I think, Jackie . . . I think the book you referred to is one of the *Grimoires,* or 'Black Books,' as they are called." He leaned back against the port side of the vessel. "There's four of them that I know of, and they are sinister books, but only sinister in their intent. Where the intention is not evil, then the instructions in the books are only frivolous, hyperbolical and paramountly foolish.

"Of course, there are other books that are better known in crackpot circles than the *Grimoires.* Be that as it may, the Grimoires are the elite in the world of the demonlovers. No doubt maniacs like C.W. Silvestter have entire libraries of such works."

"Such works are monuments of human perversity!" Phillippe de Gasquet said very seriously. "And only sick minds could believe that any good could come from evil!"

"*Goetia*—a Greek word meaning witchcraft—is the first and oldest Grimoire," Camellion said, wondering if Gasquet, since he obviously believed in a Devil, was also stupid enough to think that such an abstraction of mythology could be "contacted" via any magical operation. Well, the poor fool had a right to his opinion . . .

"The *Goetia* deals with the evocation of seventy-two powerful evil spirits who are servants of the four kings of Hell: Amaymon, Corson, Zimamay and Goap. Each of these seventy-two spirits rules over legions of lesser spirits, just like Caporegimes in the Mafia!"

The others laughed, including Gasquet, and Camellion continued.

"For instance, the spirit Focalor, so the book says, commands thirty legions. Since some demonologists give the number of spirits in a legion as two thousand-two hundred and twenty-two, this places quite a formidable army at the magician's service."

"Listen," said Harmsworth with a broad grin, "if that billionaire bastard can muster two thousand-two hundred-and twenty-two bad spirits, you guys are going to have to take the Aussie army into Queensland with you!"

"If King Solomon were still around, we could get his help," Camellion said. "According to a legend set forth in the *Goetia,* King Sol once commanded these seventy-two spirits with their legions into a vessel of brass and cast it into a deep lake in Babylon. But certain citizens of Babylon, too curious for their own damn good, retrieved the vessel and broke it open, hoping to find treasure. As from Pandor's box, the demons rushed out wailing over the land; the world has been in one hell of a mess ever since."

"It's just another stupid Jewish myth," said Wiseloggle, drawing in a long breath as though preparing to fight against a tide. "For almost two thousand years they've been babbling about a 'redeemer,' but I didn't see him coming down out of the sky in the last Israeli-Arab war."

"He was there though—in Washington, D.C.!" Camellion commented drily. "Getting guns and tanks and planes. But now, considering what is happening in the Near East, I'm inclined to think that the Allah of the Arabs might be even more powerful than the Jehovah of the Jews!"

J. Warren Kimber smiled first at Camellion, then at Pavel Telpuchovskii, who all this time had been listening with a kind of twisted sneer on his handsome face.

"That's all well and good, Camellion," said Kimber, "your little lecture on Black Magic. You have confirmed what I was trying to tell our Ivan friend here. You still insist, Pavel, that a nasty old demon can be called into a 'sacred triangle' in front of a 'magic circle'?"

"I did not say that!" Pavel intoned, holding up his hand

for silence before Kimber could contradict him. "I said that if the sorcerer had faith, if he believed strongly enough, he would see something: exactly what he wanted to see, exactly what his mind could bring to consciousness from his own dark subconscious. But you, with typical British smugness, jumped to conclusions that are all wrong!"

Kimber kept his typical British poise as he removed the cigar from his mouth. "I say, that puts a different light on the matter. Why didn't you say that you were referring to hallucinations."

Camellion said, "The devil, when seen by a crackpot sorcerer, is merely a recalcitrant part of the magician's own personality."

"Precisely," Pavel said. He had almost no hair on his muscular chest, and his skin was very white. He was truly a man who did not have companionship with the sun. "To evoke any so-called evil spirit, Devil or not, is to become conscious of some part of one's own character; to command and restrain the 'spirit' is to bring that part of the subconscious into subjection."

"Which is another way of proving that while the 'Kingdom of God' is within you, so too is the 'Kingdom of Hell,'" Camellion said in a tired voice. "And it also gives evidence that since there are so many chambers to the mind, there are also an infinite number of 'gods,' individual and equal though diverse, each one supreme and utterly indestructible. This is also the only explanation of how a being could create a world in which war and evil exist. This is because evil, like good, is only an appearance. It cannot affect the substance itself, but only multiply its combinations. This is related to mystic monotheism, but the objection to the theory is that God—and I'm speaking of the Christian concept of God—has to create things that are all parts of Himself, and evil cannot be a part of the Good-Guy God!"

"The Devil is responsible for evil!" de Gasquet said quickly, as proudly as a first-grader reciting his ABCs.

"On the other hand, the ancient philosophers thought they had the answer, in that they considered God to be a male!" Camellion said with a slight laugh. "If we presuppose many elements, their interplay is natural. It is no objection to monotheism to ask who made the elements; they are there. But God, when you look for Him, is not there! As the Ancients were prone to say: Theism is *obscurum per obscurius*. A male star is built up from the center outward; a female from the circumference inward. That's what the Ancients meant when they said a woman has no soul—which of course is a lot of bovine excrement!"

Harmsworth spit over the leeward side of the boat, wiped his mouth with the back of a huge hand, and said, "It's going to take a lot more than philosophy to wipe out Silvestter's underground city."

There was no merriment in his eyes as he looked straight at the Death Merchant. "You've said that our party will be small—just us, except for the three dudes serving as a crew, and ten Aussies. Like man, we're going to be like sheep among wolves!"

Camellion removed his sunglasses and wiped his tanned face with a handkerchief that was already sweat-wet. There was a subtle cunning and mockery in his hypnotic blue eyes.

"In that case, Jackie, old buddy, we shall have to take the advice that Christ gave to his Apostles! We shall have to appear as harmless as the dove and use the sneakiness of a serpent—and be better shots!"

Gasquet and Kimber shifted uncomfortably. They didn't like the odds, and they didn't have Camellion's confidence, nor his affinity for Death. They were afraid to die, and that was their weakness.

"Harmsworth makes good sense!" Nat Wiseloggle's voice was bitter. "Sixteen men aren't much of a force against hundreds of fanatics, most of whom will be armed! Those damned Australians! Giving us only ten men!" His face twitched as if he'd been pricked with a goad, and his thin-lipped mouth opened like a rubber purse. "Have you figured out a definite plan yet? Damn it, Richard. You're in charge of the planning, but you still haven't told us anything definite!"

"There's time enough, after we get to Brisbane," Camellion said.

He put the handkerchief back into his pocket, noticing how Wiseloggle's eyes had caught fire with anger, and the way the line of his mouth had tightened.

Pavel Telpuchovskii folded his hands over his belly, letting his body rock with the motion of the boat, and murmured, "We will not be going in on foot, or even by truck. It's almost nine hundred miles from Brisbane to Silvestter's sheep ranch and his 'New Eden.' Too bad for him we're going to have to make it a burning hell of destruction . . ."

"Provided the gods of war and death continue to smile on us and frown on Silvestter and his group of Satanists," Camellion declared quietly. "Nothing is certain until it has been accomplished."

"Those gods of yours had better smile, monsieur," de Gasquet said. "The worst sort of life is far better than the best kind of death . . ."

A chilling mystic wind blew across the outer edge of the Death Merchant's soul. A preternatural warning? A hint by the interior forces of self-preservation that he had better begin to formulate a definite plan? *I think so . . .*

Many hours later Camellion was still putting together his master attack strategy for Plan Poaka, as he stood on the fore deck of the cabin housing, staring out to sea.

At her speed, and because of good weather, *Lonely Lady* had made good progress, plowing the sea like an over anxious farmer at planting time. The water had become choppy; yet the barometer had continued to hold.

The brigantine had cruised through the Timor Sea and the Arafura Sea and was now approaching the center of the Torres Strait, the narrowest point of the entire journey. Lying between the southern coast of New Guinea and the tip of Queensland's Cape York Peninsula, Torres Strait, at its longest point, was only eighty-three miles wide.

At this moment of passage *Lonely Lady* was only some fifteen miles from land, from Mulgrave Island lying to the south, and only thirty-four miles from Turnagain Island off the New Guinea coast . . . the boat not one degree off course. Very soon she would pass through the Great Northeast Channel, on past the Great Barrier Reef, and veer southeast into the Coral Sea. Then the last leg of her long journey: She would head into the wide, blue Pacific and finally pull into the busy harbor of Brisbane.

Standing there on the foredeck of the cabin housing, Camellion thought of another body of water to the south and a bit west of *Lonely Lady*—the Gulf of Carpentaria, between Australia's Cape York Peninsula and the Northern Territory. At the extreme southern end of the Gulf—497 miles from the boat—was Woolgorang. From this small town (owned lock, stock, every board, brick, and nail by C.W. Silvestter), a two-track railroad coursed thirty-five miles southeast to the northern edge of C.W. Silvestter's giant sheep ranch. This was the main supply route, of great advantage to the psychotic billionaire and his equally crazy associates, for more reasons than one. For instance, supply freighters coming in through the Gulf of Carpentaria were under lighter custom's surveillance than those pulling into the big ports, such as Sydney, Melbourne, and Brisbane. The main advantage was the shortness of the route; it was almost nine hundred miles shorter—if supplies had come from a route leading to either Brisbane or Rockhampton, the two nearest ports of any size.

We won't be able to use surprise, thought the Death Merchant. *Silvestter is expecting us, and he'll have radar and other detection devices in operation. Steele will have seen to that! I am convinced that the answer to our success lies in high explosives and some kind of toxic gas. Hmmmm . . . vomit gas, such as diphenylchloroarsine, will do fine. Yeah, we'll use DA and—*

"Camellion! Down here, Quick!" The voice belonged to Nat Wiseloggle, who was calling from the cabin below.

His heart quickening, Camellion hurried below, where the other agents had gathered in the forward part of the cabin, around Wiseloggle, who was seated at the shortwave radio, his hands trembling as he decoded the message just received from "The Hub."

Finally, his expression as bleak as a cemetery on a rainy afternoon, Nat handed the sheet of paper to the Death Merchant, who scanned it for a moment, then read aloud:

ATTEMPT MADE ON LIFE OF U.S. PRESIDENT AT 1300 HOURS. ATTEMPT FAILED. WHITE HOUSE PARTIALLY DESTROYED BY EXPLOSIVES. PRESIDENT UNHARMED. FINAL SUNSET FOR TEN NEW DAWN ASSASSINS. PROCEED PLAN POAKA AS SCHELUDED. TAKE CHIEF DEVIL ALIVE. "The message is signed 'Blue-Boy,' which is the code name for Chuck Cleevis.' "

Spontaneous exclamations of alarm, those quick inhalations and fearful expressions, came from the men.

Jackie Harmsworth was also in the cabin, since he periodically let one of the crewmen take over the wheel.

"That's a lot of goddamn crap," he said loudly. "How in hell can the brass expect us to take Silvestter alive! Bullshit three times over! Hell, 'Blueboy' didn't even say 'please' or 'if possible'!"

J. Warren Kimber drew a long breath. "I wonder if a similar attempt was made against Brezhnev? Weren't the last two wipeouts on New Dawn's schedule supposed to be synchronized?"

A lot of eyes turned questioningly to Pavel Telpuchovskii.

"If and when an attempt is made on the life of our Chairman, Moscow will contact us by shortwave," the Russian said in a flat voice.

Now one had time to make any kind of comment, for at that moment one of the CIA crewmen thrust his head and shoulders through the topside stair opening. The man had been on watch in the bow, scanning the horizon through fieldglasses.

"There's a vessel headed directly at us," he said in an anxious voice. "Coming in from the southeast. She's too far yet to make out what kind of deal she is, but she's coming in fast!"

Lonely Lady had company!

"Jackie, break out the weapons—the big stuff, too, just in case our visitor isn't friendly!" Camellion's voice was like the thrust of an icepick, quick and to the point.

90

Turning, Camellion raced up the metal steps to the above deck, the others following him.

The Death Merchant detected His presence!

The rotting stink was there!

The Great God Death was in the area!

CHAPTER SEVEN

There was no "Tree of Life" on C.W. Silvestter's sheep ranch in Queensland, nor were there any apples for the faithful to gobble surreptitiously. The only forbidden fruit that existed on the ranch was disobedience to the laws Silvestter had proclaimed, and to transgress these edicts brought not a spiritual demise, but a physical death to the sinner. Within this 850,000-acre kingdom, Silvestter reigned supreme. As the *Chosen One of Satan,* his word was The Law, and God in His Heaven could not help those who might disobey the Chosen One—not that anyone ever did.

There wasn't anything unusual about the ranch itself, which, like other sheep and cattle ranches in Queensland (or the "Deep North" as the Aussies refer to the state), was a world unto itself, a world that raised not only sheep but cattle, the favorite breed being Brahman crossed with Herefords and Shorthorns, Silvestter's ranch doing its share of keeping Queensland the state that raises half of Australia's cattle.

Australia exports more sugar than any other nation except Cuba, and almost half of it is grown in Queensland; yet none was grown on the Silvestter ranch, although there were pineapples, coffee, peanuts, macadamia nuts, and pawpaw trees, which in the fall would be heavy with fruit resembling plump, green bananas.

The ranch was a vast treasure house of natural resources. Other than thousands upon thousands of acres of pasturage—called "downs"—lush with spinifex, wallaby and kangaroo grasses, there were also many many acres of desert, but not of the barren, sandy variety. In Queensland terminese, "desert" means timbered country! On Silvestter's "deserts" were walnut, blackwood and rosewood trees, as well as jarrah, Queensland maple, and hoop pine. Other areas of the vast ranch contained bunya and kauri pines, along with those two botanical wonders, the giant stinging tree, with large, bellicose, velvety leaves, and the ungrateful epiphytic fig, which lodges high in a host tree and then sends down a curtain of roots that enclose and strangle it.

Silvestterville was located in the northern part of the ranch; it was the small community in which the workers lived . . . entire families whose livelihood depended on what the ranch produced and exported—wool, mutton, beef, lumber, and fruit products.

But no other ranch in all Queensland, nor in all Australia—for that matter, in all the world—contained what was situated in the southern section of the ranch: New Eden, the Chosen One's underground city, the entire complex below the surface of the hot Australian earth, the construction of which had cost slightly more than $300-million American. And it was big!

Almost twice the length of a football field, New Eden was 580 feet long, 300 feet wide, and five levels deep, each level thirteen feet high, the first level beginning at a depth of thirty feet below a surface that gave no hint of what lay underground, except for the building roofing the wide entrance, and two towers, one at each end of the complex whose five-foot-thick concrete-reinforced roof had been covered with seven feet of earth.

One tower, ninety-six feet high, looked like a tall, silver pencil with a bulb on top. This was the weather-and-radiation detection center, which would be used to detect the poisonous radioactive particles from the worldwide hydrogen war the Chosen One hoped to touch off.

The other tower, only some twenty-five feet high, was a

gun tower, to be used in defense of New Eden in case something went wrong and the Australian government decided to send in troops against Silvestter and his fellow crackpots.

Next to the complex was an airfield, complete with hangars, the strip long enough to accommodate the Chosen One's Lear jet and prop-driven cargo planes from Brisbane and Melbourne. On the roof of the New Eden complex was a landing pad for the two helicopters used as transportation between Satan's center on earth, Silvestterville and Woolgorang.

New Eden contained living facilities for one hundred couples each with two children. These couples had been chosen for their fanaticism and complete dedication to Satanism and were known as "The Select of Satan." There was also ample room for the one hundred members of the New Dawn Elite Guard and the one hundred girls who had been kidnapped from all over the world. These unfortunate girls (between sixteen and twenty years of age) were the Virgins of Satan, who would, eventually, mate with the Elite Guard and, along with the one hundred other couples and their offspring, produce "superior" children, which would repopulate a dead world. All these girls were lilywhite, since Silvestter was convinced that the black, yellow and brown races were contaminated by Satan. These girls, while they were treated well, were imprisoned on the fourth level.

New Eden had accommodations that, although not plush, were adequate. There were living quarters (three tiny rooms per couple), a large dining hall, and a nursery for the small children. A fifty-bed, well-equipped hospital (there were seven doctors among The Select of Satan) was on the fifth level; repair shops on the fourth, next to the air-conditioning and air-purification machinery; this area also contained the air tanks of the city that could be completely sealed off from the surface and made airtight.

When World War III exploded over the planet, the inhabitants of New Eden would breathe uncontaminated, recycled air and drink uncontaminated, recycled water from the 150,000-gallon tank buried at the north end of the city.

There was an armory, and large warehouse rooms filled

93

with food and clothing (for those who smoked . . . plenty of cigarettes, cigars, and pipe tobacco, enough to last almost five years); on the second level a large gymnasium— it even had a small swimming pool—and "sun" rooms to keep a healthy tan on the bodies of Satan's children. There were also other recreation rooms—one had to do more than worship the Devil! Two libraries were on the third level, one for the "children," the other for Silvestter and his aides and their families, all of whom, including the Chosen One, had their living quarters—larger and more lavishly furnished than the apartments of the hoi polloi—on the second level.

At one end of the city five passenger and three huge freight elevators led to the surface; next to the bank of elevators, a wide steel staircase angled down from level to level. There was another opening from the surface: Within a circular concrete tube, a steel staircase, built around a central axis, spiraled straight down, a ramp extending outward to the stairs from each level.

The electric generators were on the fifth level, one large dynamo (direct current) and two spares.

What could be called the heart-and-soul of the city was the Hall of Conjuration, the equivalent of which in Christian terminology would have been a chapel. There was, of course, a difference between the two . . . as much dissimilarity as between high noon on a bright sunny day and midnight without a moon! Never was God mentioned in the Hall of Conjuration. Only Satan and the other demons of the hierarchy of Hades were invoked in this sanctum of evil whose motif, while disturbingly eerie, was horrifyingly beautiful.

Enormous—300 by 180 by 25 feet—the hall was the most elaborate devil-worshipping sanctuary the world had ever known. Demonologists in Rome, Paris, Marseilles and other Satan centers of the world might have to content themselves with gloomy old cellars and rooms in private homes, but not C.W. Silvestter and his group of dangerous psychopaths. They worshipped in a holy of holies a Roman emperor would have envied.

The floor, ceiling, side and back walls were of red marble, the front wall also of marble, of a pure black color; in the center of the front wall was a ten-foot square of pure white marble, on which was painted the symbolic figure of Satan: the Sabbatic Goat—a figure seated on a throne resting on the globe of the world. A loose robe covered the lower part of the seated figure, and from underneath the black robe projected the crossed legs of a goat, the cloven hooves resting on the continents of Europe and North America.

The torso was that of a male human being, the right arm bent at the elbow, the hand pointing upward . . . the left arm extended in front of the figure, the palm held open, as if beckoning . . .

From the shoulders projected black wings, outstretched on either side of the head, the ugly head of a black goat, from the skull of which grew enormous horns, each one curled and twisted. Between the horns, resting on the skull, directly between the evil eyes staring in hate and fury, was a three-pointed torch holder, in which burned a bright red flame.

Twenty feet in front of the Sabbatic Goat was a long block of black marble, the altar which was used for the celebration of Black Masses, the celebrant always being one of the three defrocked Roman Catholic priests who lived in New Eden.

In front of the altar was the Grand Kabbalistic Circle of Invocation—two black circles, perfectly round, with a space of two feet between them, in which had been painted the mighty words of Power: Adonay, Eloim, Jehovam, Tagla, Mathon and Amioram. The outer circle had a diameter of 47.3 feet. Within the inner circle a huge triangle had been painted, its apex pointed directly at the altar, the bottom points extending to the lower sides of the circle.

Three smaller circles, each one eight feet in diameter, had been painted within the triangle . . . one toward the apex, the other two on either side of the bottom points. During services Silvestter, the Chosen One, would sit in the circle at the apex, his two assistants—Steele and Ebro—in the other two circles.

A blue marble block, each side a perfect three feet,

stood between the altar and the Grand Kabbalistic Circle —the stand on which Lucifuge Rofocale would appear, when the day came that Silvestter summoned Him to appear in person!

The pews were behind the Grand Kabbalistic Circle, and ranged along the side walls were braziers, the giant bowls holding the burning charcoal, resting on wrought-iron posts, almost eight feet above the floor. In spite of the smoke given off by the fifty braziers, the temple never filled with fumes nor did the ceiling and walls become grimy with soot; the residue was drawn upward through the ceiling by large fans and carried to the surface by a special ventilating system.

On the side and rear walls were painted, in black paint on red marble, the names of all the chief devils occupying Hell—*Beelzebub, Astaroth, Canikk, Tasmin, Korubot,* and score of other powerful demons. Beside each name was the devil's special and unholy seal.

The Hall of Conjuration was truly a monument to human perversity, an enormous cenotaph to a dark demon that had never been, all of it conceived by a warped and devilish mind . . . by a man who preferred to scream hallelujahs to Hell rather than quietly sing the praises of Heaven . . . by Cleveland Winston Silvestter, who now stood in the globe section atop the weather-and-radiation detection tower, which was empty except for Silvestter, Jerry Steele, and Mason Ebro, Steele's murderous assistant.

"We are being tested," Silvestter said in an odd voice. "Satan is testing us, to see if we are worthy of His divine blessing . . . just as the swine, sewer god of the Christians tests them. That is the only explanation for the failure to kill that idiot in the White House!"

Clothed in a black silk monk's robe, the cowl thrown to the back of his neck, Silvestter stood facing one huge window, his hands folded behind his back, his eyes roaming over the countryside. Before him stretched his 850,000-acre Australian empire, and in the far distance, the blue-gray mountains of the Great Dividing Range.

Silvestter continued. "That is also the reason why our agents failed to kill the Death Merchant and the Russian in

96

the Colosseum. I know that to be true. The breath of the Master has blown across the logic of my mind!"

Unexpectedly he spun around and stared at the two men seated at a small table. "Well, do you not agree?"

Neither Steele nor Ebro did, each one of the opinion that the New Dawn agents in Rome got wasted because Camellion and the Russian had been better men. Ebro was convinced of it. After all, who could take the fantastic Death Merchant? Neither man, however, was foolish enough to tell Silvestter what he actually thought.

"Yes, you're right, C. W.," Steele said with deceptive sincerity. "Satan is putting us to the test, wanting to see how we bear up under His yoke of chastisement—right, Mason?"

"Postively!" Ebro replied quickly. "Like the Chosen One said, the Master is testing us. But Satan won't let us down when the going gets rough. That son of a bitch Camellion will get his when Astaroth intercepts him and those other swine!"

A tall, big-boned man, with a narrow, almost chinless face, Ebro had arms and legs as thick as small pillars. In his mid forties, he had been the police chief of a large East Coast city, until he was fired for brutality. A realist who loved money, women, and firearms—and in that order —he no more believed in Satanism than Richard Nixon believed in the good fairy!

Scratching his hawklike nose, Ebro glanced uncomfortably at the tower's metal floor, doing his best to avoid Silvestter's penetrating gaze, the words rolling out of his mouth. "Our being tested . . . that's probably why our boys couldn't do a number on Camellion when he and his party flew to Bombay and when they sailed out on *Lonely Lady.*"

As if reassured, Silvestter's mouth twisted into his version of a smile. He pulled out a chair from a table, on which rested a large recording hygrometer and a Richard Fréres barograph, and sat down, gathering in his robe, like a woman straightening her dress.

The Chosen One spoke gently, softly, persuasively. "Both of you, listen! It is possible that Astaroth may not

97

succeed in her mission against *Lonely Lady* . . . possible that the Master might continue to test us, right up to the last moment. *We must not lose faith in Satan!*"

"But damn it, C. W.! If the Death Merchant reaches Brisbane, we know he'll organize an expedition to wipe out New Eden!" interposed Steele in an excited voice. "And what about the scheduled attack against Brezhnev and Carrero Blanco? Do I radio our people in Moscow and Madrid to proceed as scheduled?"

Silvestter banged his fist on the metal table. "Very well, suppose the Death Merchant does reach Brisbane and does organize an attack force." he said loudly, but without inflection. "Once the force gets close enough, our radar can pinpoint it for an ambush!"

His brow wrinkled, the deep ditches of a frown making him appear even more diabolical. "Joseph! Are you losing faith in the Master? Why an army couldn't get into New Eden!"

Conscious that Silvestter was eyeing him with a slight change of manner, Steele remained unruffled. From what he had heard about Camellion, the Death Merchant wouldn't need an army. He could probably smash New Eden all by himself! That was C. W's. trouble: He had never learned that Satan helps those who help themselves!

Ebro, the perfect yes-man—and for $75,000 a year he could afford to be—said hurriedly, "That's right! An army couldn't blast their way into the city." Thinking that he might be overdoing it, he added, "But an attack might cause a lot of damage, The hangar and airstrip could be wrecked, and this tower, and the gun tower. I don't think it's very probable. Our agents in the Australian government tell us that Melbourne is only going to give Camellion ten men—And what can ten men do? Why, hell, one of our armored cars could just run out in the bush and blow them apart!"

"As for Brezhnev," Silvestter was saying, "we shall cancel our killing him, at least for the moment. We know that the CIA and the KGB are working together. We can assume that the CIA and the American Secret Service deduced our plans to kill the President with explosives, a deduction that caused our plan to misfire! No doubt similar steps have been taken to protect that fool in the Kremlin. Yes, for now we will call off the Brezhnev assassination."

"And Blanco?" asked Steele. He felt a strange little stir of cold, and it didn't come from the tower's air-conditioning system! It was the chill of tension. He didn't like the way the Death Merchant was progressing with Plan *Poaka*. Having faith in the God of Evil was a must, but blind, fanatical faith, the kind Silvestter had, was ridiculous. Satan wasn't going to pop up from Hell to help *them* any more than God was going to come down from Heaven to assist Camellion!

Silvestter blinked rapidly and put his hands to the side of his head. "Yes! *Yes!* I hear Satan whispering to me!" he said with great emphasis. "We must postpone the Brezhnev assassination!"

He rose from the chair and, with great animation, walked across to the thick window. Outside, heat waves shimmered on the downs, not too far distant, the air a furnace of 102-degree heat. In contrast the inside of the tower was a cool 70 degrees.

"The Premier of Spain is a man of unflinching habits, is he not?" intoned Silvestter solemnly, standing straight as an arrow.

"Every morning he attends mass at the Church of San Francisco Borja in Madrid," Steele replied, with suppressed violence. "Every morning at precisely eight fifteen, he leaves the damned church and his chauffeur drives him down the narrow Calle de Claudio Coello. There's a large sewer under the street, and Plan Y calls for placing a large charge of TNT in the sewer. We'll touch it off from across the street and blow the car apart when it passes over the spot. The Premier's death will naturally be blamed on the Basque separatist movement, until we have our agents leak the word to the world that it was the KGB who murdered the dear Premier."

"Yessss, a beautiful plan," said Silvestter, sneering majestically. "Those 'godless' Communist bastard will indeed get the blame for it. Yes . . . a very clever plan, and one the CIA can't possibly know about."

99

"We proceed then with Plan Y?" asked Steele. He leaned forward and lit a cigarette. "I have your permission?"

"At the scheduled time, radio our agents in Madrid to proceed as planned!" Silvestter said softly. "Luis Carrero Blanco will die as previously planned."

He turned from the window, looking proud and pleased as he pulled the cowl up over his head, then walked over to the chair and sat down again, crossing his legs underneath the silk monk's robe. He looked at his wristwatch. In a short while McKillip would be finished transcribing the reports coming in from the Radio Room.

Idly he began toying with an Isanomalous Temperature Chart lying on the table, his long finger tracing over the numerous curving lines, his evil mind knowing what Steele and Ebro had to be thinking, but had so far refrained from asking. The fools! To think that he wasn't prepared for any eventuality!

"There is a question moving around in your brains!" he said slyly, almost in a whisper. He watched the two men the way a cat tortures a mouse with its sinister gaze. "How can we formulate World War III, now that we have failed to kill the US President and have postponed the assassination against Brezhnev."

He raised his arm and pointed a finger at his two silent aides.

"That is what you are wondering! That is what you would like to ask me!" he said, his tone demanding that they comply and prove him correct.

"The problem did cross my mind," Steele admitted calmly as he lit a cigarette and looked directly at Silvestter. Long ago he had learned that the billionaire despised men who showed fear or even too much respect, but admired men who at times treated him as an equal. The secret was in knowing how not to go too far.

Steele continued in a matter-of-fact voice, "Unless Satan works a miracle, we can't expect the United States and the Soviet Union to start tossing missiles at each other. It's obvious, C. W., that we haven't fooled either nation. I'll tell you something else I've been thinking about—the Death

Merchant. He's a lot more dangerous than we thought, and if you ask me, I'm of the opinion that Satan wants us to use our own resources and not depend on Him for help in matters we should handle!"

Silvestter merely stared at Steele, who began thinking that perhaps, this time, he had gone too far. Well, suppose he had! What could Silvestter do, other than become angry? Privately though, the big man had to admit that every time he thought about Silvestter, he felt he was face to face, not with a miracle, but with a mind that was unique in its own evil and personal ambition. Steele had been to a lot of places, including the Far East where the mysteries of the spirit transcend in importance the demands of the material body. Yet even in Japan he had never met a man as diabolical as Cleveland Winston Silvestter. And the billionaire was correct about the human race: People were idiots. Doubters circle the globe without ever leaving the town where they were born. He had watched them on dozens of trips, men and women going around the little globe of a planet encased in the language, beliefs, shibboleths and traditions of their great-grandfathers. People with not an original thought in their heads! People who demand a sign for everything, have signs showered upon them and yet manage to return home, wearing the self-satisfied smirk of the undeceived. All their days these fools would be an easy mark for any divining rod, not because they believed in it, but for love of the light in the eyes of the diviner, a light that mocks all men of lesser faith! But Silvestter had never been fooled by the world and the human dung crawling over its surface. The world was a giant conglomeration of trash, an experiment in human landfill. Why in hell should anyone expect anything but blood, misery and death?

C. W. was right about something else, too: The Christians were the worst of the lot! And it was also true that Satanism made far more sense than the impossible dream of Christianity, which stubbornly denied man the right to his basic nature and would try to turn him into a superman of denial. That's why the religion of the "gentle Jesus" had been such a flop, a 1,974-year failure—it demanded that people make themselves miserable by denying their honest

101

emotions, that they suffer for their so-called sins. Christianity was nothing more than a big bag of masochistic bullshit . . . a ridiculously stupid belief that only fools, weaklings and neutrotics could embrace. At least Satanism told man to enjoy himself and to indulge his passions to the fullest. That was the difference between the two: Christianity was a religion of pain! Satanism was a religion of pleasure!

"Joseph! You are not listening!" Silvestter's voice was sharp and demanding. Steele, snapping out of his introspective reverie, became aware that the billionaire was glaring at him in irritation.

"I'm sorry, C. W. I was thinking about Plan Y," he said blandly, the lie coming easily. He crushed his cigarette in the ashtray, not failing to notice that Mason Ebro was ashen-faced, as though he had just been throughly shocked.

"I said that we will build our own ICBMs—two of them!" Silvestter said with pride, a smile twitching his lips. "The project will cost a great deal of money and it will take time to make the cash available, more time to obtain the materials, assemble the rockets, and build the launching pad. We'll launch the rockets at Moscow. I am convinced that with Satan's help the plan will work. The USSR will have to launch a counterattack against the United States!"

Steele felt a thickness in his throat and a rush of blood to his temples. His mouth opened slightly as he stared in disbelief at Sillvestter. Was it possible? Could the billionaire be insane? How could he assume so dogmatically that the Death Merchant was as good as dead? How could he assume that they could assemble two rockets at New Eden without being detected, especially by US and by USSR spy satellites? Had he forgotten that within the last year five CIA agents had penetrated New Eden, posing as dedicated Satanists? How many reports had they smuggled out before being detected and executed?

No, now was not the time to remind Silvestter of that, nor of the insurmountable problems standing in the way of building two ICBMs, which the Americans and the Russians would undoubtedly blow apart before they could even be launched! How to reply to Silvestter?

Steele didn't have to. Abruptly Silvestter changed the subject.

"Another thing, Joseph," he began, his voice angry. "This morning I was inspecting the fourth level, and in a toilet next to the medical stores area, I found not only a roll of toilet paper that rolled from the top, but also a roll of paper towels that did not roll from the bottom!"

The billionaire's voice rose in fury and he pounded both fists on the metal table. "I will not tolerate such inefficiency!" he screamed, flecks of saliva flying from the corners of his mouth. *"All paper must roll outward from the bottom!"*

Ebro looked at the floor. Steele opened his mouth to speak, changed his mind, and closed his mouth.

"You find the man or woman responsible!" raged Silvestter. "He or she must and will be punished. Find out who is responsible and put the culprit in a stand-up cell for a week, on a diet of bread, water and vitamin pills! Do you understand, Joseph?"

"I'll begin an investigation immediately!" Steele replied, trying to keep his voice normal. "Whoever is responsible will be punished."

"I want to know who did it!" Silvestter said, calming down somewhat. "I want his name and record. Any person that inefficient should be executed!"

It was then that Steele made up his mind—

Cleveland Winston Silvestter was not The Chosen One!

He was not being guided by Satan, the Master!

Cleveland Winston Silvestter was a madman!

CHAPTER EIGHT

"She's coming in fast—straight at us!" the Death Merchant said to the other men crowded on the upper deck of the cabin. Calmly, through wide-angle binoculars, he studied the other vessel, which was still almost five miles distant, but seemed to be slowing. His mouth was one grim line of sheer determination, his anger rising in pigmy imitation of the choppy waves of the Torres Strait, water that was restless and beautiful, but defiant and destructive. The water—like an impassive-faced tyrant with a sharp poniard held behind Camellion's back—called mockingly to him, jeering at him as at something stranded, as at a man in one hell of a fix—and by God, the water was right! The vessel boring in from the southeast was a cabin cruiser, although it was difficult as yet to tell her size, since all they could see was a big "V" of spray, with a steel line of prow in the middle and the glass of the bridge deck behind.

"I doubt the son of a bitch is friendly," Nat Wiseloggle said, as if talking to himself. He and the other members of the attack force were also watching the approaching vessel through powerful fieldglasses. They could hear the throbbing engines of the big boat.

Jackson Jorah Harmsworth raced up the cabin steps to the deck, his heavy black beard practically flying in the hot wind.

"Fred and I have got submachine guns, sidearms, and plenty of ammo for both," he said loudly and wrapped a big hand around the curved tubing of the railing. "We could hold off an army—maybe!"

"I say, do you think that chap yonder could be an Aussie coastal-patrol boat?" Warren Kimber asked Jackie. He lowered the binoculars from his eyes and half-turned toward the skipper of *Lonely Lady*.

"Hell, no!" Jackie growled, rolling the unlit cigar around in his mouth. "The Aussie coastal-patrol chums don't charge in the way that creep's doing. They sneak in, easy like . . . trying to get alongside 'fore you know they're there. That mother-frigger out there . . . the way he's charging, he's not going to throw us any roses!"

The big man laid a huge paw on Camellion's shoulder, the thick, knotted muscles quivering beneath the sun-browned skin of his massive arms. De Gasquet didn't like the bald and bearded man; he felt his mouth was too loud and his manner too domineering, but one look at those mighty muscles had filled the Frenchman with the kind of admiration all men feel for superhuman strength.

"Fred and me, we also brought up the Burney twenty-five-pounder and its tripod," Jackie said, taking a deep breath. "With the pitch of the boat, we'd have a difficult time firing it from the shoulder. Fred and Max are lashing the tripod down in back of the cockpit, and I'm having them and Eli put up the stern and side portions of the cabin."

Lowering his binoculars, Camellion nodded in understanding, the joy in his face like flying flags, the fighting look in his eyes like the blare of trumpets. He was about to speak when de Gasquet interrupted:

"Monsieur Camellion, if it is the enemy, do you think they will try to board us?" the French SDECE agent asked. "Or ram us?"

Wiseloggle, overhearing the remark, gave de Gasquet a pathetic how-dumb-can-you-get look and said in a matter-of-fact voice, "They won't try to board us because they know we'd cut them to pieces, and she can't ram us without doing a lot of damage to herself. Grenades! They'll use hand grenades!"

All this time Pavel Telpuchovskii had been standing straddle-legged, his body rocking with the sway of the boat, his eyes glued to the new ship.

Suddenly he spoke up, "Take a look! Our friend has turned and is slowing!"

As a unit the Death Merchant and the other men swung their eyes out to sea, to where the strange cabin cruiser had made a wide turn and, almost two miles off to port, was now running parallel with the *Lonely Lady*.

"That settles it!" Jackie muttered under his breath, his hands on his hips. "That bastard ain't the Aussie coast-guard! Man, what a yacht! She must have cost a triple bundle!"

He raised his glasses and began bringing the huge plea-sure boat into closer, sharper focus, his glabrous skull dot-ted with a billion beads of sweat.

Silence wrapped its arms around the men as they studied the newcomer. Through binoculars Camellion saw that the vessel was big, almost a hundred feet long; its length put it in the inboard-motor yacht class. A luxurious vessel, the sleek, neat-as-a-bandbox look provided by teak and ma-hogany, she was powered by either twin gasoline or diesel engines, Camellion thought. *Yes, a custom job built by a private boatyard—built for a nut like C. W. Silvestter!*

The ship had a high freeboard, her bridge also high on the two-deck mid-shelter cabin that dropped to one deck toward the stern. A two-master, one back of the bridge, the second in front of the walk-down stern hatch. Yes sir . . . everything was there for the billionaire who already had everything—*wall-to-wall carpeting, no doubt . . . a well-stocked bar and a large frozen-food storage compartment.*

The numerous wheels of Camellion's mind, well-oiled with the experience of a thousand battles, began turning in another devious direction, while he continued to study the long, trim hull, which was painted a flat, dead black and whose sides were pierced by a double row of round eye-sockets covered with porthole glass, off which the bright sun glistened.

The vessel had an ample beam, and Camellion's keen eyes could tell that the craft had a hard-chine displace-ment hull rather than the planing or semiplaning hulls found on pure sailers or motor sailers. The big, trim bas-tard was V-shaped forward, but the stern was round and almost flat.

The cut of her hull, the way she was constructed, told

the Death Merchant that while the boat could generate a lot of speed forward, it required a lot of room, a lot of ocean space to swing either to port or starboard. On turns, because of her hull, she would also pitch and roll more than *Lonely Lady*.

Richard consumed the vessel with his sharp gaze, from stern to bow. There were men along her starboard and on the bridge deck. More men were forward.

Kimber, the British agent, broke the silence. *"The Astaroth!"* he exclaimed. "What kind of a bloody name is that?"

Camellion moved his binoculars to the gold name plate on the side of the bow. *ASTAROTH* was printed in raised black letters.

"Astaroth is the Hebrew form of *Astarte,"* explained Camellion. "Astarte was the Phoenician goddess of love and fertility. The Bible Book of Bull refers to her as Ashtaroth or Ashtoreth; and since the gods of any conquered people invariably become the 'devils' of the conquerors, we find Astaroth is one of the big boys of Hell. Only the Christians changed her into a him. After all, whoever heard of a she-devil, except in married life?"

"I'll be damned!" laughed Harmsworth. "That's a hell of a note!"

Jackie returned the fieldglasses to his eyes and, with the others, saw at once how *Astaroth* intended to fight. On the forward deck of the huge motor yacht, ten feet from the bow, four men were jerking canvas from a deck cannon that appeared to be a German 5.5-cm Gerat 58, one of the finest medium antiaircraft guns in the world!

"By God," said Wiseloggle in alarm, "those son of a bitches are going to try to blow us out of the water!"

As Jackie Harmsworth brushed past him, headed for the cabin below, he glanced fearfully at the Death Merchant, as if Camellion had the instant answer.

"We're not going to stay up here and pray for rain!" Camellion sighed, giving the other three intelligence agents a brief let's-get-with-it look, then bracing himself as *Lonely Lady* swung violently to port, and back again to starboard, a split second later.

107

Harmsworth, in the cockpit below, had taken over the wheel and was zigzagging the boat, in order to make it a more difficult target to hit—and none too soon. Just as Camellion and the other four men reached the lower deck, where Fred, Max, and Eli were finishing the task of putting the port, starboard, and stern panels into place, the New Dawn slobs on board *Astaroth* opened up with 5.5-cm Gerat 58-AA gun. The first shell whizzed across the two-mile distance between the two boats and exploded twenty yards astern of *Lonely Lady,* throwing up a huge column of water.

"Damn!" Wiseloggle said. The single word had a strangled sound, and the CIA agent's eyes flickered left and right, as if seeking escape. "That damned shell could have blown us out of the water, if it had hit!"

"But it didn't!" Pavel Telpuchovskii said, with a trace of a smile. He stooped and picked up a .45 M3-A1 submachine gun that had a flash-hider and a sixty-five-cartridge magazine. "Of course, the next shell might. Let's hope it doesn't!"

The next Gerat 58-AA almost did, exploding five or six yards off starboard; the terrific explosion threw a lot of water over the ship, the concussion battered at their eardrums.

"And that one didn't either!" Pavel laughed, calmly lighting a cigarette.

Wiseloggle only glared at him. Why, the damned Russian seemed to be actually enjoying himself! He was exactly like the Death Merchant, a cold-blooded realist with a strong will to live, an attirubte that made him a hunter who could smell danger. Men who loved life but respected death were always the dangerous ones.

Kimber and de Gasquet stretched their heads up, their fearful eyes licking the reinforced panels the three CIA "sailors" had attached to the top of the port and starboard sections, over the open portion of the cabin. The Englishman and the Frenchman also saw how the top and side panels completely blocked the view of Jackie Harmsworth, an arrangement that necessitated his standing up in the cockpit.

In the section directly over the wheel there was a large, round hole; by putting his head and shoulders through the opening, Jackie had a clear vision of all thirty-two points of the compass; he was protected by a dome (really two domes, one within the other), fitted snugly over the aperture, a dome of thick mellaglass, the best bulletproof glass the Corning Glassworks could devise. Naturally a direct hit would tear the glass apart like tissue paper—not that anyone would give a damn! A direct blast on the cockpit and no one would be alive to worry about anything . . .

Kimber and de Gasquet (both men wondered how they could use submachine guns with any effectiveness—at a range of almost two miles?) were not afraid of dying. Battled-hardened, they merely calculated the odds, then did their best. No man could do better . . . Patiently they waited for the Death Merchant to give orders, watching his expressionless face and every move he made. He was unbelievably composed. Was it all a pose? No, decided both men. It was not. Nor was it that Camellion didn't give a damn. He was simply one hundred percent fatalistic. The bloody chap was one of those rare birds who would stand eyeball to eyeball with Death and snarl: *Do your best! Oui,* if today was the day that *Dieu* or the *Diable* called Monsieur *Mort Marchand* . . . so be it!

Sitting on a locker, Camellion scowled as he tied the laces of the canvas sneakers he had just put on—*This damned callus is killing me!* He stood up and, swaying with the motion of the boat, moved toward the cockpit in the stern. He felt the vibration of the engine through the deck boards, and was satisfied that—at least for the moment—everything had been done that could be done.

Another loud explosion! This one off starboard! For the last few minutes the man at the wheel of the *Astaroth* had been doing his very best to get closer to *Lonely Lady,* but his every attempt had failed, Harmsworth always swinging away.

Camellion visually inspected the five-foot area behind the cockpit. Max and Eli were mounting the firing tube of the Burney twenty-five-pounder to the low tripod, while Fred, the third CIA crew member, checked the nylon ropes fastened from the legs of the tripod and to the cleats of the stern railing. There was an opening in the stern panel that enclosed the stern—a foot wide and three feet high—through which the firing tube projected.

Woooommmmmmmmmmmmm! The Gerat 58-AA shell had been close, only fifteen feet from port, midship. *Lonely Lady* rocked violently, the eight men grabbing anything handy to keep from falling.

"See! That one missed, too!" Pavel said cheerfully. Holding onto the side of the steps, he laughed, his teeth clamped on his cigarette. "Today's not our day to die. Then again, maybe it is and it's not time yet . . ."

Fred Mancoy stood up, braced himself by grabbing a hand railing, and glanced at Camellion, then at the Burney, which resembled an oversized bazooka, except for the four Venturi throats sticking out from around the breech.

"How does this thing work?" he asked Camellion. He was a mild-mannered man in his middle twenties, built like a college athlete. "It's a recoilless weapon, isn't it? Something like a Kromuskit?"

The Death Merchant nodded slightly, saying, "The principle is based on the idea that if an equal force—after a shell explodes—escapes at each end of the barrel, or tube, they will cancel each other out, and the gun will be recoilless." He looked down and touched one of the Wallbuster shells with the tip of his foot. "You've got to use special shells or—"

Lonely Lady rocked like a cork in a typhoon, the concussion ear-splitting. The Gerat 55-AA had exploded not more than twenty feet from the port and a bit to the stern. Two tons of water slammed over the low freeboard, some of it pouring in through the cracks of the roof over the cabin.

The men glanced nervously at each other, no one smiling, not even Pavel Telpuchovskii. For a change he was also grim-faced.

Camellion moved closer to Jackie Harmsworth, whose head and shoulders were beyond the cabin roof, enclosed within the dome over the cockpit.

"Jackie, do you have the engine on full throttle, and can

we outrun the other yacht?" the Death Merchant called up.

"No to your first question," Jackie yelled down, "and yes-and-no to your second. There's no way we can outdistance the mother-frigger in a straight stretch, but we have better maneuverability. We've got a shorter and narrower hull and a lower freeboard. If we can spin on a dime, that son of a bitch will need a dollar to do it! Want me to swing our stern to her port so's you can open up with the Burney?"

"Yeah, but get in to within half a mile, and try to keep our stern away from her bow," Camellion said. "Their Gerat-58 isn't on a full-circle mount, and they can only fire the gun in a triangular pattern."

"Hang on! Here we go!" Jackie said in a deep growl. Ducking down into the cockpit for a moment, he pushed in on the throttle, making the engine roar with a deeper insistence of power.

As Jackie swung the boat to starboard, beginning a short turn—as short as he could make it—that would take him in a direction opposite to *Astaroth*, then, as he completed the loop, back again in the same direction, only a mile and a half closer . . . Camellion did some fast and furious thinking—*We cannot outrun the other boat! She will either blow us out of the water, or else we've got to wreck her!*

He studied the port and starboard panels whose port holes contained not glass, but round steel plates. But like ordinary portholes, the plates were hinged and could be pulled open.

The four other intelligence agents and the three CIA "sailors" contemplated the Merchant of Death, who at the moment resembled a philosopher pondering the secret of life. In a sense he was—only he was weighing their chances of staying alive! He continued to scrutinize the closed ports.

Hmmmmm! Astaroth has a high freeboard. If we get in too close, the slobs on board that big baby can lob down hand grenades on us. Machine guns won't matter. The slugs will bounce off our steel roof deck. We will have one advantage—should we get in close, that close: The enemy

111

won't be able to use their Gerat-58. At such close range, they won't be able to depress the barrel down far enough to be effective. The shell would sail over us and explode far off to our starboard. Ahhh, there is a catch! Hand grenades can do just as much damage as a 5.5-cm shell!

In the simplicity of his thoughts there was a suggestion of things remembered so vaguely that he couldn't place it at once . . . as though he had had thought these same thoughts in another time and in another place. He supposed that he had as his mind turned to the disadvantages facing Lonely Lady . . .

In close to Astaroth *we won't be able to use choppers because her main deck's too high for us to angle the fire upward through our low portholes.*

Yet . . . if we can stay abreast of her, at say a hundred yards, and at the same time keep our bow back along her midsection, they won't be able to lob grenades at us, nor will the Gerat-58 be able to traverse at an angle that will make it a threat. But we'll be able to rake her decks with submachine gunfire!

"What do you have in mind, my Amerikanski friend?" Pavel asked. He closed his cigarette lighter and exhaled a cloud of smoke. "Something not too risky, I hope!"

As if applying mental telepathy and reading Camellion's mind, Wiseloggle, Kimber, and de Gasquet had begun opening the gun ports, Kimber saying airily, "We might as well have a go at it, I suppose. We can't keep dodging those bloody shells forever!"

Wiseloggle looked startled, which was only natural, since he was a man who worried so much about tomorrow's rain that he couldn't enjoy today's sunshine.

"We sure as hell can't do much damage with machine-gun fire!" he said, directing the words at the British agent. "Our best bet is to keep dodging as we head in for the coast. With our low draft we can get a lot closer to shore than she can. And we don't have a stabilizing fin to worry about!"

Another 5.5-cm shell exploded, close to starboard, rocking *Lonely Lady* and throwing up a column of water that bathed her decks from midships to stern. Camellion almost fell flat on his face as he stumbled toward the Burney RCL.

Expertly Jackie had executed the turn to starboard, and now the *Lonely Lady* was headed west as *Astaroth*, still moving east, also began a turn, her skipper no doubt thinking that the seventy-five-foot brigantine was trying for an escape by racing in the opposite direction. However, *Astaroth* was much slower in turning than *Lonely Lady*, and because of her broad beam and length she also required almost three times the space in which to maneuver. By the time she had made a complete turn, her prow cutting the water toward the west, the *Lonely Lady* was again making a pivot, as if trying to do a ballet on the waves—this time to starboard—a complete roundabout that brought her bowsprit pointed at the much larger vessel. The smaller vessel charged right in at an angle as Captain Paul Weidamier, the skipper of *Astaroth*, standing on the bridge, both hands on the wheel, stared in disbelief. By God! Was the damned boat going to try to ram *him!* Of course not! She was too small a vessel for such drastic action. What then was the damned boat trying to do?

Weidamier swung the wheel to starboard and bellowed at this first officer—a sinister-faced Jap named Yumio Nama, whom everyone called Yum-Yum—to order the men manning the Gerat-58 to do a better job.

"Tell those stupid son of a bitches I want them to *hit* that damned boat!" he snarled in frustration. As if the gunners hadn't been trying to blow *Lonely Lady* out of the Indian Ocean!

As *Astaroth* went into her turn, Weidamier and Yum-Yum got another big surprise that stirred their broth of confusion—which was already bubbling.

Lonely Lady had also swung to starboard, so sharply it seemed her skipper was trying to move her in a circle. Her stern skidded on the slick pavement of sea and—*Vvvooooommmmmm!*

The shell exploded only ten feet from the bow of *Astaroth*, the giant spray caused by the blast throwing itself over the gunners as the prow plowed right through the thick column of water!

"I'll be a cross-eyed son of a bitch!" the second office of *Astaroth* yelled. "They got some kind of gun mounted in the stern—and look at that crazy housing enclosing the cockpit!"

The man had a face that would have sent Frankenstein's monster running home to hide in a cellar. His name was Pong Laut Sanghe; he was an Indonesian and an expert in Tai Kwon Do, the Korean martial art.

"Tell me something I don't know, you idiot!" Weidamier snarled, just as a second and a third shell from *Lonely Lady* exploded, the first damn close to the large round stern, the second going off close to midship, so close that water even splashed up through the open windows of the bridge deck.

One thing was very clear to Captain Weidamier, Yum-Yum, and Sanghe: Whoever was doing the firing was good, very good, and was quickly getting the range.

Cursing almost as furiously as a Brisbane prostitute, Captain Weidamier spun the wheel, to the left, to port, in a desperate attempt to dodge the incoming shells. He succeeded. The next shell fell twenty yards to the starboard stern . . .

Staring through the three-by-one-foot space of the panel in the stern. The Death Merchant was more angry than a neurotic mother-in-law. All those shots and he had missed —But how does one synchronize the movements between two boats, each dodging and weaving, each trying to kill the other?

He watched the big motor yacht turn to port, her sleek, black hull cutting through the water like a tremendous barracuda. Proving how stupid they were, the gunners manning the Gerat 58-AA sent another round at *Lonely Lady*. Another 5.5-cm shell was wasted, exploding far to starboard of *Lonely Lady*.

Grim-faced and coldhearted, the Death Merchant shoved another wire-mesh bagged shell into the breech of the Burney, closed the breech, locked it, and, looking through the crosshairs of the Werfer type sights, adjusted the alti-azimuth, his long fingers delicately moving the

114

knob on the tripod flange mount. He made a few quick adjustments, making allowances for the time that would pass between the movement of *Astaroth* and the trajectory of the Wallbuster shell. He turned the AA adjustment, elated to discover he was still optimistic in spite of the previous misses. The subconscious is always a builder, and his had built well. It had completed Camellion into the perfect manhunter, flawless in spirit and form, incredible when compared to the hopes and dreams of normal men. Most men are blinded to the imperfections of the reality in which they exist. The Death Merchant had no such illusions about life, nor about himself.

He moved the Burney RCL Recoilless Rifle, centering the crosshairs on a space fifty feet ahead of the bow of *Astaroth,* then flipped the firing lever. A *whooshhhhhhh* as the shell left the forward end of the tube, another *whooshhhhhhhhhhhh* as the gasses rushed out the throats of the Venturi tubes in the rear.

Flinty-eyed, the Death Merchant watched the results. The shell went out across the water at one angle, the *Astaroth* at another, the two almost meeting in the same general area, but not exactly as Camellion had planned. The Wallbuster exploded high, twenty feet too high, shearing off the main mast, some fifteen feet above the bridge.

Fudge! Camellion did receive a measure of consolation by reminding himself that his last shell had done more damage to Astaroth than all her previous shells had done to *Lonely Lady*.

"A damn good shot!" Jackie called down. "That last one should give them the triple shits!"

Standing up as he was, his head in the bubble of mellaglass, all Jackie had to do was swivel around to see what was happening on *Astaroth.* In contrast the other occupants of the cabin, who were limited to looking through the port and starboard gun ports, could see only empty water when *Lonely Lady's* stern was pointed at the other vessel.

Camellion braced himself when Jackie turned to port in an attempt to "stern in" again at either the port or starboard side of *Astaroth,* depending on how the big motor yacht turned.

115

There was only one thing Jackie had forgotten, although Camellion had not: Captain Weidamier, an ex-commander of a German submarine, was neither a fool nor an amatueur at attack and evasion tactics. Now that he knew *Lonely Lady* was dangerous only when she presented her stern, he carefully slipped out of the traps that lay in Jackie Harmsworth's maneuvers. The smaller craft had the advantage in the turns, requiring only a small area of water; yet Silvestter's yacht was pure power in the short, straight lunges, the bursts of speed, short as they were, giving *Astaroth* a slight edge, enough to prevent the Death Merchant from zeroing in on the big black bastard, even when Jackie did manage to swing *Lonely Lady's* stern either to the port or starboard of the much larger vessel.

The two vessels continued to dodge each other . . . circling, moving forward, executing sharp turns to port and starboard, at times bursting ahead of each other . . . two angry monsters, keeping each other at bay. Beneath a sun glaring down angrily on the churning waters, on the waves and swells whipped up by the racing hulls, the two boats continued to circle each other, like two street fighters, each afraid of the other, each getting off a round now and then, the Gerat-58 booming, the Burney RCL hissing loudly, with neither doing any damage to the other.

The big advantage lay with *Astaroth!* If she had to, she could outdistance *Lonely Lady;* all *Lonely Lady* could do was dodge and weave on the water and hope that the men at the Gerat 58 didn't get lucky and slam in a fatal 5.5-cm shell.

An hour passed, during which time the Death Merchant had reached the conclusion that if *Lonely Lady* were to survive, drastic action would have to be taken. There was no need to bully himself with a lot of questions about what could happen, with trying to unravel the past or pierce the future. It was only the present that mattered, a present in which a lucky 5.5-cm shell might blow *Lonely Lady* right out of the water.

The conclusion closed in his mind with the finality of a doomed soul sliding down the chute to Hell: *We'll never stop the black bastard playing this kind of ring-around-*

116

the-rosie! There's no other way! I'll have to board her!

He surveyed the cramped, low cabin. One of the men had opened the vent in one of the panels forming the top deck over the cockpit area, but the air was still thick with acrid fumes from the back blast coming through the throats of the Berney's Venturi tubes. Each shot only added to the bluish haze. The unrelenting sun, beating down on the steel deck roof of the low cabin, didn't increase the comfort index; it did decrease the well-being of the men, who were almost standing in puddles of their own sweat. Every day they had seen the the the sneering sun sink shamefacedly, without pomp or show, into the Western waters. They wondered if they would be around to see the sunset today! Or end up as fish food at the bottom of Torres Strait?

Based on the events of the last sixty minutes, they had the creepy feeling that Camellion wasn't about to ace out the black yacht with the Burney RCL and that sooner or later the other gunners were going to score a hit, if only be accident! Almost to a man they felt they had over-estimated the Death Merchant, attributing the wild stories they had heard, his fantastic and incredible escapes and daring exploits, to ninety-five percent exaggeration based on five percent fact. Pavel Telpuchovskii was the exception. The KGB agent was convinced that Camellion was a man who—the Russian proverb said—accepted the bare skull beneath the skin. Pavel wouldn't have been unduly startled if Camellion had announced they were going to ram the *Astorath!* But when the Death Merchant said in a flat voice that he was going to board the black yacht, that was a bowl of borsch of a different recipe!

Pavel was as genuinely surprised as Wiseloggle, Kimber, and de Gasquet. As for the three CIA sailors, they were flabbergasted. By God! The nerve Camellion possessed had to be the tenth wonder of the world!

Watching astonishment pull a blanket over their faces, Camellion reiterated his intention to singlehandedly attack the *Astaroth,* cut her crew to pieces, plant a charge of plastic COMP-C3 on board, and blow the boat to hell!

"I'm going to board the *Astaroth* because if I don't, we'll end up buried here!" Camellion said, wiping thick streams

117

of sweat from his face. More sweat dripped from his chest and back.

Philippe de Gasquet forgot and said what he had been thinking.

"You are mad, Monsieur Camellion! Absolutely mad!"

Remaining silent, Pavel Telpuchovskii didn't think so. Poor de Gasquet . . . not to realize that the impossible becomes possible only to the mad!

The French agent's opinion didn't faze Camellion, who thought of de Gasquet as a conformist fool. Had the man been an American, he would no doubt have lived in the suburbs, have had a wife who baked brownies for the PTA; he would have been afraid to correct his own brats and would have made a deep mystery out of so normal a function as sex.

"Well, if you ask me—and you haven't—I think trying to get on board that black son of a bitch is carrying patriotism too far!" Fred Mancoy exclaimed, his sweat-stained face turned to Camellion.

He wiped his mouth with the back of his hand and handed the canteen to Kimber, who took it and gratefully swallowed a long drink.

Annoyed at Mancoy's remark, Camellion snapped right back, " 'Patriotism' is a word used to make morons feel guilty if they don't 'heil' whatever political party happens to be in power."

He grabbed a handhold as *Lonely Lady* rolled from the concussion of a 5.5-cm shell that had exploded very close to starboard.

Mancoy made a noise of surprise. "Then why take such a chance?"

"Money!" said Camellion in a sugar-sweet voice. "I don't get paid unless I complete the mission—and Silvester and all his devils aren't going to prevent me from collecting a hundred grand!"

Wiseloggle shook his blond head in total disagreement. Always lanky, there was a new gauntness about him that made him literally cadaverous. Tenseness had widened his eyes and deepened the hollows of his cheeks.

"You'll only collect a lot of slugs if you try to get on

board the enemy boat!" he said, his voice fearful. He glanced around the narrow confines of the cabin. "We might as well be inside an iron coffin! How do you think you're going to get on board? Go up to our cabin deck and Jump across. Damn it, man! They'll blow you into a dozen parts with small-arms fire!"

Pavel Telpuchovskii reluctantly agreed. "You will have no protection on the upper deck," he said quietly. "If you had that protection, it would still not matter. *Astaroth's* deck would still be five to six feet *above* you!"

The Death Merchant pointed to the small doorway in the front of the cabin, and as the men turned and stared at it, he said, "I intend to go through the forward to the bow and hide underneath the overhang of the rope locker. I don't need the cabin deck."

"And what's to prevent the enemy from looking down and blowing your ass off when we get close, if we get close?" Wiseloggle asked, with a wolfish grin. "There's no real protection in the bow!"

"I'm intrigued by how he intends to leap up the ten feet to the yacht's deck!" Kimber interjected. "I say, one would have to pole vault in order to do it!" He tried to make a joke of it. "I'm sure the other chaps aren't going to toss a rope ladder to you, old boy!"

The Death Merchant ignored the remark. If Kimber were an example of British efficiency and imagination, no wonder the US had been forced to pull the "Empire's" chestnuts out of two German fires within the last sixty years!

"None of you is very observant," Camellion said, as calm as a lake in heaven. "Or maybe it's because you didn't have a clear view of the other boat. She has a metal boarding ladder attached to her portside stern. If Jackie can bring our bow up to her stern—if he can get close enough—I can leap from our starboard side, grab her ladder and, hanging on her side, lob hand grenades onto her deck. In the confusion of the aftermath of the explosions I should be able to get on board, that is, climb onto her deck!"

119

Wiseloggle inhaled sharply. Kimber and de Gasquet gaped stupidly at Camellion.

"What do you think the New Dawn boys on board are going to be doing all that time?" Wiseloggle asked. "If they don't kill you when you make the leap, they'll chop you to liver when you're on the ladder!"

"Nathaniel is right," Pavel said, a somber cast to his handsome features. "Unless you wear a suit of bulletproof armor!"

"You're both wrong!' the Death Merchant said somewhat smugly. He looked straight at the Russian. "You're wrong because you, Pavel, are going to be at the cabin's front hatch. When I signal you from the bow, you're going to open up with a submachine gun and keep the enemy engaged while I make the jump, grab the ladder, and start the fireworks!"

The Russian pursed his lips, the first glimmer of the possibilities flaming in his eyes. His mouth twisted into a smile.

"It could work," he said slowly, as if speaking to himself.

"It has to," Camellion said.

"I think you're both crazy!" Wiseloggle said, sighing deeply. "If you insist on going through with it, we can increase the odds. I'll help Pavel cover you and—"

"You will not!" Camellion snapped, with razor-blade sharpness.

Wiseloggle jerked back, a stunned expression on his face. Kimber and de Gasquet reacted in a similar manner.

"I'll tell you why," Camellion explained quickly, his eyes drilling holes in the lanky CIA agent. "I don't know how good a shot you are. Pavel's an expert marksman. He proved that at the Colosseum in Rome. Do you understand what I'm saying, Nat? If you shot too high when I jumped, you might get me!"

"Have it your way," Wiseloggle said stiffly. He sat down heavily on a locker. "It's your neck; you're the one taking all the risk."

"I won't have to risk anything if Jackie can't get us in to *Astaroth*'s stern!" Camellion said, and moved toward the cockpit. "It all depends on him!"

"If he can't?" Pavel asked, lighting a cigarette.

There was a loud explosion to port. Once more *Lonely Lady* rolled violently on her beam ends, every man in the cabin reaching out to brace himself, all except Harmsworth, who, standing, was braced in the cockpit, both hands on the wheel.

The Death Merchant turned around and gave the Russian a big smile.

"That was your answer," he said. "If Jackie can't get us close to *Astaroth*, we'll end up permanently dead. Doesn't God let it rain on the just as well as the unjust?"

CHAPTER NINE

Can the dead weep? Can tears roll from the sightless eyes of a corpse? Strange thoughts trickled through the mind of the Death Merchant. Healthy flesh, no matter the color, can have the same fine-pored texture of marble, but a steel slug, once it enters that flesh, can begin a process of rot that consumes faster than cancer.

Crouched down in the bow, underneath the foot-wide overhang of the rope locker, the DM was as prepared to die as he ever would be, his only other protection the small, wooden ornamental walls on each side of the deck, curving inward toward the base knot of the bowsprit.

Patiently he waited for Harmsworth to spear the bow of *Lonely Lady* alongside the fat, round stern of *Astaroth*, a maneuver that Jackie, when Camellion had proposed it to him, had accepted as a challenge to his expertise at seamanship. "I'll put our bow up the Captain's hind end if you want me to!" he had confidently reassured the Death Merchant.

The only trouble was Jackie wasn't doing it! He had

tried! For the last fifteen minutes he had attempted to stab in his bow at the stern of the other vessel, alongside it; for the last fifteen minutes the two yachts had fenced with one another, churning the water with their turns, lunges and rushes, in a ballet of death that could only end with the loser sliding into an eternal dream, from which he would never awaken.

In spite of his lack of success Harmsworth had the advantage, in that Captain Weidamier still believed *Lonely Lady* was scooting all over the place in an effort to get in a stern shot. Twice Jackie had come very close to *Astaroth,* his bow within three feet of the black devil's stern—but it had been her starboard side!

Then God smiled on *Lonely Lady* and the Devil turned away from the *Astaroth.* At the wheel, so furious he had reverted to cursing in high German, Captain Weidamier guided his vessel east at almost full speed, while Jackie pointed *Lonely Lady* northeast, a direction that would bring his port across the big yacht's bow. It was a collision course, but Jackie was gambling that at the last moment the other captain would veer off, not wanting to risk any kind of damage that could possibly sink him. It was a gamble of life and death, and Jackie won. At the last moment, when it seemed the black ship would have to ram the port bow of the *Lady,* Captain Weidamier turned to port, a sharp turn that, when completed, would take *Astaroth* due west. At the same time Jackie turned slightly to starboard to avoid the swinging-around stern of *Astaroth.* Quickly then Jackie turned to port in pursuit, his bow right behind the stern of *Astaroth.*

Feeling like a mole whose tunnel had been uncovered and exposed to sunshine, Camellion was pleased with Jackie's success. *He's done it—almost! If our speed holds, he'll be able to put our port bow right up to her starboard side. If I miss the leap, I'll either be crushed between the two hulls or sink like a double anvil!*

The Death Merchant wasn't all that weighed down. He had strapped on two .45 Colt automatics and on the same belt carried a Marine combat knife and a long canvas holster filled with two spare submachine-gun magazines. A canvas utility bag was on his left hip, its strap over his right shoulder. It contained hand grenades and a two and one-fourth-pound/eleven-by-two-by-two-block charge of plastic COMP C-3, which was far more powerful than TNT and could only be electrically detonated. Attached to the block of military explosive was a ten-minute timer with five-second gap intervals.

The Death Merchant glanced toward the small hatch opening of the *Lady's* deck cabin. There was Pavel Telpuchovskii, ready with his submachine gun, giving him the high sign, thumb and finger in an "O." Good deal! The Russian was all set!

Camellion looked in the opposite direction, toward the bow. There, to port, was the stern of *Astaroth,* now only ten feet from the *Lady's* bow. Higher forward, was the double-decked midship housing, men on the second deck staring in hate at the approaching *Lady.* Men were also on the stern deck, standing by the walk-in hatchway housing.

If only our speed holds!

The speed did! And Jackie did: He began closing the gap, bringing his port bow to the starboard stern of *Astaroth!*

All at once, Pavel Telpuchovskii opened up with his M3-A1 submachine gun, the big .45 slugs raking the stern deck and midship housing of the large yacht.

This is it! It was then, at that split second in eternity, that the Death Merchant wished he had chosen a less tempestuous line of work! He didn't have to do it, but he did . . . as the bow of *Lonely Lady* slid alongside the starboard stern of the *Astaroth.* With his heart rammed up in his throat to his ears and the skull head of Death grinning in his face, he jumped to the portside bow of *Lady,* crouched for a moment—listening to the aria of Pavel's .45 slugs as they screamed an opera over his head—then leaped out into space, his eyes on the starboard ladder of the other vessel, his hands reaching out.

A tiny moment of time—too short for even God to calculate—and Camellion was a creature of the air, suspended in nothingness . . . boiling sky above, racing water be-

123

low . . . water untroubled by the antics of any human being.

This is going to be easy! Well .——. all play and no work makes no jack! All set for the turmoil of an angry sea, he had jumped across waters that had the tranquility of a fishpond, the wind, more illusion than force, created by the sensation of speed.

The transition became complete, and Richard felt his feet skim water, and his hands touch racing black hull . . . the whining of Pavel's ricochets a marvelous concerto to his ears—*Yeah! Telpuchovskii's Concerto in "M3-Al" minor!*

Another half-second and one hand found one rung of the starboard ladder! *I've made it!* Camellion laughed, pulled himself closer, thrust his arm between the rung and hull, while holding on with the other hand, and pulled up his feet. He hung on tightly, one hand dipping into the utility bag dangling from his hip. *Astaroth* was about to be blessed with hand grenades!

Perched on the ladder—like some kind of half-naked parasite about to feed on steel (or in this case, a termite about to gobble teakwood!), Camellion, as fast as he could, flung three grenades to the stern and rear midship deck of the vessel, trying to space them at least ten feet apart.

As the grenades exploded, one after another, Pavel stopped firing and *Lonely Lady* dropped back, Harmsworth turning to starboard. The Death Merchant was on his own . . .

The echo of the three explosions were still laughing hollowly across sky and sea when Camellion—who wasn't singing "Onward Christian Soldiers"!—pulled himself over the side railing onto the deck, his M-3 submachine hungry for the enemy.

The grenades had not done too much damage, having exploded in an open area, the force of the blast going upward. They did blow apart most of the stern hatch housing, make kindling wood of a lot of deck chairs and kill one man standing by the hatchway. A second man, his left leg blown off at the knee, lay unconscious and bleeding to death. The three grenades had accomplished their main purpose: They had forced other New Dawn killers, on the second deck of the midhouse, to drop down flat. By the time they recovered their wits, the Death Merchant was aboard, scrambling to safety behind the remnant of the blasted hatch housing whose top on all three sides was a mass of jagged, protruding splinters.

His mouth pulled back in a sneer, he reached the back of the housing at about the same time the topside crew recovered from the shock of the three explosions . . . snuggling down to avoid the vicious blasts from half a dozen Austen Mark-1 9-mms—submachine guns of Australian manufacture.

A lean, mean machine, Camellion almost felt the hot breeze of the slugs slamming outward across the fat-ass stern of the boat, the burning streams of metal going over and around of what remained of the housing. More 9-mms punched into the thick, hard wood, chipping off more splinters. Glancing down, Richard saw that one slug had penetrated the wood of the back wall—almost —the steel point barely sticking through the wood, pointed directly at his stomach!

Fudge! As Jackie would say, this is a lot of goddamn crap, and I'm going to do something about it!

Cold fury turned Camellion into a maniac, not a madman hitting out in all directions at once, but a brutal physical mechanism controlled by a clever, calculating mind that knew from past experience just what to do . . . all the proper moves to make.

I can't remain here, pinned down . . . with no place to go, but Hell or into the sea!

He took out a grenade, pulled the ring, and tossed it over the jagged top of the housing, toward midship, his mouth a twisted line as he heard the terrific detonation five seconds later—*And the meek shall inherit the earth! Yes indeed! Like the dumbbells who scream "Peace" the loudest but are the first to get war, the meek will inherit the earth—six feet of it, and one casket to each gutless idiot!*

He counted then, took out another grenade, pulled out the ring, and tossed it in the same direction. This time he

125

would be the aggressor! The moment it exploded he stuck his head around one side of the hatch housing, his finger on the .45 M3-Al submachine gun.

The second deck of the midship housing was empty. So was the doorway, as well as the hatchway of the first-deck housing. Then men rushed from both doorways, but they never had a chance to open fire. Half rising, the Death Merchant did a long number on them, playing a vicious symphony of slugs, an orchestration of Death, the lines of .45 slugs slicing into screaming flesh, smashing, ripping, tearing.

Death caught three men on the top deck ten times over, a flood of slugs meat-grinding them into eternity. They knocked one man back against the wall, after tearing out his belly and chest. Bloody and butchered, he collapsed to the catwalk, a zero in the cosmos!

Two more New Dawn dummies pitched over the second-deck railing, one man's face shot off, the other half-wit's heart and lungs laundered with a dozen .45 slugs.

It had become Morgue Day on the *Astaroth,* and the corpses were piling up, celebrating the festival of the Great God Death!

The men who had run out of the first-deck hatchway also got a bath of .45 slugs that tore them into bloody nothings and shut off their souls forever . . .

"The Death Merchant! He's—on board!" The guttural voice floated up to Camellion from below, through the hatchway whose housing was protecting him, the man who had spoken sounding as if he had a mouthful of rocks! The voice crashed into the Death Merchant's brain like a cleaver, filling him with more anger. Savagely he knocked off two more men on the top deck, exhausting the last of his shells from the magazine of the submachine gun. Quickly he reloaded, then calmly dropped two hand grenades over the back wall of the hatch, smiling as he heard them plop-plop-plop down the steel stairs, humming a part of Brahms Academic Festival Overture as they exploded, making the deck under his feet tremble and shake.

While dropping the two grenades, he had put the odds and arguments (For *vs.* Against) through the logic circuits of his mind; now he had the answer: *Attack!* To give himself cover, he lobbed another grenade at the stern end of the midship cabin, waited until it exploded in a flash of red and orange, then charged across the deck, which was rolling with the ship. He was aware of *Lonely Lady,* a few hundred yards off starboard. She was still dodging Gerat-58 shells fired from the bow of *Astaroth* and occasionally getting off a shot of her own. J. Warren Kimber had taken over the Burney RCL—but his aim was about as effective as a tissue-paper umbrella in a hurricane!

Camellion was only six feet from the first-deck doorway of the cabin when two New Dawn agents, dressed in blue shorts, loomed up in the hatchway, their mouths falling open in alarm and terror, their mouths closing as Camellion stitched their stomachs with two slugs each, both men looking as dumbfounded as a new bride who had just discovered she couldn't boil water without burning it! Instantly they stopped looking surprised; they merely died!

Once inside the cabin Richard saw he was in the radio room. He also saw the three men in front of the cabin, to the left, coming down the stairs that led up to the second deck—and they saw him! They also fired before he could raise his M-3 and zero in on him.

"Kill the son of a bitch!" shouted a tall creep with a shaved head and wide staring eyes! All three tried, Tall Creep using an Austen Mark-1 submachine gun, the other two firing Browning 9-mm pistols—all three missing, their rain of steel whizzing by Camellion, who had flung himself to the other side of the cabin. As incredibly quick as he was, two slugs did come within half an inch of his head, while another grazed the top of his right shoulder, leaving a cut that would heal smoothly . . . on a body already a crossword puzzle of scars.

Tall Creep was a lousy shot. All his slugs did was wreck the shortwave radio set, ending its life. Camellion, firing as he moved, terminated the breathing of the New Dawn members on the steps.

To save ammo he cut them down with short spitting burst, his slugs covering them like a burning blanket. Tall Creep got four slugs in the face and fell without features!

127

He didn't have a head nor any brains either! And because the Death Merchant had fired upward from a crouching, sideways position, the second and third got the fatal business high up. A dozen slugs chopped into clavicles and breastbones—one joker got his throat torn out—and the two idiots pitched forward, dumb, useless, and dead!

The Death Merchant didn't give them a second look. The hell with the 10,001 clay pigeons! He wanted the wild duck—*And Silvestter, in New Eden, is a long way off!*

Richard drew in a long breath, straightened up and, preparing to jump over the bodies on the steps, looked up toward the bridge house. Beneath him the deck throbbed from the engines in the vessel's bowels, a steady hum that didn't mesh with the stink of burnt gunpowder and the sweetish odor of blood and spilled brains.

Thinking that the place needed a good deodorant, Camellion caught sight of the man staring down at him! Lying on the floor, the slant-eyed simpleton was peering from around the opening at the top of the steps—a Jap who jerked back as Camellion let fly a short burst that missed, the slugs ricocheting off the ceiling of the bridge deck.

"The bastard's killed all of them!"

Camellion felt a warm, tingling pleasure at the scared-stiff sound of the Jap's voice.

Yes, sir! It's gung-ho all the way! Stepping lightly over the three corpses, Camellion padded softly up the steps, ever so often triggering off short bursts that sent the slugs in through the top opening at an angle that prevented the men on the bridge from standing close to the stairway and firing down at him.

How many were waiting for him on the bridge, their weapons pointed at the opening? As if he'd be dumb enough to trot on up the steps and let them butcher him with a blast of steel!

As my old pappy used to say—or was it George Washington?—to be prepared for war is one of the most effectual means of preserving peace! It also prevents the enemy from blowing out your brains!

Pausing, almost at the top of the steps, Camellion took

two grenades from his utility bag, two he had specially prepared on board *Lonely Lady*. A truly uncomplicated device, a hand grenade is nothing more than a lot of shrapnel built around a main bursting charge touched off by a fuse. You pull the ring that releases the striker pin that detonates the primer. In turn the primer triggers the five-second fuse that ignites the main bursting charge. The result is a lovely explosion, but only if you have a main bursting charge. These two hand grenades didn't. Camellion had removed their screw plugs, at the bottom of the grenades, and poured out the main charge, rendering them harmless, except for the small detonating charge in the copper-tube fuse. In effect, he had converted the grenades into nothing more than large firecrackers.

Smiling like an imp, bracing himself, he flipped both grenades over the opening onto the floor of the bridge deck, spacing them so that they fell on each side of the cabin.

"Grenades!" a voice screamed.

Another voice, jabbering in Japanese!

"Throw them out the windows!" A third voice . . . brutal, fearful.

Then the same voice, cursing in German!

The Death Merchant made his move. Knowing that the grenades would momentarily divert the attention of the men, he charged up the final seven steps—over the top, going in low, weaving like an animated pretzel! And firing!

His first burst caught an ordinary seaman full in the chest, a handful of slugs that smacked the slob instantly into the supposed "world beyond." One of the .45s also shattered a gold-plated chronometer!

At a glance Camellion saw that his ruse with the grenades had worked! The men on the bridge had been caught with their pants down, and their shorts on crooked!

To pile confusion on confusion, one of the hand grenades exploded with a big loud bang, the primer in the fuse having gone off.

The explosion demoralized the New Dawn dummies even more!

Half-turned to the wall, his arms over his face, Pong Laut Sanghe looked utterly astonished when after the explosion he found himself unharmed, unriddled by splinters of shrapnel . . .

Yumio Nama, the Jap first officer, appeared terrified. Down on one knee by the binnacle, a NATO AR-16 rifle in his hands, he glanced up at Camellion, the cast of his eyes ninety-eight parts fear and two parts disbelief.

There was both fear and rage in the squared jawed face of Captain Weidamier, who, half-turned to starboard, had just tossed the first grenade out the window. He looked like an idiot when the grenade exploded in midair, over the ocean, with a bang that wouldn't have frightened a girl-scout. Realizing then that Camellion had tricked them, Weidamier bellowed in rage.

"Du schweinhund!" he screamed, and tried to bring up the Walther P-38 in his hand. It was the last movement, but not the last motion, of his life.

"Auf wiedersehen, you dummy of a *Dummkopf!"* Camellion said and gently squeezed the trigger of the M3-A1 submachine gun.

The stream of hot metal flowed all over Captain Weidamier, bursting him open like a watermelon that had lain too long in the boiling sun, the blast banging him against the starboard wall of the bridge. One of the big .45 slugs even tore off his right shoulder-board captain's insignia. The others lifted away his life. Mouth as wide as the Grand Canyon, eyes staring into Hell, he dropped to the deck, blinked once—the last motion of his life—and died.

Yumio Nama followed a moment later. Cursing in Japanese, Yum-Yum lifted the Ar-16 rifle with amazing speed and snapped off two shots at Camellion, who jumped sideways and triggered the .45 M-3, the shower of slugs raining all over the Jap jackass, turning him into instant sukiyaki, but without the chicken and vegetables. This mess was only bone, blood, and chopped flesh. Yum-Yum dropped to the deck, and he was just as dead, too, as a grilled eel!

Pong Laut Sanghe surprised the Death Merchant by jumping to his feet, but *not* yanking the .38 Webley revolver from his belt. Curious as to what the huge ugly mountain intended to do, Camellion did not fire. He soon found out what the Indonesian had in mind.

Pure naked rage had made the goof forget both the Webley and the submachine gun in Camellion's hands. A simple soul, he reverted to his trained instincts that revolved around Tai Kwon Do. His only thought was to pull Camellion apart with his bare hands!

The hidiously ugly man screamed *"Kai-ieee!"*—the attack yell of an expert, and instantly went into a *Chunbi Sogi,* a ready stance. Then he charged, with all the speed of a brakeless ski train roaring down a mountain, his fists and arms all set for a *Sangdan Chirugi,* a terrible high punch that could have flattened a young, healthy bull!

What the bullet-headed boob didn't know was that Richard Camellion was also a master of the Oriental fighting arts—all of them, from the highly secretive *Choy Lay Fut Kung Fu,* the greatest of the Chinese martial arts, to Japanese *Ninjitsu!* The Merchant of Quick Dying was also five times faster.

"You've seen too many movies and have watched too much telly!" laughed Camellion. With incredible speed he stepped aside and at the same instant let Sanghe have a *Gamori Chungdan Apchagi* in his solar plexus, a bit to the right, a middle-front snap kick with a foot that could very easily break four one-inch pine boards. The same foot broke Sanghe, stomping his liver to brown jelly!

The wind shot from the Indonesian's lungs, his eyes widened, and his mouth formed a big "O." He made one last feeble attempt to grab the Death Merchant, who had become busier than a hungry hog rootin' in a turnip patch! Pivoting to the rear of the already dying Sanghe, Camellion followed up with a terrible *Empi* elbow smash in the right kidney area, then finished him off with multiple-fingered *Nukite* hand stab to the side of the neck, the terrific shock shaking Sanghe's brain like an earthquake.

Pong Laut Sanghe flowed to the deck, as lifeless as warm wax. He had fought his last *Tai Kwon Do* match. He had gambled with his life and had lost out to Death—*Well, that's life!*

No time for self-congratulation! The Death Merchant

131

had work to do, such as silencing the Gerat-58, whose crew was still trying to hit *Lonely Lady*. Whether it was their poor marksmanship that prevented them from scoring or Jackie Harmsworth's rich talent for seamanship was a moot question! What small luck the gun crew might have had ended when Camellion cracked open a forward bridge window, stuck the barrel through the opening, and cut loose. It was like bowling, the big, blunt .45 slugs knocking over the men with one long strike of death. The four corpses were still toppling to the deck as another group of crewmen tried to come up through the forward hatch, five feet behind the AA gun. They, too, walked into a rain of steel death. Camellion cut three to pieces, made the fourth jump over the port side into the sea, and caused the fifth man to fall backward down the narrow steps of the hatch, in his haste to reach safety.

Click! The firing pin of the .45 M-3 fell on empty space. The breech was empty! Hurriedly Camellion rammed in his last magazine and moved to the rear of the bridge deck, stopping on the way to pick up the AR-16 rifle. Why let the enemy's ammo go to waste?

Fudge—and burnt at that! Men were pouring from the stern hatch, racing in like attacking wolves, but dying like ordinary men—scared stiff—as Camellion opened up with the Nato rifle, the stream of darting 7.65-mm slugs dropping them quicker than Hell could sizzle tissue paper!— except for two or three New Dawners who had made it to the first-deck doorway of the midship housing before Camellion could splatter them. He knew what the "old chaps" were trying to do, what they had to do—kill him. They had no choice. He was in control of the boat.

For the hell of it Camellion spun the wheel to port, twisting *Astaroth* around like some kind of sea monster skidding on the waves. The sudden reversal rocked the pleasure yacht on her beams and caused the hull to shudder in protest as the bow swung left and the stern jerked to the right. The unexpected maneuver didn't help the three men who now were in the radio room and about to race up the steps to the bridge deck; it knocked them off their feet. The hand grenade Camellion dropped down the steps did even less to assist them! And this one wasn't a blank! It exploded in a flash of red and orange, killing one man outright. He fell backward, while his head rolled across the deck. The other two men had been blown across the room, one creep minus an arm, which, making like a birdie, had flown across the cabin and fallen on the demolished shortwave set. It lay there, dripping blood on a power pack whose power had been pulled with slugs.

The third son of a sad slut had been flung against the wall, with a force that rattled him from hook nose to navel; and by the time he had recovered his senses—*surprise!*—there was the Death Merchant, standing middleways on the stairs, his lips moving.

The man didn't hear the "Bye-bye, Dummy!" The blast of the grenade had made him as deaf as the mummy of Pharaoh's mother! But there wasn't anything wrong with his eyes. Very clearly he could see the deadly muzzle of the submachine gun in Camellion's hands!

The Death Merchant felt sorry for the silly sap. Why, gee, golly, gosh! The slob looked more frightened than Macbeth flinching before the ghost of Banquo! Then he looked dead-dead as Camellion sent him and the other drip to hell with a short burst of .45 slugs. *I've done them a favor! The world is a stinking place to live in!*

With no one at the wheel on the bridge *Astaroth* had become a vessel without purpose and direction, helpless, at the mercy of the water; she wobbled from port to stern, as if trying to make up her mind, cutting the water aimlessly.

Camellion stumbled to the doorway and looked out toward the stern, which was empty of Life but brimful of Death, the corpses piled around the splintered hatchway. To be on the safe side he tossed his last two grenades, waited until they exploded, then stumbled to the starboard funnel-type ventilator. He took a bottle of shark repellent from one section of the bag, opened it, and poured the contents over his body. He then removed the block charge of COMP C-3. and turned the small knob of the timer to four minutes, after which he dropped the brown oil-paper-wrapped charge down the funnel mouth of the ventilator.

A last look around the boat! He ran to the portside railing! Another look to make sure no one was trying to aim in on him! Over the railing then, a long dive far over the side. He cut the warm water with his hands, went under, rose, and began swimming toward *Lonely Lady,* which was coming in from the southwest.

The Merchant of Death turned and looked at the *Astaroth,* which had veered slightly to starboard. The sea had a deserted air, its emptiness as loud as a scream. Watching, he luxuriated in the water, the way a pig takes to a wallow. It oiled his tired muscles and calmed his nerves.

He was pouring another bottle of shark repellent into the lapping, all-embracing water when the COMP C-3 went off in the bowels of *Astaroth,* with the subdued *whoommmm* that resembled the angry belch of a Titan. Lazily *Astaroth* rolled over on her port side, down by the head, and took her terrible rest while the mounds of water pillowed her and washed her quietly. Like a disarray of complete weariness, starboard davits on the main deck dangled rope and swinging white life boats. She had her twin screws clear, pinned like two metal flowers on the stern, on either side of the swinging rudder.

There she lay in motionless lethargy, and then without pause or warning, she began to go. The shooting swell rose in a hill, rolling over her bows, Her funnel (it was there only for decoration) inclined. Water poured freely into it and into the high hoods of her ventilators. Like a pool, the dark gully of her small promenade deck filled forward. A great sigh of the wooden hull, a final shudder of surrender, and *Astaroth* slid under, down to her final deep sleep. The waters folded over her, and then there was nothing, nothing but some floating debris, a dozen or more corpses, and the kind of deadly quiet that comes after an air raid.

The past day had been calm, too calm. Once *Lonely Lady* had passed through the Coral Sea and was in the wide Pacific, Camellion and his men knew they were on the last lap of their long journey. Tomorrow afternoon, with any luck, they would dock in Brisbane—and it would take not only luck but seamanship to ride out the approaching squall, although they had been assured by Jackie Harmsworth that the *Lonely Lady* could withstand the wild winds of the Pacific. With the exception of Camellion, who didn't give a triple damn, the other men weren't at all convinced. After all, the caprice of winds, like the wilfulness of men, is fraught with the disastrous consequences of self-indulgence. The southwest wind is worst of all. He breathes his rage in terrific squalls, and overwhelms his realm with an inexhaustible welter of clouds; he strews the seeds of anxiety upon the decks of scudding ships and makes the foam-stripped ocean look old.

Preceding the fury of the elements had been a mysterious gloom, like the passage of a shadow above the firmament of blue-black clouds. That evening the red ball of a sun had dipped into an ocean already restless, as a vast curtain of velvet was being drawn across the wide bowl of the sky. The wind rose gradually, the drops of rain falling separately, each one a tiny blow, each one a tiny preview of what was coming. When the darkness was complete, the wind became stronger, the clouds denser and more overwhelming, the crashing thunder followed by jagged streaks of beautiful blue and purple lightning. The rain thickened. The waves grew longer, larger and more threatening. The hours, whose minutes were marked by the crash of the breaking seas, slipped by with the screaming, pelting squalls smashing at the *Lonely Lady* as she ran on, her decks dripping, her hull tortured . . . Jackie fighting the wheel. The water fell in torrents, and it seemed that the ship were going to be drowned before she sank, as if all the atmosphere had turned to water . . .

The Death Merchant sat fingering a small vial of "Destroying Angel," a mushroom poison that was very deadly . . . his mind looking ahead to the state of Queensland. He wasn't worried about the squall. They would either survive or they wouldn't. If they did, there would be no problem. If they didn't, they'd be dead, in which case there still wouldn't be a problem!

The other men were not so philosophical. Silently they sat, hunched down, listening to the roaring of the wind and the crashing of the waves over and across the slim needle-like hull of *Lonely Lady*. And the news they had received

earlier over the shortwave—directly from The Hub—
hadn't done anything toward making them feel cheerful:

Señor Luis Carrero Blanco, the Premier of Spain, had
been assassinated that very morning in Madrid . . . blown
to bits by a bomb, the force of the blast lifting the car like
a toy, throwing it five stories high, over the roof of the
church rectory and onto a balcony overlooking an inner
courtyard.

Blanco's power in Spain had been exceeded only by that
of his political mentor—Generalissimo Francisco Franco.

Another score for Cleveland Winston Silvestter, the
Chosen One!

CHAPTER TEN

Shielded from the unrelenting sun by a light brown Aussie bush hat with a leopard band, Richard Camellion
watched the Globemaster cargo plane being unloaded,
wishing it could have landed closer to C. W. Silvestter's
ranch and New Eden, both of which were fifty-eight miles
to the northwest. But the Bjelke-Petersen Chalk ranch was
Silvestter's nearest neighbor. Either Camellion and his boys
landed at the B.-P.C. ranch or not at all!

Very carefully the pilots had set down on the sun baked
airstrip, fearing they might not have the needed length.
They hadn't had any room to spare; however, the big-bel-
lied cargo plane had landed safely. There would be no
trouble taking off, since she would be tons lighter.

Watching the Humbler armored car being driven down
the ramp from the rear of the Globemaster's fuselage, Richard knew that their next move, now that they were here,
would be to get to there, to Silvestter's giant sheep and cattle ranch—get there and utterly destroy New Eden! Take

136

C. W. Silvestter alive and make the CIA brass happy—
bovine excrement! There was more of a chance that the
Pope would turn Jewish!

There was a road of sorts, twisting through the bush to
Silvestter's empire, but in the 100-degree heat progress
would be torturous. The virgin roughness of the Queensland countryside would impede the trek in no small way,
contribute only misery and a thirst for cool comfort.

Already Camellion felt he was in the middle of nowhere,
which he wasn't! He was in the northeastern section of
Queensland—only one step away from nowhere! All he
had to do was look around him to increase the feeling that
he was a settler in the "outback." A couple hundred feet
from where the Globemaster squatted like a giant pregnant
duck, a huge 180-foot-tall King Karri tree reached for the
sky, heavy with tumbling cumuli; and beyond it, a mile distant, was a flock of seven-foot-tall, flightless emus, moving
about aimlessly on the downs. High up in the King Karri, a
kookaburra bird occasionally burst into crazy laughter, as
if the damn fool bird were thinking that Camellion and his
men were making fools of themselves!

Maybe we are! But I doubt it! Camellion's icy blue
eyes, protected behind very dark sunglasses, became mere
slits as he thought of the past few days . . .

A bruised and battered *Lonely Lady* had made port, five
hours late—still better than not at all. At a glance Camellion saw that Brisbane (pronounced "Brizbun") had not
changed one iota since the last time he had been there. It
was still the same misproportioned down-under city—
850,000 people in an area larger than all of New York
City. The people were the same—young women with brats
on their back . . . young men swinging in and out of coffee bars; the same fierce traffic, in a city where the summer
"uniform" for many businessmen was white shirt, tie, hat,
shorts, and kneesocks. The same "Casket" signs were
there, but instead of advertising the kind in which corpses
are buried, they referred to the state lottery, which ridiculously enough was called the *Golden Casket Art Union,*
this curious appellation coming from the old British continental practice of raffling off works of art.

Another oddity that always amused Richard was the affinity the people of Brisbane and those of its hinterland had with one aspect of the Soviet Union: their abnormal preoccupation with culture. Desperately did the people of Brisbane went to be considered "cultured," and the Russian word *nekulturny,* indicating the pervasive stigma attached to nonculture, was understood by almost everyone in Brisbane.

Only two hours after docking, Camellion and his five companions were conferring with two representatives from the central government in Canberra and with Hector Geffling, the Australian intelligence officer who would be in charge of the Aussie commandos going along on the mission—not ten men as originally pledged, but twenty tough fighters, one of whom was a tall, burr-headed half-caste "abo," with the unlikely name of Roosevelt Windsor Jones! Camellion wasn't at all surprised; he knew that the 75,000 aborigines (almost 50,000 were half-castes) left in Australia lived in all stages of evolution—everything from cavemen to jeep-riding cowboys and soldiers.

Right off Geffling explained that he was responsible for getting twenty men instead of ten. "I told those blokes in Canberra that if we didn't 'ave the proper 'elp, there wouldn't be any use in 'aving a go at Silvestter's fortress!" he said.

A wiry little blighter, with an open windburned face that sported a long mustache curled upward at each end, Geffling had large hands, an insatiable appetite for beer, and a "bushie" manner, indicating he was used to getting things done.

He had certainly done his job with the Australian Defense Ministry, and because he had, the Death Merchant was now watching the giant Globemaster disgorge all kinds of death-dealing goodies.

One of the commandos drove the Humbler armored car down the ramp and parked it close to one side of the four-engine aircraft, not far from where Nat Wiseloggle and Jackie Harmsworth were standing. Pavel Telpuchovskii, J. Warren Kimber and Philippe de Gasquet stood on the other side of the plane, parallel to Camellion, who noticed

138

how Pavel was sizing up the Globemaster. The KGB agent would have a lot to report to the Kremlin—if he got back to the USSR.

Camellion watched the unloading of the cargo plane. *Yeah, the Humbler is a nice piece of equipment!* A squat, three-man, six-wheeled vehicle with a low-silhouetted turret, from which protruded a brace of 35-mm Oerlikon cannons. A .30-caliber Owens machine gun was mounted to the rear of the back hatch.

Following the Humbler down the ramp were four jeeps (one had a 105-mm recoilless gun mounted to braces behind the rear seat); at last came the armored half-track scout car, to which was mounted a rapid-fire 40-mm Bofors gun, its barrel depressed over the cab of the vehicle.

Commandoes carried other vital supplies from the plane —food rations, jerry cans of fuel and water, cases of shells, hand grenades, tear gas, smoke bombs, and small-arms ammo, all of which the men began carrying to the half-track, until Geffling ordered them to distribute the supplies among all the vehicles.

A good man! He doesn't want to risk putting all our eggs in one armored basket!

There were other supplies and weapons, including three recoilless rifles of the Burney type. The Death Merchant also noticed three wooden cases the commandos were carrying—green cases with large white "X's"—DM—Adamsite—gas, every bit as good as the Diphenylchloroarsine that Camellion had originally wanted to use. One tiny whiff of DM and the victim because intensely nauseated; then came the terrible vomiting, hours of retching that left him exhausted. There was no protection against DM, which also interferred with vision and equilibrium, except a special-type gas mask, of which Camellion and his men had an ample supply: two per man.

Finally the men carried the main demolition explosives from the aircraft: eight-pound blocks of TNT, three blocks per haversack, four satchels per wooden case. Enough explosive to—*yeah*—to blow New Eden all the way down to hell and back up again to heaven!

Smoking a cigarette, Geffling walked over to the Death

Merchant and pushed back his hunter's bush hat, sweat running down his leathery face.

"I say, old buster, we're almost set to head out," he said in a husky voice. "At least we've got some bloody good weapons, which don't make me the least bit un'appy!"

He waved a large hand toward the half-track and other vehicles.

"Patterned after American design, you know! You've some smart lads in your country, matey!"

"Yes, we have," Richard said, smiling slightly. "For instance, we have one genius named Kennedy. He's one of our Senators. He's so 'intélligent' he thinks the crime rate can be reduced by taking all hand guns from private citizens. Any fool knows that as long as criminals are petted and pampered by the courts, crime will not diminish no matter what is done about hand-gun laws."

Thinking the remark unusual, Geffling regarded Camellion with a curious eye. He had heard any number of incredible stories about the Death Merchant, but he hadn't heard that the bloke was anti-American.

"You don't like your government?" Geffling ventured. He glanced toward Pavel Telpuchovskii, Kimber, and de Gasquet, who were headed in his and Camellion's direction.

"I don't like stupidity and hypocrisy," Camellion replied harshly. "In most nations drug pushers are even given very long sentences or else executed. Not in the United States, the land of 'equal-opportunity crime'! In the US drug pushers are usually given five years, then paroled in two—turned loose to prey on society. Does that make sense to you . . . 'Old Buster'?"

No, it did not, but before Geffling could reply, Pavel Telpuchovskii addressed himself to the Aussie, using the intelligent agent's nickname.

"Comrade Heck, I trust that since you are the man in charge of food and medical supplies, you did not forget anti-venom in case of snakebite? I have read of the taipan snake, which is very ferocious and will attack on sight. This deadly species exists in Queensland, does he not?"

Geffling dropped his cigarette and stubbed it out with the heel of his heavy leather boot.

"You don't 'ave to worry about the taipan," he said cheerfully. " 'E's a rare sort of bastard. In me whole life I've seen only one. Blew the blighter's 'ead off with a shotgun. It's the bloomin' tiger snake we 'ave to watch out for! 'E's thick as fleas on a 'roo's back in these parts, and the father north we get, the thicker 'e'll get. 'E's a bad-tempered old fart and twice as poisonous as the taipan! Strikes so fast you think 'e's jumping!"

Kimber swallowed, his golfball of an Adam's apple bobbing up and down. "I say, the tiger snake—is that dangerous?" he said.

" 'E sure is!" Heck said. 'But 'e'll run if 'e can. There's not much danger we'll meet a tiger, unless one of you chappies gets to poking around off the road. If you do, your leather boots won't be worth half a bobbin'! The tiger 'e strikes high, mates. Up almost to the hip. They will protect you against the death adder. 'E's a little bastard, only about two feet long."

Pavel, who had the same kind of phobia about snakes that Camellion had about rats, shifted uncomfortably and cleared his throat.

"But we do have antivenom?" he repeated anxiously.

"Sure we do, mate, for all the good it would do if one of us got bitten!" Heck said. A chain-smoker, he paused to light another cigarette, using an old-fashioned kitchen match. "You see, these snakes are so poisonous that by the time you could get the serum into a bloke, it would be too bloody late. It would only take 'im longer to die! The secret is in knowing 'ow not to get chawed on by a snake. When you walk through the grass, you make a lot of bloody noise and watch where you step!" His mouth became a large quarter-moon of a smile. "And if a snake does bite you . . . well, mates, you can pray. But it won't do you any good!"

Every one of the men, including Camellion, took to heart what Heck had said, especially Pavel (who wished he were back in the Soviet Union). Many hours later the Russian KGB agent was still pondering the possibilities of his

141

being bitten by a snake and—from the side of the half-track in which he rode—looking down suspiciously at the knee-high kangaroo grass, as if a tiger snake might rear up on stilts and strike out at him!

The attack force—it numbered thirty-one men—moved northwest toward C. W. Silvestter's vast ranch and his underground city of Satan—New Eden. The road was hardly more than two wide tracks that twisted and turned through a savanna of wallaby grass, just as the column of vehicles twisted and turned over the so-called road. Camellion, Wiseloggle, and Geffling were in the lead jeep, Heck doing the driving. Next in line was another jeep, in which rode Jackie Harmsworth and the three agents from Great Britain, France, and the Soviet Union; this jeep also carried one of the two shortwave radios. Every hour Geffling contacted Canberra and gave headquarters a progress report. The Humbler and the half-track were next. Behind them, the last two jeeps made up the rear guard.

The odds were against the column's being ambushed by New Dawn fanatics. Far from being fools, Silvestter and Steele realized that to attack the column outside the boundaries of the ranch would be an open invitation to the Austrialian government to move in with force, with perhaps a battalion of heavy weapons. Even so, Camellion and Geffling did not take that first chance. Silvestter was stark raving mad—And who could predict what a madman might do? Scouts were always sent ahead when the column approached any "desert"—timbered—area. Not once did the scouts see another human being, nor did Camellion and the others in the main column. (They didn't see any snakes either.) Not that the primitive countryside was devoid of life!

At the noisy approach of the column, dingoes ran off and watched suspiciously. There were kangaroos, hundreds of them. They would bound away from the column, the source of their alarm, then pause, stock-still, to see what the danger was.

Emus by the score! Those ostrichlike birds that according to Heck were the dumbest creatures alive.

"They can run forty miles an hour," Heck explained,

"but are so bloody stupid they 'aven't the sense to stop for a fence! The dumb bastards run right through it!

There were other animals but not a single human being in this area that was so sparsely settled it contained only one person for every eight miles. This was the "outback" that city-dwellers spoke of . . . the "bush," the "never-never," the "back-of-beyond." And the Death Merchant and the thirty other men were "fair dinkum diggers"—on a mission of Death.

The column halted for the night, the vehicles drawn in a circle on an open "desert" of tussocky grass—like wagon trains of the Old West in America. But unlike old-time settlers, these travelers had all the conveniences of modern science, including a wire that, laid flat on the ground, was drawn in a circle around the vehicles, a wire plugged into a gasoline-driven generator. Any snake crawling over the wire would be instantly electrocuted. Nonetheless, Pavel announced that he was going to sleep in the half-track. He wouldn't be alone! Jackie, J. Warren, and Philippe said they would join him in the carrier!

The darkness came quickly and quietly, in layers. Here in the outback, on moonlit nights, it could be as thin as gauze, fighting the eye with a translucent flood. That night there was no moon and the darkness was complete, a blackness that lay over the camp like a weight, in spite of the Coleman lanterns burning in the large Alamo wall tent. Guards were posted, watching the area around the camp through night glasses and infrared sniper-scopes, thereby eliminating any possibility of a night attack.

"We're safe enough 'ere, gents," Heck said. "Besides, there's almost no possibility that those New Dawn blokes could even get close without our spotting them."

Nat Wiseloggle, who hadn't been in favor of stopping in the first place, was the only dissenting voice, stating that in his opinion they should have bored straight in to New Eden and attacked, using the darkness as a cover.

"It's ridiculous!" Wiseloggle said angrily. "Why in hell should we lay over for the night when we're only twenty miles from that madman's ranch? What we should do is—"

"Thirty miles," Warren Kimber corrected. "We're twenty miles from the dingo fence that surrounds the entire ranch. Beyond the fence we have another ten miles to go before we reach the underground city."

"All the more reason why we should have kept going!" Wiseloggle countered. "We could have been there by two in the morning at the rate of speed we were going. We could have taken them off guard. Instead we're sitting here on our asses, like a bunch of 'white hunters'!"

Camellion's eyes swept Wiseloggle, who was sitting across from him. "Nat, I sometimes wonder how you ever got into the CIA!" he snapped. "Haven't you stopped to think that Silvestter has every alarm device known to modern science—floodlights, invisible beam alarms, the works, including radar on the gun tower. If we were stupid enough to attack in the dark, the darkness would be our enemy, not our friend!"

Reluctantly the lanky CIA agent was forced to agree. Moving his hand slowly over his stomach, he got up from the aluminum folding table, walked over to the medicine chest and took out a bottle of Alka Seltzer. He poured water into a paper cup and dropped a tablet in, then stood watching it fizzle.

"What the hell, do you live on those damn things?" Jackie Harmsworth asked, turning and looking at Wiseloggle. "That's the fourth or fifth you've had since chow! That's a lot of goddamn crap. They'll ruin your stomach!"

"I don't feel so hot," Wiseloggle said dully. He shook the paper cup. "My stomach's been bothering me ever since we landed at the Chalk ranch this morning. I don't know what's wrong . . . I even feel like I might have to vomit . . ."

Some of the men nodded sympathetically, but not Pavel Telpuchovskii, whose face looked positively sinister in the shadows cast by the lantern hanging from the center of the tent.

"What time do you estimate we'll reach the dingo fence?" he asked, sounding almost sullen as he regarded Heck Geffling, his eyes full of unanswered questions. The Russian then took another sip of Blue Chip beer, drinking it directly from the can.

De Gasquet interjected, "I'm curious about the method we'll use in attacking the underground fortress itself. We'll have to eliminate the gun tower first of all."

He kept giving Pavel darting little glances, all the while wondering how Pavel and Heck could guzzle warm beer.

Warren Kimber yawned. "We can blow the fence," he said. He looked expectantly at Geffling. "How tall are those fences the ranchers put up to keep wild dogs away from their sheep?"

"We won't have to blow the fence," Camellion said. "It's only wire, not more than eight feet tall. The personnel carrier can run right over it."

"What time will we reach the fence tomorrow?" Pavel asked again. His voice was louder this time and more insistent.

Heck Geffling leaned forward over the table and put the tip of his finger on a spot on the map. The other men around the table looked down at the map.

"Now, pay attention, laddies," Heck said. "'Ere we are —right 'ere. And 'ere"—he moved his finger a very short distance—"is where we're going in. We'll leave at dawn and get there . . . I should say about ten o'clock!"

"You mean to the fence?" Kimber asked.

"You 'ave it!" Heck nodded. "To the fence. And—"

"And after we go through the fence—that's anyone's guess as to how long it will take us to reach New Eden!" Camellion said.

Harmsworth seemed puzzled as he sat stroking his black beard.

"It shouldn't take us long to cover ten miles!" he said loudly. "The ten miles from the fence to New Eden! What the hell! According to the map it's all pretty much open country."

"You figure the New Dawn sons of bitches will be there to meet us?" Wiseloggle asked, giving both Camellion and Geffling brief glances. He had finished his Alka Seltzer and was returning to the table.

De Gasquet, thinking the remark amusing, laughed. "We'll know when we get there, won't we?"

"According to what information our agents were able to

145

smuggle out, Silvestter has three armored cars—British Saladins," Camellion said roughly, piqued by the Frenchman's comment and feeling a quick flash of guilt when he paused to think why: He didn't like de Gasquet. He didn't like the man because he was religious. Long ago Camellion had learned that it was dangerous to depend on truly religious people, who were always unrealistic . . . emotional leaners who depended on prayer instead of common sense.

Heck scratched his head and took a sip of beer, looking worried.

"Those Saladins, those twelve-ton bastards will give us a lot of trouble," he said solemnly. "They 'ave seventy-six-millimeter guns—could blow a hole right through our carrier and Humbler."

"We've got the edge," Pavel said. He ground out his cigarette in the grass with the heel of his boot. "Our Oerlikons can fire ten times faster and those steel shells can go right through them, and so can our Bofors and recoilless weapons." He spread his hands out over the table. "So what's the problem?"

"Staying alive while we blast them!" the Death Merchant said drily. "Like Heck said, a seventy-six-millimeter can do a lot of damage. And don't forget the gun tower! That's our biggest problem. If our information is correct, there are four German eighty-eighty-mm Flak thirty-six war-surplus guns in that mess of concrete, not to mention heavy machine guns. We won't have to worry about the machine guns, but the eighty-eights will be deadly. If only one shell connects, that's it! Then it's bye-bye life and hello death."

"There's also four German PAK thirty-eights guarding the entrance of New Eden!" Wiseloggle said. "They'll be just as dangerous as the eighty-eights."

"How are we going to do it?" Kimber asked. A suspicion had been growing in his mind, and now he was almost convinced that most of them were as good as dead. The Death Merchant would no doubt survive, for Camellion was a man favored by Death, used by Death, and loved by Death.

"If you're referring to the gun tower, there's only one

way," Camellion said. "I'll get up to the side of the tower, using the Humbler, plant the TNT, and blow the damn thing off the map! Anyone know a better way?"

There was no mistaking the sweep of that declaration of an individual independence, and Kimber felt a twinge of envy for his self-sufficiency. It came to him that he had nothing in common with the Death Merchant. None of the men had, with perhaps the exception of Pavel Telpuchovskii, who also killed like a well-oiled machine . . . efficiently and without any kind of human feeling. In fact they were partners with Camellion only outside themselves and beyond a mystic border. In the everyday world they remained as separate as cause and effect, his lot to command and theirs to obey. At the same time Kimber often discovered a sadness in Camellion . . . a pale echo of nostalgia.

Nat Wiseloggle got up from the table, his face pale and tortured.

"Whatever you decide, Camellion, you'll have to do it without me." His voice was as full of misery as his face. "I've got to throwup . . ."

Hurriedly he left the tent, Heck calling after him, "If you go beyond the wire, watch where you step, laddie!"

Jackie Harmsworth looked out past the open tent flap. "Man, that poor guy's in a bad way! I wonder what the hell's wrong with him?"

The Death Merchant said in a quiet but serious voice, "Here is what I have in mind regarding an attack plan—and I'd appreciate your suggestions . . ."

Out in the black night, not far from the camp, a lyrebird called to its mate, its cry mournful and lonely . . . like a requiem to the dead and to those who would soon die . . .

CHAPTER ELEVEN

Cowards never came, and weak men didn't last long!—that's what the old timers said about the Queensland outback. Neither were the Death Merchant and his thirty helpers cowards nor weak, but—as their vehicles rolled over the dingo fence and headed toward New Eden—they couldn't help but speculate over the odds, how long they would last after the battle began . . . a battle "between Good and Evil, between Satan and God," as de Gasquet had so eloquently phrased it—*the damn fool!*

Standing high in the turret of the Humbler armored car, leaning forward, his arms folded over the top of the curved armor shield, Richard didn't feel that "God" was on their side, nor that "Satan" was against them. Their only ally was planning, strategy based on experience. He did have a lot of confidence. You had to have that feeling of winning. That was a prime requisite! Without it you were nothing, nothing but a candidate for instant corpsehood—and that's what the whole human race was waiting for, only the poor slobs didn't know it. *Instant annihilation! They're all working to bury each other!*

We'll take New Eden, but luck won't have anything to do with our success!

Know how and equipment would! The Humbler for instance! It was a nice little kill-car, a fast little blob of a bastard that could attain a top speed of sixty miles per hour and run circles around the enemy's heavier and more clumsy Saladins, especially with a wild maniac like Jackson Jorah Harmsworth in the driver's seat! But Jackie was exactly the kind of man Camellion wanted in the driver's seat—a man who wasn't afraid of dying, a "blighter" who wouldn't argue with himself as to what he should have done! Jackie would know and would do it! Or a man like Pavel Telpuchovskii! A natural-born killer, but with a big flaw: He enjoyed it. *Some day his sadism will cause his death!* Sadist or not, Pavel was a damn good man to have around, even if he was a Russian "pig farmer"!

They were all good men, including Philippe de Gasquet —*If believing that "God" is on our side gives him courage and confidence, I'll even say a rosary with him!*

Nat Wiseloggle was another matter, not that the CIA agent didn't have know how or wasn't brave. His CIA record proved that he did and that he was! Only Wiseloggle wouldn't be in the battle! During the night he had become violently ill, his stomach an agony of hideous cramps. There were also vomiting and diarrhea. In no way was it possible for Wiseloggle to accompany the party when it moved on at dawn. They had left him, and a commando to watch over him, in the vicinity of the night's campsight, under a tall and solitary bottle tree whose swollen truck resembled a huge wine cask.

The six vehicles of the Plan *Poaka* attack force were four miles past the dingo fence, and still no sign of Silvester's New Dawn Elite Guard. The Satan simpletons couldn't be waiting in ambush because there wasn't any place for them to hide. Already parched under a merciless midmorning sun, the land was flat and pastoral, a thick carpet of 'roo and wallaby grass, dotted with knobs of saltbushes. The area wasn't exactly a plain. There were clumps of mulgas trees and scribbly gum. But nowhere could a Saladin armored car find refuge; there simply wasn't enough cover.

Wishing he had a glass of cold tomato juice (and he had, in a thermos at his feet, only the damn Humbler was bouncing around too much for him to pour it), Richard checked on either side and behind him to make certain everything was as it should be and that everyone was in line. It was and they were—the six vehicles spread out in a large V-formation, with the Humbler taking the point. Twenty feet behind the Humbler rumbled the armored personnel carrier, manned by commandoes, and driven by Roosevelt

Windsor Jones (whose fair dinkum-digger of a father had been a fanatical admirer of both Franklin D. Roosevelt and King George of England), the heavy tractor treads of the half-track chewing up the grass a hell of a lot more efficiently than a hundred sheep could!

The four jeeps, in back of the personnel carrier, formed the sides of the "V," the last two jeeps a hundred feet from and parallel to each other. J. Warren Kimber, the British Secret Intelligence Service agent, rode in the first jeep to the left of the carrier; Philippe de Gasquet, the French SDECE agent in the first jeep to the right, which was being driven by the gutsy Aussie intelligence agent, Heck Geffling.

All four of the jeeps had been enclosed with armor plate, of a thickness that while it wouldn't stop an 88 or a PAK 38 shell, would deflect large-caliber machine-gun slugs.

Geffling's jeep contained the 105-mm recoilless weapon, which could be loaded and fired from behind the rear seat. Its eight-foot firing tube lay lengthwise across the armored roof of the jeep.

The three Burney RCLs were mounted on the roofs of the other three jeeps and could be fired by a commando standing between the seats—all of it a makeshift arrangement and completely untested. Would it work? *It had damn well better!*

The Death Merchant swung around in the cramped turret and glanced down at Pavel Telpuchovskii, whose head and shoulders were protruding from the rear hatch opening, the KGB agent's hands resting lightly on the brace of thirty-caliber belt-fed Owens machine guns, the two long barrels pointed upward.

Itching for action, Pavel was as nervous as a green fly on his first mission to a cesspool. Like Camellion, who wore his twin .357s in shoulder holsters, Pavel also wore his 9-mm machine pistols under his armpits, his ten-pocket cartridge belt filled with spare clips for the Stechkin APS. In a bag, the strap slung over one shoulder, were spare magazines for the Owens sub-M. Demolition grenades and canisters of DM—Adamsite—dangled from another belt crossing his broad shirtless chest. Another bag, on his hip, contained not one but two gas masks as protection against the deadly DM, each mask having a spare sestonium-treated filter.

There comes a time when human planning must cease, when all that can be done is done. *We've done all we can! We're all set to do it! All set to go in and die!*

Camellion thought of Nat Wiseloggle and the commando with him, now more than fifteen miles back. They'd be safe, and so would the two shortwave radios removed from the jeeps and stashed in the bush.

He looked down at what lay next to his feet, next to the stacked magazines of 35-mm shells—three satchels, all told seventy two pounds of TNT, more than enough to blow New Eden's gun tower off the face of the earth, even though its concrete walls were three feet thick.

If I can get close enough to dump the satchels off! There was every possibility that he wouldn't! The TNT block charges could not be touched off by ordinary small-arms fire, not even by machine-gun slugs, but a direct hit by an 88 or a PAK 38 shell would furnish the sufficient shock to explode the charges.

A direct hit! Camellion laughed out loud! If the Humbler took a shell direct, he wouldn't be alive to hear the TNT go off!

Stooping slightly, he reached down and picked up the combination headphones and throat mike, with which he could enter into two-way communication with Jackie in the driver's seat and Pavel in the after-compartment. He removed his Aussie hat, took out a gas mask and slipped it down over his head around his neck, slipped the phones and mike in place, then put on a commando steel helmet with a thick plastic windbreaker visor.

"We're getting close, boys," he said to Pavel and Jackie. "You'd better have your wills written!"

"The hell with a will! That's a lot of goddamn crap!" Jackie's voice came back through the earphones.

"Good luck, my Amerikanski friend!" Pavel said cheerfully.

151

Camellion picked up the walkie-talkie from its frame rack in the turret and contacted Heck Geffling.

"Heck, how far are we from Silvestter's underground hell on earth?"

A low laugh and Heck's crusty voice floated back over the W-T.

"You don't 'ave to worry none, old buster! We'll be seeing the two towers any minute—and 'earing the bastards no doubt!"

Camellion heard Heck click off his set and, although he expected trouble at any moment, he still jumped when he heard the deep *vvveeroomm* of an 88 FLAK-36 gun, the short scream of the shell, and then the explosion, only twenty five yards to the right! Further to the right, a large flock of sheep, frightened out of five years' growth of wool, began bleating in fear and running in a direction opposite to the thunderous noise.

New Eden had spotted the attack force!

There was nothing left to do now but race on in and do it . . . zigzag at the gun tower, blow it to bits, turn the Saladins into blasted junk, attack the entrance of New Eden, go underground into the city, and kill everyone in sight!

Uh huh! That's all we have to do!

Just as in the already-worked-out strategy, the Humbler, increasing speed, raced ahead, the jeeps—their drivers throttling up—moved farther apart from one another, every vehicle moving in a snake-wriggle course, zigzagging. Every man was prepared for instant action, the commandos ready at their recoilless weapons and at the 40-mm Bofors rapid-fire gun on the half-track . . . only waiting to get within range.

Then, as more 88 shells screamed in at the attacking Plan *Poaka* armor, the Death Merchant and the remainder of the men got their first look at C. W. Silvestter's New Eden, not more than a half mile away.

Camellion had wondered why they hadn't seen the two towers miles away; now he saw the reason. From their angle of approach the view of the men had been obstructed by a stretch of tall heavy-leafed coachwood trees. Now, as

152

the charging war machines moved past the line of trees, New Eden loomed up clearly, in all its hellish glory—not that there was a hell of a lot to see!

But enough! Twice the size of a football field, a tremendous rectangle of a mound, the four sides of which were not quite a foot high, and whose surface was covered with short grass clipped as neatly as the green of a golf course!

The Death Merchant wasn't thinking about golf as he dropped down into the turret, slammed the cupola hatch, and settled himself in the gunner's bucket, putting his feet on the turn bar of the turret control. To him the surface of New Eden resembled a gigantic grave, a well-kept, neatly trimmed mound of death that was waiting to be crammed with corpses.

And I intend to fill it! Both hands on the guide handles of the Oerlikons, Camellion looked at the two towers through the eight-by-four-inch periscope plate of the turret. The weather station, with its slim tower and bulb of a housing, reminded him of a tremendous electrostatic generator—*The hell with the hundred-foot bastard! It's the gun tower we have to worry about!*

The gun tower was at the other end of the mound, an evil-looking cube of concrete (painted green! the color of Satan!) that measured twenty-five feet in height and width, the long, slim barrel of a German 88-mm FLAK-36 protruding from an opening in each side. On the roof was a seven-foot-high parapet ringed with loopholes, through which heavy-caliber machine guns could be fired. There were more gun ports farther down, several on each side of the 88-mm FLAK openings.

It was the 88-mm FLAK in the south side of the gun tower that was tossing the shells at them, firing first at the Humbler, then switching to the jeeps and the personnel carrier, the shells, while missing, coming dangerously close. At the speed with which Camellion's armor was traveling inward toward the mound, the man doing the sighting at the 88 could not get a fix. By the time he sighted in on one degree of elevation and azimuth, the vehicles were no longer there.

Spread out in a crooked, weaving three-hundred-foot

153

line—the width of New Eden—the armored machines of death roared in toward the surface of the underground city, the slower moving half-track in the rear, Roosevelt Jones zigzagging the carrier with all the ability at his disposal, which was considerable. Three times, by his expert swerving, he had saved the lumbering metal monster from an 88. Three times a Sabot shot-shell had exploded so close that the half-track rocked like a giant cradle.

Camellion sized up the airstrip next to the mound. A helicopter and a two-engine, prop-driven cargo plane were parked on the runway. No danger from that area!

What he next saw made him feel as anxious as a virgin bridegroom on his wedding night! As if they had been miraculously created by the waving of some sorcerer's wand, the three Saladin armored cars of the New Dawn Elite Guard appeared!

They hadn't popped out of thin air—or fat air for that matter! They had rolled up from the long concrete ramp that slanted down gradually to the main entrance of New Eden, which was fifty feet wide and twenty-five feet high, the top ten feet below the surface of the mound.

Almost twice the size of the Humbler (and even the stubby 76-mm cannons in the turret were painted a bright grass green!), the Saladins immediately spread out and roared toward Camellion and his machines, which by now were within a range that would permit them to fire at the tower, not that their weapons could do any real damage to the reinforced-concrete sides, but the explosions from the recoilless rounds, as well as from the Bofors and Oerlikon shells, would certainly interfere with the aim of the 88-mm FLAK gunners.

Almost at once, the south-side 88-mm ceased firing, its crew not wanting to risk hitting one of the Saladins, all three of which were rumbling to intercept the six vehicles of the Death Merchant's force. Their mission was simple: Destroy and kill!

Swerving—"making the Z," as tank men call it—the Saladins began moving into firing positions, the turrets moving as the gunners got the range and compensated their 76-mm cannons for altitude.

The two opposing forces charged each other—*"The forces of Good* vs. *Evil, as de Gasquet would say! God against the Devil!"* Bullshit!

Wwwwoooommmmmmmmmmmm! The 76-mm round came close, the giant blast rocking the Humbler, so close that the stink of TNT was instant-fresh and practically hot! *By God! A man could get hurt out here!*

Down in the driver's seat Jackie Harmsworth twisted the wheel, turning the Humbler at an angle, away from the Saladin that had just fired, while up in the turret, Camellion stared into the periscope plate, waiting for that split-second moment.

"Hold on, guys!" Jackie called through the communications system to Richard and to Pavel. *"I'm going to get between two of the bastards!"*

He then skidded the Humbler to the right, to avoid another Saladin whose turret was swiveling toward him. The Saladin fired, but Jackie had proved he was as good on land as he was on water. The 76-mm exploded behind the Humbler, its damage nil . . .

Jackie's maneuver had been a masterpiece of quick thinking, for it put the Humbler in a position that—at least for the moment—made it impossible for the two Saladins to fire at the Humbler without risking their own deaths.

As the Humbler shot between the two Saladins, Camellion pushed down on the control bars, swung the turret, and opened up with the twin Oerlikons, filling the cramped space with an ear-splitting roar (and the clank-clank-clank of empty shell casings hitting the deck) and raking the side of one Saladin—forty feet to his right—with a tornado of 35-mm shells that while they didn't penetrate the armor, caused the driver to veer off sharply.

The gunner of the other Saladin armored car quickly revolved his turret, to get off a rear shot as Jackie, having sped the Humbler between the two big Ss, skidded to the left.

Another big *woooommmmmmm,* the 76-mm exploding so close to the Humbler that as it rocked violently, Jackie almost lost control. But he didn't. He cut behind the Saladin at a right angle.

155

I shall make of your house a history written in blood!
—And the Death Merchant, aiming in at the four-foot-long barrel of the 76 through the crosshairs of the periscope plate, opened fire, the two Oerlikon spitting out ten shells each, a rain of explosive death that made the gunner of the Saladin think he had been caught in the jaws of a steel trap whose teeth were razor blades! Camellion's aim had been perfect. He had accomplished his purpose: He had wrecked the cannon! The shells had not penetrated the turret's armor, but they had jammed the gun mounting, at that point on the outside of the turret where the housing ring was mounted and through which the barrel protruded. The concentrated Oerlikon fire had twisted the ring, jamming it between barrel and turret, so that the barrel could not be raised or lowered.

The third Saladin armored car was having all sorts of problems. It had fired at the personnel carrier—and missed! Then at one of the armored jeeps—and half-missed, the shell, coming in low, blowing off the left front wheel. The jeep careened like a wounded animal, the driver desperately fighting the wheel. The jeep finally came to a swerving, sideways stop, its protruding axle digging a deep scar across the sun-baked grass. There it rested, a lopsided sitting duck! Working like madmen, its commandos tried to get their Burney RCL into action, unscrewing it from its roof mount.

The Saladin moved in for the kill. Confident that it would have an easy victory, the Saladin began a quick, angled maneuver that would give it another shot at the disabled jeep. While the driver bored in at a sixty-degree angle, the gunner adjusted the turret and the alti-azimuth of the 76-mm cannon. It was a mistake! In their enthusiasm to knock off the crippled jeep, the Elite Guard crew of the Saladin had diverted their attention from the half-track!

The personnel carrier had not forgotten them! Cursing in the gobbledygook language of his Aborigine ancestors, Roosevelt Windsor Jones swung the large armored monster to the right, and the man at the powerful 40-mm Bofors gun, mounted behind the cab, opened fire—*Bur-roommmm-burroommmm-burroommm-burroommm!* One-

156

two-three-four 40-mm shells hit the Saladin—in turret, driver's compartment, front glacis plate, and one "Arrowhead" shell digging in at an angle on the left side.

A giant fireball! A thunderous ear-crushing explosion! For just a billionth of a second it seemed that the Saladin had swollen to twice its normal size as turret, sides, back, and front of the vehicle moved away from each other! Then the Saladin literally disintegrated, broken, bloody men and twisted, smoking metal flying outward and up! The turret and its 76-mm Hogge cannon were blown twenty-five feet into the air, and a couple of wheels went sailing backward toward the entrance of New Eden. The gunner also went backward, minus his head and arms! They rocketed skyward! But they'd never reach the stars, only the wallaby grass. The other three crewmen died just as quickly, amputated straight into the Hell of the Satan in whose name they were fighting—and had died!

In the meanwhile the Saladin that had been forty feet to the Death Merchant's right had headed a short distance south, made a sharp right turn, and was now headed at a zigzag toward the half-track, a path that would take it—if it continued to move forward—between the personnel carrier and the disabled jeep.

Roosevelt Jones swung the half-track to the right, in an effort to avoid a head-on shot from the 76-mm Hogge. The crippled jeep, however, got off a round at the Saladin, but the Burney-RCL shell only skimmed the top of the turret, and so did the shell from another jeep, the one in which J. Warren Kimber was riding. The Saladin was simply moving too fast for anyone to sight in, unless the man doing the sighting were an expert.

No fool, knowing that his most dangerous adversary was the deadly 40-mm Bofors, the gunner in the Saladin's turret reacted accordingly. Before the half-track could get into a position to fire at the Saladin, the New Dawn Elite Guard gunner opened fire, aiming point-blank at the half-track.

The 76-mm hit the cab dead center and exploded with a tremendous flash of bright red flame, blowing the steel driver's section into pieces of twisted, smoking junk, and with it Roosevelt Windsor Jones, the commando in the cab

157

with him, and the two men manning the Bofors. The top and sides of the cab sailed outward—and so did Jones and the other commando—the huge front bumper turning over and over in the air. Like a tired old man, the half-track settled down and died—cabless, manless, and cremating itself, the entire carrier a mass of flames and very black smoke. A big *whooshhhhhh* as the gas tank exploded. It was a quick, easy way to go . . .

The driver and the gunner of the Saladin were good! The driver angled sharply to the right, neatly avoiding another Burney RCL, and the gunner zeroed in on the disabled jeep.

Whoooommmmmmmm! The high hidious howl of a 76-mm shell, a crashing explosion, a bright flash of flame, and then, where the jeep had been, there was nothing but smoking wallaby grass, which quickly became covered with parts of jeep and parts of bodies . . . an arm . . . a head . . . a few fingers . . . a lower leg, the combat boot blown off the bloody foot, and a small paperback Bible. Evidently God had not listened to the prayers of its owner . . .

The crew of the Saladin were elated. Why, for such accurate shooting Silvestter Himself, the Chosen One, would probably give them His personal blessing! Then their luck ran out!

It's engine roaring, the Saladin was turning to zero in on the jeep in which Heck Geffling and Philippe de Gasquet were riding when Heck's gunner—the man at the 105-mm recoilless cannon—made a slight adjustment on his Alconsight and triggered the firing lever.

Whoossscchhhhhh! The Sabot shell shot from the long tube of the 105-mm recoilless. Of all the weapons used to kill tanks and armored cars, the Sabot shell (also used in the deadly SAM-6 and Shrike missiles) is perhaps the best. On leaving the barrel, the shell discards everything, except the tungsten subprojectile; the throwing-away process gives the subprojectile a good staying power to penetrate at long ranges.

This Sabot did just that! It struck the advancing Saladin at the spot where the bottom part of the turret—in the front of the vehicle—revolved in the main body of the armored car, boring through the steel plate with the ease of a high-powered rifle slug tearing through tissue paper!

At almost the same time J. Warren Kimber got off a Burney-RCL round from the jeep in which he was riding, and his shell also found its target, chewing through the steel right above the driver's hatch.

The two explosions sounded as one, a giant tremendous *blooie!* that blasted the Saladin not to any Kingdom Come, but all the way past Limbo and an unpretty Purgatory—straight into the subbasement of Hell! No one leaves this world alive (astronauts excepted!), and the crew of the Saladin-56 was no exception. One moment the four men were hopeful and alive, the next second—oblivion!

"I say, a damn good show!" Warren Kimber muttered to himself, hanging onto the side braces as he stared at where the Saladin had been, but where now there were only smoking pieces of assorted junk.

Heck Geffling turned the wheel of his jeep to avoid the wreck of the Saladin . . . and raced after the Humbler, which was in pursuit of the remaining Saladin. Speaking into the walkie-talkie hanging around his neck, Heck barked orders at the drivers of the other two jeeps.

"All right, lads, let's follow the Death Merchant, but keep a sharp eye at the gun tower and the entrance. Those bloody bastards 'ave PAK thirty-eights mounted down there in that 'ell!"

Minutes earlier the four saps of Satan in the Saladin had decided that since the housing ring of their 76-mm was jammed, they had better head for home, which meant the underground security of New Eden. But first the big car had to maneuver past the enemy and turn around.

Camellion and the Humbler shot past the Saladin, which was roaring south. Again he raked the monster with a half-dozen 35-mm Oerlikon cannon shells, his rounds exploding on the side of the car and on its turret. The shells burned off a lot of green paint and made the four New Dawn idiots think they were as close to being dead as they would ever get—without doing it!

Another blast of 35-mm shells, the inside of the Saladin

ringing with all the clashing and clanging sound of a thousand huge bells—or so it seemed!

"Get us out of here!" the gunner screamed in fear through the mike to the driver. *"Or every goddamn one will aim in on us!"*

The driver turned the wheel, skidded the rear of the car west, turned east, swung back to the north, and headed at top speed toward the entrance of New Eden. God wouldn't help them, and the Devil couldn't. They were in one helluva fix!

Jackie Harmsworth turned the Humbler, skidding it all over the place. Quickly he righted the armored car, pressed down on the gas pedal, and shot after the Saladin, peering through the narrow slit in front of him.

Up in the turret, the Death Merchant had become a pair of red eyes, inflamed by smoke, the fumes of burnt TNT, and sweet-sour bouquet of Death. He was a brain, working at top speed, a mind that knew exactly what to do and how and when to do it. He was without anger, without hatred, consumed only by a deadly purpose.

Staring at the back of the fleeing Saladin, he smiled. *The Christian God is more concerned with justice than with mercy! Yes, sir . . . He will 'smite the sinner'! Only he's too slow. I better do it for him!*

Again he opened up with the Oerlikons, sighting in on the right rear wheel, the 35-mms practically blowing the rubber apart. The Saladin swerved crazily, left to right and back again. Camellion's next five shells exploded harmlessly against the rear glacis plate.

Jackie began twisting and swerving the Humbler, doing his best to stay directly behind the Saladin, which was now bouncing over the forward section of the concrete ramp leading downward to the entrance, on each side of which were two PAK-38 antitank cannon, the long barrels pointed upward toward the end of the runway.

Camellion reasoned that his party now had the edge on the deadly 88 in the south side of the gun tower. The gun could not fire down at them without blasting a hole in the roof of the underground city—Unless the roof is reinforced concrete! *I wonder if it is?*

160

He got his answer a few seconds later. An 88 shell came screaming overhead, exploding far to the left and doing no damage to either the Humbler or the three jeeps behind it.

It is! The roof's reinforced concrete! And on this narrow, fifty-foot-wide runway we don't have much room to maneuver in. With the PAKs in front of us, we're in a rather difficult position!

The Death Merchant was about to tell Jackie what he wanted him to do when the bearded man called up to him, his voice anxious through the innercom system: "Like man, what the hell do we do now? We going to follow that green beetle in or what? Once that muther-frigger's out of the way, the PAKs will have a clear shot at us, as sure as God made little green apples!"

"Swing to the left, Jackie, enough for me to get a clear shot at the two PAKs to our left. I can splatter them before they realize what's going on. It will take only a few seconds and surprise will be on our side!"

Jackie's reply dripped with skepticism. "Uh huh! What about the PAKs to the right. Their gunners ain't going to be sittin' on their duffs playin' pocket pool!"

Pavel Telpuchoskii chimed in. "Once we swing around, I can splatter them with this Owens. A PAK has only a small front armor shield!"

"The minute the Saladin roars into the entrance, I'll open up on the right-side PAKs," Camellion said. "There's no other way!"

"Suppose it doesn't work?" Jackie asked.

"Then we're dead!" Camellion replied.

"Hang on! Here we go!" Jackie said resignedly. He swung the Humbler armored car sharply to the left, and there, for a brief moment, the Death Merchant saw the two PAK antitank guns . . . directly in front of him, not more than 125 feet away. The barrels were pointed directly at him, their muzzle-brakes sneering and looking hungry. Another glimpse—of white terrified faces . . . of gun crews crouched behind the low shields mounted over and around the barrels.

The Death Merchant barely touched the firing buttons, and the deadly Oerlikons belched a rain of explosive death

—more than thirty shells that demolished the PAKs and their four-man crews. The thin protective-armor shields offered no protection against the 35-mm shells, which literally blew the men apart, like blood-filled balloons.

Hot, sticky sweat plastered Camellion's shirt to his back and chest. More sweat ran down the sides of his face and the back of his neck as he swung the turret and the Oerlikons to the right. A few more seconds and he could splatter the PAKs on the right side of the entrance. A few more seconds and—surprise!

The Saladin—not more than twenty-five feet ahead of the Humbler and seventy-five feet in front of the entrance —blew up with a tremendous roar, the flames of the fireball almost licking at the Humbler!

There was no great mystery about what had happened, nor had God in His Heaven created a *deus ex machina*.

Heck Geffling had! Heck had ordered two of the jeeps not to go down the ramp. "Lads, you stay at an angle to the southeast corner of the gun tower," he told his commandos. "That way, neither the east nor the south eighty-eights will be able to traverse enough to fire at you. You 'ave that, laddies?"

The laddies 'ad! Geffling, however, with nerve tempered by common sense and experience, had followed the Humbler down the ramp, and when Jackie swung the car to the left, giving Heck a clear view of the enemy Saladin, his gunner opened up with the 105-mm recoilless! A *whooshhhhh!* The round left the tube, the Sabot shell boring far down in the turret of the Saladin, in the rear. A giant explosion! Then twisted, smoking junk and mangled bodies!

Even while the wreckage of the Saladin was still falling, Heck's gunner got off another 105-mm shell, which whizzed over the two PAKs to the right and blew apart a truck parked fifty feet inside the entrance. Then Heck turned the jeep around and headed it back up the ramp, thinking that the Death Merchant was one hell of a brave man. Crazy, but nervy! *'Ell! The Blighter 'as to be a little off to go all the way in like that. No! 'E 'as to be a lot off!*

The DM didn't miss! The instant the Saladin blew

162

apart, Jackie slowed the speed of the Humbler, knowing that they would have to make a run for it, now that they were exposed to the two PAKs on the right side of the entrance. Jackie swung to the right, beginning a turn that would take the Humbler back up the ramp—and that's when Camellion fired! A blast of 35-mm, a *boop-boop-boop-boop* that did what it was supposed to do! The two PAK 38s became twisted junk, their crews dismembered corpses, the whole mess spraying the area with chopped flesh, blood, bone, and ripped metal. A wheel rolled into the entrance! A PAK barrel sailed almost forty feet upward and, falling back down, landed on the green-grass roof of Satan and Silvestter's underground city.

"Jackie, take her back, all the way into the entrance, at least about twenty or thirty feet!" Camellion shouted into the mike. "I want to soften up those 'sinners' for later and dump some DM gas in their laps!"

He reached up and flung open the hatch cover, a foot above his head. It clanged back against the turret, giving Camellion a view of clear blue sky.

"This is a lot of goddamn crap!" Jackie shouted back in a rough voice. "Hell, this is bad for my weak heart! But hang on. Here we go—*wheeeeeeeee!*"

His gloved hands twisted the wheel, and his foot eased up slightly on the gas. The Humbler swung around, and once again headed south for the entrance of New Eden. Inside New Dawn Elite Guards and the Select of Satan began running so fast their shorts almost had to catch up with them!

The hand of God shall weigh heavily upon thee! Chuckled the Death Merchant, watching the periscope viewplate as the Humbler shot through the entrance of the underground city, the first level of which was lighted by huge arc lamps strung out along the ceiling.

Parked not far from a bank of elevators were several large bush jeeps and four trucks, which appeared as fat, delicious targets in the viewplate. Richard swung the turret slightly and opened up with the Oerlikons, raking the vehicles as Jackie turned the Humbler—which was not fifty feet inside the entrance—and raced back in a southern direction, toward the ramp leading upward.

Boop-boop-boop-boop-boop! The trucks and bush jeeps disappeared in the viewplate, and in their place there remained only flames, black smoke and twisted metal.

All right! Give those "sinners" some gas! Camellion began flipping canisters of DM—Adamsite—through the open hatch above him. He wasn't concerned that he wasn't wearing his special gas mask. At the Humbler's rate of speed the gas could not drift to the car—not yet. And when the Death Merchant and his kill crew returned, they would be wearing their special masks.

Toward the entrance the Humbler sped, its rear end pointed north, in the direction of the long first level, which seemed to stretch out into infinity. Weird! A two-block-long, short-block-wide area of lights and activity . . . men in green uniforms moving up guns and other equipment. Unfortunately for the New Dawners right inside the entrance, Pavel Telpuchovskii was an expert. They weren't! They were only fanatics who had faith in a madman and his equally mad dream . . . faith that now was beginning to wear goddamn thin! Where in hell was the help of Satan? The forces of the Christian swine god had already blown up the three Saladins and were now inside New Eden, something that the Chosen One had assured them could not happen! But it had!

Their faith dissolved completely when Pavel cut loose with the thirty-caliber Owens machine gun, his head and shoulders sticking up from the open hatch of the rear compartment; yet he was protected from small-arms fire, even from heavy machine-gun slugs, since his front and two sides were armored by two-inch plate attached to—and moving with—the machine-gun mount.

The canvas belt jumped and the .30 shells exploded in the breech—at the rate of 350 per minute—as the KGB agent brought final salvation to anything that moved. A dozen figures—were two of them women?—were chopped to pieces before they could dive to cover. Those who didn't die soon wished they had when they got the first whiff of the drifting red clouds of DM!

If Pavel and his .30-Owens had been Purgatory, the Adamsite (a type of nerve gas that interferred with the delicate function of the autonomic nervous system) was pure Hell—and not the kind inhabited by the Devil and his legions. This earthly kind was much worse!

One tiny whiff brought instant God-awful, Devil-terrible misery! Instantaneous nausea, a qualmishness more hideous than Death could ever be! Came the instant vomiting, a disgorgement of breakfast, lunch, and dinner that would not stop . . . a puking that instead of decreasing increased with each slobber of a second!

Gasping (and wondering why they had ever believed a nut like Silvestter in the first place!), the defenders of Lucifer's underground lair staggered around like drunks, the DM also having an intervenient action on their vision and inner-ear centers of equilibrium. Terrified, the silly Satanists became frantic, thinking they were going to die!

Compounding their fear and misery was their deep sense of shame and embarrassment when the DM relaxed their anal sphincter muscles and they began to defecate! A crapping they could not control! Dammit to Hell! It was bad enough to die, but who wants to shit his pants before he goes bye-bye and jumps into the "Great Beyond!"

What in hell could the Satanists do? They didn't know! Those who exposed themselves to Pavel in the rear compartment of the Humbler got their answer—a hot blast of .30 slugs that instantly cured their terrible sickness. The slugs also broke their lifelong habit of breathing . . .

Leaving Death and misery behind it, the Humbler bounced out of the entrance onto the concrete ramp, its heavy shock springs screaming in protest. Like some monstrous gray behemoth, the armored car raced for the surface—right through a thick cloud of boiling black smoke coming from the burning Saladin, the rancid stink of burning rubber hanging heavily in the air. And the hot, not unpleasant odor of dead flesh being barbecued!

Three of the crewmen of the Saladin had been blown apart, but not the driver, who, strapped in his bucket seat, had been splashed with gasoline and catapulted twenty-five feet into the air! He came back down half-cooked! Now he sat in the seat—the seat flat on the concrete—a charred corpse that would have made an excellent "long pig" banquet for the Sepik cannibals of New Guinea.

Then the Humbler was on the surface, the wide rubber tires tearing the grass as Jackie swung to the southeast, taking a course that would—once the car was at an acute angle from the southeast corner of the gun tower—make it almost impossible for the south-side FLAK 88 to zero in on it.

Richard's orders to Jackie Harmsworth were simple: *Charge in at the tower from the southeast*—"And put on your gas mask. You, too, Pavel!"

His orders to Heck Geffling and his men were equally uncomplicated: *Go in at the same angle, but keep at least a hundred feet from the tower. Plaster it with Burney-RCL and 105-mm recoilless shells*—"And make damn sure you fire high, at least on the same level as the eighty-eights! And put on your gas masks!"

Jackie's voice floated through the headphones. "What the hell do we do about grenades?" he asked, swinging the car around. "If you get one down your open turret hatch —man, that'll be all she wrote!"

Reaching up, Camellion jerked down on the lever, and the hatch cover closed with a loud clang. He replied to Jackie by speaking into the mike to Pavel.

"Pavel, it's too risky for me to toss out smoke and DM canisters. Grenades and small-arms fire will be too thick. You can do the job by thrusting the canisters through your side ventilators. Open them as wide as you can and take the screens off. Shoot 'em off if you have to. What I want you to do, you push the canisters through the vents when Jackie—after he gets in close—begins the turn away from the tower. Do you 'ave that, old chap?"

"Yes, me boy! I 'ave it!" Pavel joked back. "I'll 'ave a go at it as soon as you shoot me down some smoke and DM."

"Coming up, old buster!" Camellion cracked. Scooting down low in the seat, he shoved the wooden cases of Adamsite and white phosphorous smoke grenades across the turret-well deck to the square door that opened inward to the rear compartment. Opening the door, Pavel pulled the two cases into his own hot, cramped compartment. The door slammed. Then a series of muffled machine-pistol shots. Pavel had blasted off the ventilator screens.

Jackie Harmsworth called up, "Hey, Camellion, you clown! You want me to make more than one run, don't you? God damn it! Tell me something. I can't read your mother-friggin' mind!"

"Don't get excited, me boy!" Camellion said in an easy manner. "You make two runs. On your first charge get in as close as you can, say, within ten feet of the wall, that's the southeast corner of the tower—and that's cutting it close. Pavel can drop the smoke and gas when you make your outward turn. On the second run I'll toss out the charges through the turret. By then the smoke and gas should have done their work, and we shouldn't be in too much danger. The odds will be on our side at least. Take her in, Jackie!"

"What the hell do you think I'm doing down here—drinking tea!" Jackie snapped annoyed. "Take a look!"

The Death Merchant examined the viewplate of the turret's periscope. Ahead of him, at a distance of perhaps 450 feet, was the grim, green gun tower—a bunker above the ground. Good old Jackie! He was angling in with such expertise that the sharp southeast corner appeared to be centered between the two barrels of the 35-mm Oerlikons! Yes, sir! Damn good driving . . .

Richard turned the 'scope knob and changed the view pick up to the rear of the Humbler. There was Geffling's jeep, fifty yards back and a bit to the left, enough to the left to give the 105-mm gunner a clear shot at the southeast corner of the tower.

The other two armored jeeps were strung out behind Geffling, the first one to the right. It would send RCL-Burney rounds at the east side of the gun tower. The last jeep, in line with the Humbler, would wait until the three other vehicles had charged in and had turned away; then it would fire at both the east and south sides of the bunker. But for now it could veer neither left nor right, its firing trajectory obstructed by the three other machines.

Jackie steered the Humbler straight at the southeast corner of the gun tower whose defenders were laying down a vicious rain of heavy-calibered machine-gun fire, the muzzles of at least a dozen .50 Brownings pointed at the Humbler and at the three jeeps behind it. The east and south 88 FLAK guns also boomed, although their crews, unable to move their weapons to the proper degrees of traverse, fully realized the shells had only an annoyance value. It didn't work! Camellion and the other men were too experienced; the exploding fireballs were ignored.

Then the 88s became silent. Placed to fire at armor attacking at a distance, the antitank guns were almost ten feet above the ground, and their barrels had been cranked down to the lowest degree of vertical traverse. To continue to fire the guns would have been a sheer waste of shells, which would have exploded hundreds of feet behind the charging Humbler and the other three vehicles.

A terrible rain of big fifty-caliber slugs poured down on the Humbler, the racket sounding as if giants were tossing tubsful of steel balls at the front and sides of the armored car. Almost immediately the periscope "eye" was shot away, and Camellion had to resort to the narrow two-by-ten-inch slot in front of the turret; his vision was limited, tunnellike. The range became even more narrow and short when, in order to prevent a stray slug from zipping through the slit, he quickly cranked down the armored awning over the slot as far as it would go; the action limited his vision even more, to a mere twenty feet in front of him. Yet he didn't have to have a full view of the tower in order to fire at it. Using an uncanny sense of distance and direction, he opened up with the Oerlikon 35-mms, the shells exploding all over the corner of the east and south wall, making the walls look as if they had just healed from a severe case of smallpox. Then several larger explosions as Geffling's gunner gave the thick concrete walls two large pockmarks with two 105-mm rounds.

By now the Humbler was not more than fifty feet from the southeast corner of the gun tower, the bunker so close it filled the view in front of Jackie, who yelled into his

168

mike, "Watch it, you blokes! I'm going to turn this mess of hot metal and head back. Get ready, Pavel!"

He cursed to himself. His back itched, but how in hell could he reach around and scratch it? The hell with it!

He began slowing the Humbler, his sense of timing working on all twelve and one-quarter gears. When it seemed that the big steel bumper of the car would have to slam into the concrete, he braked, jerked the wheel to the left, and did a lot of hoping! The Humbler skidded around in an arc, the rear end spinning around in a half circle, the hook ring on the back bumper almost scraping the wall, missing it by only a few inches!

Pavel was ready. He had been for the last minute. The very second the Humbler began its skid, he began thrusting DM and smoke canisters through both vents—the smoke to the left, DM to the right. By the time the armored car had made the complete turn and was twenty-five feet from the wall, headed in the opposite direction, he had managed to thrust a dozen of each type of canister through the vents.

Thick white smoke poured from the canisters, along with a red mist from the Adamsite grenades, both drifting upward . . . floating up through the large and the small gun ports . . . up to the couple dozen members of Silvester's Elite Guard, who were hastily pulling standard gas masks over their heat-flushed faces.

That's when the crews of the 88s and the machine-gunners received a sickening surprise. The masks were one-hundred percent ineffective against the red gas! *Satan help us!* The Devil didn't! And no other myth could!

The terrible vomiting and insidious sickness started seconds later, the miserable sons of Satan eliminating waste matter from both ends, mouth and rectum.

The DM drifted to the roof and the machine-gunners suffered the same fate. They puked! They staggered, unable to see clearly, unable to keep their balance. They shit their pants and wished they had flung hand grenades over the parapet at the god-cursed armored car. The grenades would not have inflicted any serious damage to the Humbler, but the explosions might have prevented the men inside from tossing out the deadly gas. But the commander of the bunker had forbidden the use of grenades, fearing that one might bounce back through one of the large 88 ports and explode inside the tower. The nuisance value was not worth the risk. For the same reason, Molotov cocktails had not been used—and for another reason: If the car were loaded with high explosives and blew up close to the bunker—what then?

Within a few minutes the men inside the bunker and on its roof were immobilized. They rolled on the floor, leaned against the walls, slipping and sliding over spent shell casings, and wondered why Satan had not helped them. The stink of vomit, fecal matter, smoke and gas mingled together, all sprinkled with the fumes of exploded shells. The bunker did not smell like a rose, and the shells exploding against the sides of the bunker—fired by the three jeeps—didn't instill confidence in the violently ill men.

In the meantime the Death Merchant and his expert crew of Death givers rolled merrily on their way, riding either to hell or glory, depending on who was doing the judging. No one was, except a pair of bowerbirds in a manna gum tree, far in the distance. They watched the battle, thinking that while the cleverness of Man was only slightly less than that of the Angels, he was still the only creature who slaughtered his own kind because of a lust for power and a difference in political and religious beliefs.

"Back again we go!" Jackie Harmsworth shouted in his mike and again skidded the Humbler around to the southeast. His foot slammed down on the gas and the car shot toward the corner of the bunker. Thick white smoke obscured the south and east walls, smoke laced with the red gas of Adamsite, through which the muzzles of the 88s stuck out like pale tongues. But the guns were silent, including the Browning heavy machine guns. The DM had done its work well.

Heck Geffling and his men did not follow. The three jeeps had parked at the top of the runway leading down to the underground city and were firing at the entrance with the two Burney RCLs and the 105-mm recoilless.

170

The Death Merchant had prepared the three satchels of TNT, setting the three timers for three minutes. He threw open the turret hatch, and sat ready, the three satchels in his lap—*Another half-minute to get there! Two and a half minutes to get away!*

He heard Jackie's anxious voice through the headset— "Get set, Camellion! We're almost there!"

He felt the Humbler slowing, but this time Jackie did not make a skidding turn. Instead, he made a slow, proper turn, taking the chance that no one would rain down hand grenades. No one did. The Elite Guards were too ill to even think of the armored car.

NOW!

Working at top speed, the Death Merchant shoved the three satchels through the opened hatch—one! two! three! and the seventy-two pounds of TNT were gone, all three packages falling about four feet from the corner. Jackie pulled away, his foot heavy on the gas pedal. Then he turned west when Camellion told him to head for the airstrip next to the mound of New Eden.

"I'm not going to take that first chance on Silvestter or Steele's getting away," he said. "We'll blow the aircraft."

The Humbler rolled across the hot grass and Camellion, first cranking back the awning over the firing slit, opened up with the Oerlikons. It took only one 35-mm shell to turn the helicopter into a mass of all-consuming flames . . . three shells to explode the fuel tanks of the prop-driven cargo plane.

The TNT satchels exploded, with a roar that sounded like half a dozen A-bombs! A brief giant flash, a tremendous fireball shooting skyward, and then a smaller roar as the southeast corner of the bunker dissolved.

The Humbler seemed to have been caught in a powerful wind! For a moment, its ten tons swayed from side to side, at the complete mercy of the shock wave rocking it. Jackie slammed on the brakes, parking sideways on the airstrip, raised the driver's hatch and looked out at the bunker, Camellion rearing up through the open turret, Pavel through the hatch of the rear compartment.

"Thank God!" Jackie said in awe. "We did it!"

"Thank TNT," Camellion replied drily.

"And this British-built armored car!" Pavel added, lighting a cigarette. "But ours in the Soviet Union are just as good . . ."

Without further comment Jackie removed his helmet and headphones and wiped his sweaty, powder-blackened face with a hand towel. He had never doubted, not for an instant, that they would succeed in blowing the bunker. With the Death Merchant bossing the show, how could they fail? Camellion couldn't be killed, not on this hot day! People died only when they had something to live for . . .

Apparently the Elite Guard in the bunker must have had a helluva lot to live for! The terrible blast and concussion had killed every damn one!

The gun tower itself now resembled the ruins of a medieval castle . . . the ruins of a smoking medieval castle! One corner had been completely demolished, to the extent that only half of the east and south walls remained standing, and they sagged, the east wall inward, the south wall outward, twisted reinforcement rods sticking out from the jagged ends.

The two 88 antitank cannons had been blown from their mounts, one lying thirty feet in front of the east wall, the other, whose barrel had been bent back to form a "U," hung at a grotesque angle from the west side of the sagging roof! The whole blasted mess smoking! Chunks of concrete, some as large as a jeep, had been blown as far as fifty feet; they, too, smoked . . .

"What's our next move?" Pavel asked, in the process of reloading his machine pistols. "As if I didn't know!"

The Death Merchant smiled.

"Let's go kill Cleveland Winston Silvestter," he said.

172

CHAPTER TWELVE

The agony I must suffer! The trials and tribulations I must undergo for the glory of the Master!

In the operations room—the room adjoining the Hall of Conjuration—Cleveland Winston Silvestter, dressed in his red, white, and green sorcerer's robe, sat stupefied from the events he had been forced to witness during the last half hour. Television cameras on the weather tower and on the ceiling of the first level had recorded the battle, and what the Chosen One had seen, the Chosen One had not enjoyed!

An enemy half-track and one of its jeeps had been destroyed. Fine! Bless the Master! Satan had won! Had he? Within minutes, two of the Master's Saladins had been blown apart! Five minutes later, the remaining Saladin was shot out of existence, almost inside the very entrance of New Eden! Absolutely impossible!

With his top aides—Steele, Ebro, and McKillip—the Chosen One had been forced to watch the Humbler race through the entrance, destroy trucks and jeeps, and throw out deadly DM gas! Another impossibility! Oh! How the Master was testing His children!

The frantic call from one of the Elite Guards on the first level:

"Th-This gas!" the man had managed to gasp. "It's—this sickness! Oh God! I can't stand it!"

Then the guard quit talking and the line went dead!

By now, utterly demented, Silvestter jerked toward Steele, his large brown eyes blazing with an unholy hatred, and screamed at his Chief of Security. "Put that man in front of a firing squad! He mentioned the swine god of evil! For that he must die. No! Don't shoot that sinner! Strangle him with wire . . . very *slowly!*"

Jerry Joseph Steele did not reply. Too busy watching the television screen, his own gray eyes flickered with fear and disbelief, his block of a body as taut as a drawn-too-tight guitar. The hell with Silvestter and his ridiculous orders! Let *him* go up top and put a slug in the poor guard!

The bitter truth was that Steele was more disgusted with himself than with Silvestter. He too had gambled with the forces of Fate . . . gambled that *Astaroth* would sink *Lonely Lady* and everyone on board. Even if the Death Merchant escaped—and he certainly had!—Steele had still another line of defense: the three Saladin armored cars and the heavy stuff in the gun tower.

A ring of emotional fire had held him fixed within a cosmic storm, and all reality had been smashed when he had seen the Saladins destroyed and a short time later the precious gun tower blown into useless rubble!

The Death Merchant will now attack the city itself!

He and his men will now come after us!

There was only one line of defense left: the remaining Elite Guards and the Select of Satan. If they failed to stop the incredible Death Merchant and his men—?

Never had the big ex-CIA agent known an antagonism so instantaneous or more heartily reciprocated! How he hated Richard Camellion! He sensed a battle that eclipsed the two combatants as separate entities, a battle that was bigger than either he or Camellion. Steele accepted the challenge. If the Death Merchant managed to get past the various levels, if Camellion aced out the New Dawn Elite Guard and the Elite of Satan . . . if the son of a bitch got to this very bottom level—*I'll kill him if it's the last thing I do!*

For now, Steele decided, they were safe. The operations room, the long guard room beyond it, and the Hall of Conjuration had already been hermetically sealed off from the rest of the city, their own air-circulation plant running smoothly. Should a flaw develop in the system, they would still be safe from the deadly DM gas, should the Death Merchant use it throughout the various levels. Having pre-

174

pared for any eventuality, Steele had an ample supply of special gas masks, a supply that also included his personally picked New Dawn agents, the twenty men waiting in the guard room.

The big man thought of the only avenues by which the Death Merchant and his men could approach the sixth level: From the fifth level stairs led down to the room beyond the north end of the Hall of Conjuration. From the opposite end of the fifth level a double ladder led down to a long, wide hall that led to the guard room. The Death Merchant could come from either direction, either from the north or the south. *Let him! Let the son of a bitch use explosives! He can blow himself to hell with us! His only choice is to attack with small weapons! So let him! Mason and I and the hand-picked twenty will be waiting! If that madman Silvestter has other plans*—Steele suddenly felt like laughing—*he can go straight to hell!*

But he remained silent . . . thinking . . . staring at the screen of the television set.

Mason Ebro was also quiet. Holding a SIG-AMT 7.62 automatic rifle in his lap, the tall, big-boned man sat glued to the screen, watching the Elite Guards stagger around all over the place on the first level, a look of incredulity on his almost chinless face. The memory of how the gun tower had been demolished was still fresh in his mind, as vivid as a schoolgirl's remembrance of her first kiss.

Scott McKillip merely looked like a man who was trapped in the middle of a hideous nightmare, which he was! Sweat dripped from his round face, and his small dark eyes kept glancing at Lucifer II, the black billygoat standing stupidly next to the Chosen One, who was holding the end of its gold-mesh leash in his hand. Scott hated the animal, this living symbol of the Sabbatic Goat. Imagine! Putting perfume on a goat!

"What are we going to do?" Scott asked timidly, thinking of how the entire complex had been shaken to its foundations when the gun tower had exploded. He looked first at Silvestter, then moved his ferretlike eyes to a sullen-faced Steele. "How are we going to stop the Death Merchant!"

Silvestter glared at his personal secretary. As in every mortal contest between warring individuals, he was dominated by the conviction that he stood for righteousness and Richard Camellion for evil. Temper dulls the mind; madness breeds not only cunning but more madness! The Romans had made gods of their emperors, and the Christians —those cancerous vermin!—continued to make "saints" of mere men! But *he*—Cleveland Winston Silvestter—was the Chosen One of Satan! There could be no defeat. Didn't Scott know that?

Silvestter stood up to his full height, his voice a high screech.

"Satan is testing us! The Master is chastising his Children because *you,* Scott"—he pointed a finger at the awe-stricken man—and *you,* Joseph, and *you,* Mason"—again the finger stabbed out—"have not shown the proper faith. But the Master will not abandon us in our hour of need! He will not turn His head and give us over to the evil of the Christian god! I shall go into the Hall of Conjuration and summon Satan personally to strike down our enemies! I shall perform the Rite of Lucifuge Rofocale and Satan will appear in all His Glory! With a wave of His hand He will cast lightning bolts at His enemies! We will be saved, and the Master will carry the Death Merchant back to Hell with Him!"

Silvestter paused, catching his breath, spit dripping from the corners of his mouth. "This is the day!" he thundered. "The Master will appear! World War III will begin before this day is over and humanity will destroy itself. I, the Chosen One, have spoken! I feel the Master whispering in my brain!"

He stared at Scott McKillip, who was gaping at him, his mouth wide open in astonishment.

"Come along, Scott. You shall assist me in the Rite of Lucifuge Rofocale. You will burn the incense and help me chant the invocation to the Master!"

Looking as if he might be on his way to a masquerade ball, in his red, white, and green robe, Silvestter marched to the steel door that opened to the vast Hall of Conjura-

176

tion, Lucifer II tagging along after him. Scott McKillip followed, too dazed to refuse.

With straight faces, Steele and Ebro turned their heads and stared after the "Chosen One," who, when he reached the door, looked back at them.

"Fear not!" he thundered in a loud, ringing voice. "Satan will appear and save us!"

"Baaaaaaaaaaaaaa . . ." Lucifer II bleated.

After Silvestter, Lucifer II and McKillip had left the operations room, Steele lit a cigarette and, snickering, asked his aide, "Mason, do you believe in Santa Claus?"

"He's as nutty as a truckload of walnuts!" Mason whispered, his lips curling in disdain. "If we survive this, he'll end up in a funny farm for sure—or kill himself! If we survive, the whole damn world will be looking for us!"

Ebro was acutely conscious of a conflict within himself, as clear a warning as ever a man had that Fate was not giving him a choice. He was *here! Here . . .* at the very bottom of New Eden. A prisoner whose freedom was blocked by the Death Merchant—and he knew it! That was the difference between him and Steele. Steele didn't know it! He didn't realize that he, too, was as helpless as any lush in the gutter. All the treasures he had sought with murder were being filched from him and he didn't even know it!

"We're not beaten yet!" Steele spit out in a low, but vicious voice. "So far, Camellion's been lucky. That's all. Don't think he's some kind of superman. He can bleed and die like any man. And if he doesn't die upstairs, he'll die down here!"

Watching the television screen, Ebro did not reply.

The armored car and three armored jeeps had just rushed through the entrance of New Eden.

The Death Merchant was on the first level!

Mason Ebro wondered: *How does it feel to die?*

CHAPTER THIRTEEN

The day had become Christmas for man's oldest enemy (or oldest friend, depending on one's own private philosophy of existence!)—*Death,* at whom Richard Camellion and his kill experts were throwing presents: the fresh, bloody corpses of New Dawn Elite Guards . . . the fresh, bloody corpses of the Select of Satan!

The Humbler armored car in the lead, the three armored jeeps following, the Death Merchant and his men had charged through the entrance of New Eden and were attacking the first level, with a strategy so simple it was almost idiotic—if it moved, *kill it!* The members of Plan *Poaka* were doing precisely that, the four vehicles roaring up and down the 580-foot length of the first level . . . up one side and down the other . . . submachine guns, and the .30 Owens mounted on the rear of the Humbler, spitting like vicious tiger snakes!

The attackers—every member of the eighteen-man attack force wearing a special gas mask with a sestonium-treated filter—had ceased using their recoilless weapons. There were no enemy vehicles left to blast! What trucks and jeeps had been on the first level were already destroyed and burning, filling the area with clouds of sticky black smoke, which was reluctantly being sucked up to the outside by five large fans in the roof. Those Elite Guards and Select of Satan who hadn't managed to escape to the second level, either by the elevators or the stairs, were gunned into the Big Nothingness . . . presented to Death by Camellion, who stood in the turret of the Humbler and worked an Owens submachine gun, sending to Hell any Satanist sap who exposed himself—or *herself!*—and tried to

178

fire back. There were some women, too, on the first level, those dumb daughters of the devil who had put their trust in Hell, but now were receiving the judgment of Heaven.

Camellion did not make any distinction between the sexes. Nor did Pavel, firing from the hatch of the rear compartment, and the other attackers, slamming slugs from the gun slits in the armored sides of the jeeps. A woman pulling the trigger of a submachine gun is just as dangerous, just as deadly as a man.

Within ten minutes there was nothing left to shoot at, nothing left to kill, the first level having been turned into one tremendous morgue, thick with twisted corpses. There wasn't anything left for the attackers to do but assemble by the bank of elevators not far from the entrance and plan their next move. Camellion and his men knew where they would be going and what they would have to do to get there, their knowledge of the complex based on the reports of agents who had managed to infiltrate the city. The Hall of Conjuration was at the very bottom of New Eden, and that's where C. W. Silvestter and his top aides would be.

And that is where they are going to die! Camellion thought as he pored over a map of the city, drawn to scale from at least a half-dozen reports received by the CIA. "We will attack from two sides," the Death Merchant told his men. Heck Geffling and his commandos would attack from the south side, using the stairs by the passenger and freight elevators. The loss of one jeep and the half-track had whittled down Geffling's Aussie force, but he still had twelve men left, every one of them tough and confident with knowhow. Camellion, Jackie Harmsworth, and the British, French, and Russian agents would attack from the north end. They would go down into the bowels of the complex via the double ladders that led from level to level —so it was marked on the map. The attack would be two-pronged, a giant pincer movement that would prevent any of the enemy from escaping. The Satanists wouldn't be able to come from below on the elevators because there would be no elevators!

They checked their weapons, put on bulletproof vests that resembled inflated lifejackets, blew apart the elevator doors with Burney RCLs, and dropped hand grenades down the eight shafts, satisfied when they heard screams of agony from far below. The two groups then went their separate ways, Heck Geffling and his twelve commandos charging the stairs by the wrecked elevators, while the Death Merchant and his four men raced in the Humbler and a jeep to the north end of the first level.

Camellion and his men got their first setback when, going past the door marked EXIT, they discovered the map had been wrong. There were no double ladders going from level to level. Instead, much to their regret, there was a giant concrete tube that led straight down, like a chimney, within which was one long flight of steel steps twisted around a central axis. A ten-foot walkway, with steel-tubing railings, led from each level to the stairs.

Standing in the doorway, they stared in disgust at the lonely-looking ramp, Jackie muttering, "Man, this is a lot of bullshit. If we get on those mother-friggin' steps, we'll be completely exposed. Those Satan saps would chop us into pieces finer than frog hair!"

Carefully Camellion stepped to the edge of the doorway, poked his head out and looked down into the long, lighted emptiness. He instantly jerked his head back, in time to avoid the blast of submachine-gun slugs that streamed up from below.

"Well, now, the enemy is not a fool!" Pavel remarked, twisting his mouth in a half-sneer. "He is ready and no doubt waiting!"

"All men are God's fools!" Philippe de Gasquet said slowly.

"We'd be bigger fools if we stepped out on that ramp!" J. Warren Kimber said. "We'll have to have a go at it from the south side, or those chaps below will cut us to pieces."

The Death Merchant didn't believe in defying the gods, but it wouldn't hurt to give them a laugh or two.

"We haven't time to use the south-side stairs," he said humorlessly. "Anyhow, we can't leave this avenue of escape open. We'll flood the tube with DM and use this first-level ramp!"

"And smoke grenades should give us plenty of cover!"

180

Jackie thrust in, his eyes watery behind the glass of his gas mask.

They dropped half a dozen canisters of smoke and as many DM grenades down the tube-well and—when the smoke and gas had drifted upward—they charged the first-level ramp, going across it one by one. Then, while Kimber and de Gasquet kept up a constant fire at the door of the ramp opening to the second level, they ran down the twisting steps, across the ramp to the door and dived in, firing a blast of slugs that was almost a solid wall of steel.

The passageway beyond the door was empty!

A few minutes later, after Kimber and de Gasquet had reached the foyer fronting the main corridor of the second level, Pavel dropped a two-pound charge of TNT down the tube-well; when it exploded far below, they rushed the channel of the second level.

Coming to the end of the corridor, they found they were in—of all things—a *gymnasium,* complete with swimming pool!

The Elite Guards and the Select of Satan, all—even women!—dressed in green uniforms that resembled jump suits, were waiting, crouched down behind exercising equipment, every fanatic clutching some kind of weapon —a pistol, revolver, rifle, or submachine gun.

The Death Merchant and his four men spread out, diving in low, firing short, arching bursts, blasts that blew blood and bone from floor to ceiling. Three devil dummies tried to zero in on Pavel, but all they got for their effort was instant annihilation, from J. Warren Kimber who razored open their bellies with a burst of .30 Owens sub-M slugs, while Pavel gave the last rites to another group trying to smoke Camellion and de Gasquet, sprinkling them with holy lead from his blessed submachine gun. They dropped into Hell faster than the Pope can say God bless you!

The Russian raked them with a long stream of fire, his slugs whipping into the Guards, killing four and winging one. When the wounded man flopped to the floor, a bullet in his leg, Pavel ripped his chest apart with half a dozen slugs that bored through the slob and hit a 150-pound barbell on the floor. The slugs ricocheted off the weight and whizzed off into the fume-filled air. The KGB agent then swung his Owens to another nitwit who suddenly lost his nerve (and his faith in C. W. Silvestter—*that crazy bastard!*) and threw up his arms in surrender, his eyes asking to live! He would have had better luck asking Satan for holy water! Pavel exploded the man's head with a blast of 9-mms! *Kill your enemies and mistrust your friends!* Pavel was a devoted believer in this KGB dictum.

Almost side by side, Camellion and de Gasquet—dodging, weaving, zigzagging—advanced toward the swimming pool, and with each step they triggered off short, sure bursts, constantly moving the muzzles of their submachine guns like a couple of firemen spraying flames, only these nozzles were flooding the area with a tidal wave of steel death . . . slugs that butchered a dozen sinners as rapidly as the shadow of a cloud skims across the ground. From then on, the devil dunces would have to do their calisthenics in Hell . . .

As Camellion and his men advanced, the Satanists fell back, tripping over, dodging behind, and dying beside various kinds of body-building equipment. One group of Guards and members of the Select of Satan had even retreated as far as the swimming pool . . . lying flat, or down on one knee, firing!

Dressed in short, tight shorts and green halter, a woman jumped up from behind a rowing machine and, using a big .44 Magnum, snapped off a shot at Camellion, the big slug passing not more than two inches from Richard's head.

Bless you, baby! I'm going to make you the guest of honor at your own funeral! Camellion barely touched the trigger of his Owens, and the chain of hot metal amputated the doll's breasts and terminated her life. Backward she went, crashing into one of the legs of a parallel bar frame, her long red hair flying. She looked very surprised, as if she had just discovered the Holy Grail was only a myth. Then she looked dead . . .

Not far from where the woman had died, a man and a woman jumped up, each with an Armalite .233 semiautomatic carbine, and tried to do a double number of Jackie Harmsworth, who caught only a quick flash of their faces as he gave the woman a new facelift with a couple of Owens' slugs, dissolving her features with one short blast. The man—the old bastard looked about as intelligent as a high-school football coach—died just as he pulled the trigger of the AR-233. Jackie had dropped, firing as he did so, and the old man's slug had sung over his head. Jackie's own blast disemboweled the elderly nut. He gagged blood, spun, and toppled across the corpse of the woman, who appeared to be in her early twenties.

What the hell! thought Jackie. *The old tub of crap has it made! In old age it's more comforting to smell perfume than liniment!*

Looking around, he saw that there were hardly any Satanist defenders left, except twenty or more semicircled around the east side of the swimming pool, and they began dying so fast they became spiritual gate-crashers without knowing it!

One man—he was a Negro, as black as tar—had even backed out on the diving board, the low one that was level with the pool, acting as if he had some place to go! He had! Down into the water already dyed red with blood from a half-dozen corpses floating face down! And that's where the Elite Guard went when de Gasquet slug-cut him, from belly to breastbone! De Gasquet did a bit of thinking —*What was that American expression? Oui! A spade is a spade!*

This spade was a dead spade! He made a big red splash as he hit the red water! At about the same time the remaining Satanists began their death dives—and all without a diving board!—kicked into the water by the Death Merchant and his four assistants.

Having emptied his Owens and not having time to reload, Camellion had resorted to using his .357 Magnums, Pavel his machine pistols. Harmsworth, Kimber, and de Gasquet had also exhausted the ammo in their Owens submachine guns and were using sidearms, 9-mm Browning high-power pistols.

As the big booms of the Magnums mingled with the sharper cracks of the Brownings and the two Stechkins, the Satanists began taking long walks off of very short piers.

Like drunken acrobats practicing a new act, they toppled into the water and rose to the surface . . . coming up red-wet and thoroughly dead.

In close proximity to Camellion and his men, the last six Satanists still alive, out of ammo, came charging with their bare hands . . . charging and screaming curses—four men and two women, all young, in their twenties, well-built and determined to die for Satan. Why not accommodate them?

For the hell of it, Jackie knifed one man in the belly, then picked him up and pitched him into the pool. Kimber blew another man's head off, while de Gasquet—surprising everyone—snapped the spine of a third Satanist, using a Judo *Sasae Tsurikomi Ashi* hold! In contrast, Pavel calmly shot the two girls in the legs, laughing with all the enthusiasm of an aborigine as the screaming girls fell to the wet floor. Moaning, they rolled close to the pool.

One Satanist sap came at Camellion with his arm upraised, his fingers wrapped around the handle of a long-bladed knife. The Death Merchant felt sorry for the "bloody bloke." How stupid can you get?

Richard snap-kicked the dummy in the solar plexus, grabbed his arm, snapped it at the elbow, chopped the idiot across the side of the neck with a *Shuto* side-hand blow, then picked him up and pitched him headfirst into the bloody swimming pool. The water of his splashing was still falling when Pavel kicked one of the wounded girls into the pool, her long wail of terror terminating in the glub and gurble of drowning. A lot of bubbles and she was wet-dead.

The Death Merchant searched the smoky gymnasium, now as quiet as an undiscovered tomb. The place was empty of enemy life, but full of enemy dead. As for his own force, there had been one casualty: J. Warren Kimber had skinned his left knee in diving to the deck!

Richard was conscious of another fact: Kimber and de Gasquet were not at all pleased with Pavel's marblehearted sadism. Even Jackie Harmsworth, usually as coldblooded as a crocodile, was glaring disapprovingly at the Russian KGB agent, who was pointing a machine pistol at the girl's

184

forehead and asking her, "Bitch, where's your big man Sil-vestter and the rest of the big devils?"

More afraid of dying than an oldtime Catholic was of sex, the girl did not stall for a single second, thinking that if she talked, the men might spare her life. They might even put a tourniquet on her leg and prevent her from bleeding to death. With effort she sat up, her eyes as wide as an owl's.

"He's in the Hall of Conjuration, on the sixth level," she whispered weakly. "Please don't ki—"

The machine pistol roared, and the girl's blond head jumped outward! Dribbling brains, she fell backward, spraying blood as she flopped through the air with the greatest of ease and fell awkwardly into the bloody pool.

"*Da!* We know where Silvestter is!" Pavel said proudly. Calmly he holstered the machine pistol and proceeded to slam a new magazine into the Owens submachine gun.

"I say, you're a bloody son of a bitch!" Kimber snapped. He shoved his face to Pavel's and glared malevolently at the Russian; he turned then to Camellion, his voice rising in rage.

"Are you going to stand there and permit this Russian butcher to kill defenseless women? After all, we chaps aren't bloody torturers!"

"That's the trouble with you damned Britishers!" Pavel said, with a low, spiteful laugh. "You're always putting mercy, the gentlest of the virtues, into a double go-cart with the spotted snake of indifference. That's why your nation has ended up thinking it is wheeling twins, and that's why you lost your empire!"

"I don't approve of useless killing," Richard said, in the process of inserting a full magazine into his own Owens sub-M. "On the other hand, I'm not in the business of spreading morality! The way our Russian comrade wastes the enemy is his business, as long as his methods don't interfere with the mission!"

"If and when they do, what will you do?" asked Kimber in a cattish voice. "Reprimand him? Complain to the KGB? The Kremlin?"

Camellion began checking one of his Magnums. "I'll put

185

a 'bloody' bullet in his 'bloody' head," he said with deceptive politeness, "and yours, too, 'old chap,' if you get in the way!"

Not only J. Warren Kimber looked surprised, but also Pavel Telpuchovskii, who merely smiled in a crooked, fatalistic sort of way.

"I'll tell you something else, Kimber, 'old bean'! I believe in that part of the Bible that advises one not to cast his pearls before swine! Don't argue with me—any of you. Now keep your damn mouths zippered and follow me. Let's go find the stairs to the third level!"

Finding the stairs that led down to the third level was not difficult; they were situated in the main north-south corridor, toward the center of the second level, where the main east-west hallway intersected. But getting to the stairs was not without problems.

Camellion and his men had approached the four-way stop of the intercrossing corridors, the Death Merchant standing at the northwest corner, looking down the western length of the east-west passage, de Gasquet standing next to him, to his left. Pavel, Jackie, and J. Warren were in the eastern section of the east-west corridor, staring down its silent, ominous length. It was the silence that was disturbing, a soundlessness that was actually a warning.

Then hell roared, and the Elite Guards opened fire, not only from the steps in the main corridor, but from the doorway of a room, to the left, past the steps.

A fraction of a moment before the Satanists opened fire, de Gasquet spotted the movement at the top of the stairs, as a few heads bobbed upward and as the barrels of several submachine guns were shoved around one corner of the doorway.

"The stairs! Down!" the Frenchman shouted in a frantic voice. Jumping sideways, he shoved Camellion violently against the shoulder with the heel of one hand. Instantly Richard dived to the right, to the west side of the east-west passageway, his Owens swinging upward. De Gasquet also hit the deck, firing as he fell.

The Frenchman's keen eyes and quick thinking had

saved the Death Merchant's life. A delay of one second—if de Gasquet hadn't shoved him out of the way—and a dozen slugs would have streamed into him; and since the Satanists, crouched as they were on the stairs, had fired from an upward angle, most of the 9-mms would not have bored into the bulletproof vest, but into Camellion's groin—had they reached him. Not one had!

Richard's own lines of steel cut on target, slicing into the three Satan saps exposed at the top of the stairs, the storm of steel almost decapitating them. Spurting blood from jagged jugulars and cut carotids, the dummies rolled all the way down the stairs, as dead as Fidel Castro's dream of South American revolution.

The three guards who had jumped from the doorway were equally unlucky. Two of their slugs had zinged into de Gasquet's bulletproof vest as he feel to a belly-flat position on the smooth concrete floor. But then Camellion's lightning quick chain of slugs had made them hesitate in reflexive fear and surprise. By the time they realized the Death Merchant was not firing at them—it was too late! Almost as quick as the Death Merchant, Philippe de Gasquet sprayed them with a cure for all of life's problems, a couple dozen 9-mm Owens slugs that knocked the guards straight into the darkness of death. They looked like drunken ballet dancers as they jumped, spun, twisted and died! They would never do another dance . . .

Camellion rolled to the opposite wall of the east-west passage as the French agent sprayed another knot of nitwits who were stupidly trying to charge from a doorway to the right, in the southern section of the north-south corridor. The four guards tumbled like tenpins, the slugs cutting them to ribbons. One slob screamed and shouted, *"Satan help me!"* But Satan didn't. Death did, and the man dropped to the deck—dead!

More demonologist dummies were dying thirty feet in front of Pavel, J. Warren, and Jackie. Hearing de Gasquet's shouted warning, they had thrown themselves prone, just as a dozen Elite Guards appeared ahead of them; the Lucifer lunatics rushed out of a room down the hall, holding thick plastic shields in front of them. However, the shields did not cover their ankles and feet. The Guards wished the plastic had when Pavel swept them at floor level with a blast of bullets, while J. Warren and Jackie took them off balance by throwing up a barrage of steel against their shields.

Howling in agony, their feet shot out from under them, the Elite Guards, amid a tangle of arms, legs and shields, crashed to the floor, then fell into Hell as three Owens submachine guns punched dozens of holes in their green jumpsuits. They had tossed the dice with the devil, but had lost the game of life to God. One man lost a bit slower than his buddies. Gasping in pain, he tried to raise himself up on one elbow, his eyes staring straight at Pavel.

"Take a good look, *gluchinik*," Pavel snarled. "You've only got one left!" The Russian agent then blew the man's face apart with three well-placed slugs.

Again a terrible brain-battering silence descended over the fume-filled hallways, fumes that bit into the nostrils of the Death Merchant and the other men who had lowered their gas masks.

Keeping a wary eye to his rear, the Death Merchant got to his feet, thinking that de Gasquet was full of unexpected surprises. He may have been a superstitious god-lover, but the Frenchman killed with a deadly, professional efficiency —*I have to admit: I was wrong about that joker. He's a rather handy frog to have around . . .*

"Merci Monsieur," Camellion said. "I owe you one."

Philippe merely nodded. He wondered what the Death Merchant would have thought if—he knew I was thanking God? *Oui, he would feel as sorry for me as I am for him . . .*

The attackers tossed a couple of fragmentation grenades down the stairs and moved to the third level of New Eden, encountering only slight resistance as they sought out Satanists who had decided to retreat. Those who decided to attack died as quickly. Camellion and his men killed a dozen in the library rooms, and Pavel, branching out on his own, wasted five more who had hidden themselves in an apartment belonging to a Select-of-Satan couple—using hand grenades.

In the distance, toward the southern end of the fourth level, there was more gunfire and the *thump-whommm* of hand grenades! Heck Geffling and his boys were making excellent progress! The DM found out how much progress when he contacted Heck on a walkie-talkie! Heck and his commandos had just aced out the Elite Guards protecting the Virgins of Satan. Screaming, the kidnapped girls had fled in fear. They had been rescued, but didn't know it!

In the Hall of Conjuration, finding Silvestter and Steele was the dominant drive controlling the Death Merchant; yet he knew better than to let overanxiousness ax into his judgment.

He spoke into the walkie-talkie, giving precise orders to Geffling:

"I'm convinced that Steele will have guards in the room south of the Hall and in the two rooms at the other end," the Death Merchant said. "You'll attack from the south. We'll go in from the north. But wait on the fifth level until you get the word, I want to synchronize our two-pronged attack."

Down to the fourth level moved the Death Merchant and his men! They stormed through the repair shops, then tore apart the guards, with machine-gun fire, in the air-conditioning and air-purification centers, tossing grenades at the air-conditioning machinery. *Let the bastards sweat before we send them to hell!*

Down to the fifth level . . . through the tangled mess of rooms of the complex, including the infirmary where doctors, nurses and patients tried to fight it out, but lost the battle. Two patients in bed were too ill even to hold weapons, but that didn't prevent Pavel from giving them shots not called for on their charts—a prescription of 9-mm slugs guaranteed to cure any ailment! No one ever complained against the dosage, nor asked for his life back!

Finally they stood at the top of the steps that led down to the guard room at the north end of the fifth level. The metal steps slanted into the huge concrete silo that contained the staircase spiraling to the surface of the city. The last three levels and their ramps were only twisted steel, reduced to uselessness by the two-pound charge of TNT Pavel had dropped down the escape tube. Nevertheless, the explosion had not harmed the steel, rivet-studded door of the guard room, over one corner of which a TV camera pointed its single, bleak eye at the Death Merchant and his anxious helpers.

With an easy motion, Richard drew a Magnum and blasted the camera to junk. Beyond that door was the guard room . . . then the operations room . . . and finally, the Hall of Conjuration.

That's where I'll find C. W. Silvestter!

Richard Camellion smiled to himself, looked at the steel door, then glanced thoughtfully at the big .357 Magnum in his hand—

Yea, though I walk through the valley of the shadow of death, I will fear no evil: For thou art with me; thy barrel and thy trigger they comfort me . . .

"Gentlemen, let's send Silvestter and his boys to hell!" Camellion said . . .

CHAPTER FOURTEEN

If I were the damned Death Merchant, how would I attack? A very clever man, Jerry Joseph Steele concluded that there was only one logical way the hit could be executed: *I'd divide my forces. He's already done that! TV monitors don't lie! To get into the Hall of Conjuration, I'd have half my force hit the south guard room and the other half concentrate on the north side. That's how I would do it, and I believe that's what Camellion will do! But I could be wrong.*

Steele wasn't! The Death Merchant employed the only

strategy possible: Heck Geffling and his nine commandos (three had been wasted in the force's reaching the fifth level) attacked the south end. The Death Merchant and his four men stormed in through the guard room in the north.

An extremely intelligent man who always knew his enemies, Camellion had sensed that Steele would also divide his forces—*And he will deduce my plan of attack. A moron could!* Accordingly, he told Geffling as well as his own four men not to expect any guards in the rooms after the steel doors were blasted—"Steele and his boys will retreat inward and wait for us! Use DM gas but don't count on it to help you out. Steele and his men will have masks. He's the type of guy who'd fall into hell wearing an asbestos suit and carrying two fire extinguishers!"

The attack was synchronized almost to the second by walkie-talkie. Charges of TNT were placed against the hinged side of the doors and detonated, the thunderous explosions blowing off both doors and those sides of the wall that had supported the huge hinges. Hand grenades were then tossed into the smoking guard rooms, followed by smoke canisters and DM-gas bombs. The attackers charged in . . . diving in low through clouds of thick protective smoke, firing in front of them as they dived sideways and hit the floors.

Both guard rooms were empty, but the lack of the enemy troops surprised neither Camellion nor Heck Geffling. As the Death Merchant had predicted, Steele had split his hand-picked force into two groups, sending ten to the south end of the Hall of Conjuration and keeping ten with him and Mason Ebro in the north end operations room.

The Satanist troops in the south end of the Hall, crouched down between the thick wooden pews and waited, their submachine guns aimed at the steel door through which Geffling and his commandos would have to charge. Now and then the ten Satan Elite Guardists looked in awe toward the front of the weird 300-feet-long by 180-feet-wide hall.

There was the Chosen One and his acolytes—Silvestter and McKillip—standing within the *Grand Kabbalistic Circle,* facing the Sabbatic Goat painted on the front wall.

191

They were chanting in loud voices the invocation to Satan—
    "Lucifer-Ouyar-Chameron-Aliseon-Mandousin-Premy-Oriet—"

Lucifer II stood stupidly to the left of the black marble altar, the black billygoat looking bored with the whole business. But even though the gas-masked Elite Guards were frightened, they were determined. They knew it was the Chosen One's last stand—and theirs! They looked around the giant Hall of Conjuration, their eyes playing over the red marble walls and ceiling . . . watching the flames leap from the large bowls of the charcoal-burning braziers. Sweat poured from the men! The air-conditioners were no longer functioning. Suppose the Death Merchant wrecked the ventilating system? Would the men then suffocate from the thick smoke given off by the braziers? They wondered, and they worried!

Why didn't Geffling and his commandos attack? The ten Elite Guards had no way of knowing that Heck and his troops were waiting for the Death Merchant and his four-man army to complete the attack on the operations room.

"We have to go through two rooms at this end," Camellion had told Heck, "in contrast to your one. Wait for us, or you'll be chopped to little bitty pieces. We'll charge together and make it a two-pronged attack. I'll give you the word on the walkie-talkie."

The Elite Guards in the pews waited nervously. In the west wall of the Hall there was another door, almost 200 feet to the north of the door that opened to the south-end guard room. This was the door of the operations room. The guards stared fearfully at it. They sweated, waited, worried, and listened to Silvestter and McKillip:

"Emperor Lucifer, Master and the Prince of the Rebellious Spirits, I adjure Thee to leave Thy abode and come hither and appear and communicate with us. I command thee by Power of the Divine Adonay, Eloim, Ariel, Jehovam, and by the whole hierchy of superior intelligences. Venite! Venite! Submiritillor Lucifuge, or eternal torment shall overwhelm thee, by the great power of mine blasting rod. Come, Lucifer, Come! I implore Thee to appear and strike my enemies and—"

Most of the guards were of the opinion that if Satan were going to appear and help them—he had damn well better hurry up and do it!

On either side of the steel door in the wall separating the guard room from the operations room, the Death Merchant and his four men prepared for the final assault on the heart of New Eden. First, they blew apart the steel door, after which they tossed a half-dozen fragmentation grenades into the operations room, hearing another door clang shut as the echo of the grenades wilted away. The room was empty, except for demolished furniture. Jerry Steele and his Elite Guard had fled to the Hall of Conjuration.

Studying the closed door at the end of the room—Pavel was already attaching blocks of TNT to the hinges—Camellion contacted Heck Geffling on the walkie-talkie. Yes, Heck and his grim and determined commandos were ready and waiting in the south end guard room. Yes again! The door was ready to be blown. Just say when!

The Death Merchant glanced at Pavel. The Russian nodded. The explosives on the operations room door were ready. All Pavel had to do was set the timer.

Camellion's orders to Geffling were simple: "Heck, set your timers to three minutes. After your door blows, throw in smoke and grenades, then charge the Hall. They'll be waiting in the pews. They have to. That's all the cover they have!"

Three and a half minutes later there were two terrific explosions, and two steel doors went flying outward from the west wall of the Hall. Another half-minute and, amid chunks of marble still falling from the wall, smoke canisters and hand grenades came sailing through the blasted doorways, both falling and exploding short of the pews because Camellion and his attackers—not daring to stand in the openings and expose themselves to the streams of submachine fire—had been forced to throw around the corners of the jagged openings.

So now we do it—and how many of us will die? The Death Merchant and his group of four charged through the smoke, through the north end doorway, Geffling and his nine commandos through the south end entrance. They dived in so low they almost tripped and fell on their sweat-filled faces . . . dodging with all the ability that comes from years of experience . . . weaving and running a very crooked course. Through the cover of thick smoke and the frantic, angry snarling of submachine guns—both sides were firing as fast as they could—Richard Camellion and his force of fourteen rushed into the giant Hall of Hell, slugs of all sizes and calibers screaming all around them.

A commando got unlucky and took a slug in the mouth. He gagged, choked on blood, fell backward, and died. Three slugs slammed into the Merchant's bulletproof vest, the force rocking him. Another hot piece of steel cut across the left side of his crash helmet. A sharp, burning pain cutting across his right hip—a deep graze! *Damn it and fudge twice!* A sting along his left inner thigh! Another cut—and deep! The warm blood sticky! *A man could even get killed doing this! But the hell with it. Dying is less painful than being born, only you don't remember the tight pop-out squeeze of birth! And you don't remember the pain and fright! And what you don't remember can't hurt—but neither can the myths about death!*

The long charge continued, the Death Merchant and his thirteen men—high now on the juice of danger and the violence of battle—tossing more smoke canisters and hand grenades as they closed in on the pews.

Jerry Steele wasn't about to be tricked by such a tactic. When Camellion and his men dropped, Steele and his men also stopped firing and huddled down between the pews, the steel splinters from the grenades peppering the pews like five thousand icepicks. More smoke bombs! And by the time Steele and his guards raised up and prepared to fire, the incredible Death Merchant and his men were upon them. Curses! Cries of rage as, through drifting smoke, the two sides crashed into each other, each man on his own, his only thought being to kill the enemy and to save his own life while doing it. Both Camellion's men and Steele's had exhausted the ammo in their submachine guns, and there was no referee to blow a whistle and call *"Halt! Time to reload, gentlemen!"*—not in this game of Death.

Within the smoky pomp of red marble and the persistence of pestilence, the two opposing forces clashed in hand-to-hand combat, using fists, knives, sidearms, and anything else that was handy. The edge wasn't with the Death Merchant and his troops, although they had been trained in methods that made for quick extermination of life. Steele's men were all hand-picked, the deciding factor in his choice had been their marksmanship and proficiency in karate; and since the Elite Guards outnumbered Camellion's force by nine men, the odds were that Richard and his troops would be buried in New Eden—outnumbered by *eleven* men, counting Silvestter and McKillip.

The Chosen One and his ass of an acolyte had not joined Steele and the Elite Guards. They had stopped their ridiculous chanting, their insane invocation to the "devil," and had taken up positions behind the black block of a marble altar—a wise move on their part! Let the Death Merchant waltz through a hail of slugs to waste them—the son of a bitch!

At the moment the "son of a bitch" had only one thought: Get to Jerry Joseph Steele and Mason Roger Ebro and kill them, then go after Silvestter—*The hell with The Hub's order to bring him back alive!*

Dominated by the ambition to kill Camellion, Steele and Ebro began searching for him, but doing it at a safe distance. Why be a goddamn fool and walk into a buzz saw when you could take a side course and shut it off from ambush. Steele and Ebro began crawling underneath the pews, toward the side opposite the fighting, toward the ends of the pews facing the east wall of the Hall. Hell, yes! They would crawl all the way around the south end of the pews and machine-gun the bastard! Sneak in from the south and ace him out.

For the time being there wasn't anything Camellion could do about it. He had other problems to solve. An Elite Guard was rushing at him like a bulldozer, the Satanist simp holding an M-4 carbine bayonet knife down low, his arm drawn back, all set for an inward stomach stab. He was swinging an empty Owens submachine gun in his other hand. The slob acted as if he were going some place—he was!

The Death Merchant moved so fast he amazed the angels and astonished the devils—first giving the joker a *Sil Lum Kung Fu* flying foot kick, a *Fay Gerk* that, landing in the slob's solar plexus, sent his bayonet and submachine gun flying, the blow so intense—and the pain—that it clicked off all his strength.

Camellion followed with a *Pow Chow*—the knuckle of the middle finger held outward—to the mouth, the cannon punch making the man think he had been whacked with the barrel of an 88-FLAK gun! The blow broke off half his teeth, made him taste a flood of blood, and numbed his brain with shock. Gagging in pain, he wished he were at the North Pole. A moment later he began going to a much hotter place!

Richard used a *Nukite* to finish him off—a bunched finger stab to the throat that mashed the halfwit's Adam's apple. Choking to death, the goon dropped! And none too soon! Two more idiots were coming at Camellion, both aiming 9-mm Browning pistols at his head and neck! They pulled the triggers too late! Camellion ducked down and the slugs sang by him, almost hitting Heck Geffling who had just ripped open the belly of a Satanist with a Fairbairn commando knife. Heck then shoved the man away and began defending himself against another guard who had the idea he could shove the muzzle of a Browning into Heck's side and tickle his lungs and liver with a couple of 9-mm slugs. The men suddenly got the disturbing idea he was dying when Heck grabbed his wrist, jerked his gun arm upward, and slit his throat, at the same time belly-pushing him backward with a foot to avoid the tidal wave of blood boiling from the big, grinning mouth in the man's neck. Gurgling, his arms flapping like the wings of a decapitated rooster, the Satanist fell against an Elite Guard who was doing his damndest to blow up Jackie Harmsworth.

Jackie grabbed the moron's wrist, twisting the gun hand inward. Jackie's other set of fingers closed around the terrified guard's gun hand, and the high-powered pistol roared, the slug plowing into the man's heart.

196

Three other Elite Guards flung themselves at the giant of a bearded man, two—with Browning pistols—rushing him from the front, the third from the rear, a Mark II Gerber combat knife in his hand. Jackie aced out one slob by blasting him in the chest. The other boob got it twice in the belly, two 9-mms that collapsed his colon and severed his right external iliac artery. He didn't die saying his prayers!

Jackie's time on this planet had run out! Before he could swing around to the attacker coming at him from the rear, the man had flung an arm around his throat and plunged the Mark II Gerber into the small of his back, the blade slipping in the right kidney area. In spite of the agony—it was like the thrust of a blue-hot poker—Jackie managed to put both hands on the wrist of the forearm pressing into his throat. He twisted, a tremendous movement that almost snapped the arm of the guard, who had pulled out the Mark II-G in preparation for another kidney thrust. With his hate ten times stronger than his pain, Jackie turned, jerked the astonished man to him, grabbed his knife arm, and with one last effort pulled the knife downward and inward, the bloody blade plunging into the man just below his breastbone. The Satanist made a choked cry and for a very brief instant his gaze locked with Jackie's. It was over. Both men wilted to the floor, blood pouring from their mouths.

This is—all of it—a lot of useless goddamn crap . . . And it was! Jackie fell into the Big Blackness and became nothing, as if he had never existed . . .

Fifteen feet from Jackie's cooling corpse, Pavel Telpuchovskii was very much alive—a wild, laughing maniac of feet and fists who was using his Stechkin machine pistols as clubs, not only because he wanted to save his ammo, but because he enjoyed battering the boobs. Four Elite Guards had closed in on the Russian, and the five of them now fought in an area close to the west wall of the Hall. In fact the entire battle had spread to an area between the pews and the west wall.

They came at the Russian from all directions, trying to slice him to ribbons with knives and clobber him with their fists. Good they were, but Pavel was a lot better. He slammed one man across the jaw with a Stechkin and, when the man went down against the wall, elbowed another in the gut with a vicious bone-busting elbow *Empi* blow. He tapped the third across the temple with his other Stechkin M-P, laughing when the dummy dropped to join his buddy by the wall. The fourth Elite Guard tried a right uppercut, missed, and walked right into the tip of Pavel's left foot which had connected with the Satanist's sex machine. Gasping loudly from the terrible pain and shock, the man sank to his knees, his hand clutching his mashed-to-pulp balls. He reminded Pavel of a dog getting ready to howl at the moon, as the KGB agent spun and slammed a machine pistol against the head of the man he had previously jabbed in the stomach with his elbow. The Elite Guard fell sideways, stumbling off toward the pews, then collapsed to the floor.

Pavel turned to the two goofs against the wall and the silly sap on his knees, holding his balls. The man—he was "Oh-oh-oh-ing" all over the place—rocked back and forth, his head almost touching the floor.

With a big, wide grin of enjoyment, Pavel shot the man in both feet, and when the slob screamed and rolled over on his back, he shot him once in the belly, hoping it would take the son of a bitch a long, long time to die.

One man by the wall—Pavel shot him in both knees and made splinters of his shoulder bones with two more well placed 9-mms!

The second sinner by the wall—Pavel coldbloodedly and deliberately shot off his ears and then zeroed in a slug to the right knee! The man screamed and rolled over. Pavel hesitated, trying to make up his mind to place the fourth slug.

But the Russian's love of pain had caused him to make a fatal mistake. He had turned from the last man he had slammed against the side of the head. He should have checked to make sure the man was out. He hadn't! Now, behind Pavel, the Satanist drew a small .25-Obler automatic from his boot and let the Russian have it—two slugs in the center of the Russian's broad back. And since Pavel's bullet proof vest covered only his chest, the two .25s went into his flesh, into his lungs. Pavel spun around, his face an open book of shock, surprise, and pain. The man on the floor then emptied the weapon at Pavel's face. Two slugs missed! Three did not. One caught him in his half-opened mouth. Another zinged into the center of his forehead, the third going through his left eye.

One quick thought popped into Pavel Telpuchovskii's dying mind:

My God—I'm dead!

He was! His brain clicked off forever! He fell backward against a brazier and crashed to the floor, taking the brazier down with him. The brazier hit the floor with a loud, ringing clang, the blazing charcoal flying out of the bowl, some of it landing on a dead commando and setting the corpse on fire.

The guard who had smoked away Pavel quit congratulating himself when J. Warren Kimber blew his head off with two Colt-.45 slugs. Kimber then turned to help the Death Merchant, but found himself facing a Satanist who was charging directly at him!

J. Warren had worried needlessly. The Death Merchant was merely taking his daily constitutional! After dropping and dodging the two 9-mm slugs from the two guards, he jumped up, grabbed one man's gun arm, jerked it out and up, and let the man have a high snap-kick in his left armpit. The pistol fell from the man's hand, his entire left side paralyzed! With almost the same motion Camellion reached out for the second Elite Guard, who was trying desperately to swing his pistol toward the Merchant of Death. It was a good try, and that's all it was!

Richard grabbed the man's gun arm with one hand, pushing the weapon ceilingward, and let him have a four-fingered *Bul Jee* to the face with the other, the terrible Kung Fu strike punching out the moron's left eye. The man screamed, staggered, and died, Camellion's follow-up Shuto hand-chop strike breaking his neck! He died easy, like an old woman who had gone to bed and forgotten to live . . .

Not to be diverted from his main purpose of finding and finishing off Steele and Ebro (and he hadn't forgotten C.W. Silvestter), Camellion scooped up an Owens sub-M, dived between two rows of pews and hastily inserted a full magazine into the weapon, after which he stood up, looked around, and instantly dropped—in time to save his life! A stream of submachine-gun fire sizzled over his head, the slugs so close some of them chipped wood from the back of one pew.

Fudge! Jerry Steele and Mason Ebro had fired from the south, only thirty feet away. Crouched behind the last pew, the two men were both determined to fill the Death Merchant with a couple of pounds of hot lead.

The snarling of another submachine gun! This tornado of slugs came from Philippe de Gasquet who, spotting Steele and Ebro, had dived into the pew behind Camellion, firing as he did so.

Now that they had been discovered, Steele and Ebro weren't about to be stupid, make a forward charge, and have Camellion and the Frenchman blow them away. Live cowards had it all over brave corpses, any day of the week and three times on Sunday (four times on Holy Days of Obligation)!

"We'll go back up the other side of the pews!" Steele whispered to Mason Ebro. "If we can't kill them from the other side, we'll made a dash for the altar. There's no way they can rush the altar without our cutting them in two, and C.W. and Scott can help us."

Clever as he was, Steele then made a very bad mistake. As he and Mason crawled toward the other side of the pew section, in the direction of the east wall, he periodically threw up his machine gun and fired in the direction of Camellion and de Gasquet, the chattering of the weapon broadcasting the direction in which he and Ebro were traveling.

The Death Merchant and de Gasquet immediately crawled out and, in a low crouch as they ran to the area in back of the pews, sprayed a blast of slugs that would have chopped a herd of elephants into hamburger. By then, however, Steele and Ebro had reached the east side of the pews and were running like mad toward the altar. By the time Richard and Philippe discovered them and began run-

200

ning up the east side of the pews in pursuit, Steele and Ebro had reached the altar and were diving behind it!

Knowing that Steele and Ebro would now open fire, since they were protected by the large block of black marble, the Death Merchant and de Gasquet also sought safety, choosing to dive between pews six or seven rows from the front. Any closer and the 9-mm slugs could zip right through the wood into Camellion and the French agent.

The slugs came fast and furious from the altar as Camellion and de Gasquet snuggled down, but not to do any praying! A veritable cloudburst of slugs, raining the hot hail of death down on the pews—from at least four submachine guns!

If I weren't a religious man, I'd curse! Camellion did some stupid thinking: Steele and Ebro were behind the altar; that was for sure. And Silvestter and McKillip are probably with them. Fine! I'll smoke all four of the son of a bitches at one time!

How to do it was the problem! How to cross the seventy-foot space, from the first row of pews to the altar, without being blown away the first five feet—that was the problem!

Grenades might do it! Richard looked into the utility bag hanging from his shoulder. No grenades. He did have five smoke canisters.

As if reading the Death Merchant's mind, de Gasquet said, "I am also fresh out of hand grenades, monsieur. I do have a half-dozen smoke canisters."

This is going to be one of those days! Camellion told himself, then proceeded to tell the French agent how they would take the altar.

They'd saturate the entire area with smoke, and while de Gasquet kept up a steady stream of fire at the altar, Camellion would make his move. Naturally the four chief devils behind the altar would know that Richard was about to attack, and they'd spray the area with a deadly fire. The catch was that Camellion would zigzag in at an oblique angle, a slant charge that—at least for three-fourths of the distance—would take him away from the altar. With de Gasquet's fire covering him, by the time the four realized what was happening, Camellion would be on them—or stone-cold dead on the cold red marble!

"Let's do it, Philippe," Camellion said easily. Nodding, the Frenchman smiled. It was the first time this strange man of death had addressed him by his first name.

Richard and Philippe tossed the eleven smoke canisters out into the wide area, spacing them carefully, then crawled toward the west end of the pews. There was no way Richard would be able to crawl out through the east side, nor de Gasquet rise up and fire, not with the blast of steel that was sure to come from the block of black marble. The blast came . . . as the smoke—as thick as the fires of Hell—fumed out, clouds of it, rolling, boiling, as if you could slice it with a knife.

Here I go! Magnums fully loaded, stripped of all his gear, except for his Marine trench knife and Owens submachine gun, the Death Merchant crawled out the opening between the pews at the west end, and—zigzagging, down low, cutting first an obtuse angle, then a crooked path at an acute angle—charged the altar.

Behind him, de Gasquet's submachine gun roared, the Frenchman raking the top and both ends of the marble block, chopping up a helluva lot of marble, chips flying. The Frenchman stopped firing on the count of seven, to make sure he didn't accidentally hit the Death Merchant.

This day was not the day that Richard Camellion was fated to die! By the time Steele, Ebro, Silvestter, and McKillip realized how neatly they had been tricked . . . by the time four frantic men stuck the barrels of their weapons across the top of the slug-pitted altar, the terrible Death Merchant was upon them!

De Gasquet—*mon Dieu!* he should have remained behind!—came racing in behind the Death Merchant!

The smoke was boiling, but every one of the enemy was wearing a gas mask, and they could see the Death Merchant as easily as he—now behind the altar—could see them!

Mason Ebro, who was closest to Richard, let out a wild scream of rage and tried to swing his submachine gun around. It was the last movement of his life!

"Go to hell, stupid!" Richard snarled. He pulled the trigger of his own chopper, the muzzle not more than a foot from Ebro's face, the big blast blowing off the man's head—an explosion of blood, bones, flesh and brains that gave not only the Death Merchant a bath, but Steele, Silvestter, and McKillip as well!

The three men jumped both in terror and horror! Recovering quickly, they might have blown Camellion up in smoke, but just then de Gasquet dived across the top of the altar, crashing into Scott McKillip!

The Death Merchant swung his submachine gun to Steele and Silvestter and pulled the trigger. Nothing happened! The Aussie-made weapon was jammed.

Fudge—and Goddamn it! In less than a second Steele and Silvestter would cut him in three with slugs, even before he could draw his Magnums. Richard did the only thing possible: swinging his submachine gun, using it as a club, he charged C.W. Silvestter and Jerry Joseph Steele, his arching swing knocking the weapons from their hands.

"Satan will save us!" Silvestter screamed and, Karate and Kung Fu, expert that he was he raised his arms, his right hand held poised like a snake about to strike, his left hand and forearm horizontal to his chest—an open-hand block and reverse-punch stance!

Snarling curses, his gray eyes gleaming with insane hate, Steele prepared to meet the Merchant, his right hand drawn back for a *Shuto* hand chop, his left fist prepared for a pulverizing *Hiraken* blow. All of it was a half-trap! At the last moment Steele intended to step sideways and give Camellion a powerhouse hook kick in the belly. The only thing wrong was that although they knew the Death Merchant was very good, they had still underestimated him. Now they found out he was the best!

Steele let fly with the hook kick as Silvestter attempted a right *Nukite* to the Death Merchant's throat. Either the kick or the *Nukite* would have sent Richard to sleepy-bye land, had they landed. Neither did. Camellion now counterattacked.

As he grabbed Steele's foot and ankle with both hands

203

and twisted violently on the leg, Camellion arched himself to one side, dodging Silvestter's *Nukite*.

"*Die in the name of Satan!*" Silvestter screamed. He drew back for another try, his chestnut hair wild and mussed and his eyes gleaming insanely behind the two glass lenses of his gas mask.

Quicker than a Christian can condemn a prostitute to hell, Richard let Silvestter have a Kung Fu *Lung Tow* blow, a Dragon Head knuckle punch that connected solidly with Silvestter's chest, the explosive power knocking the madman backward, almost to where de Gasquet and Scott McKillip were battling for possession of a submachine gun.

Silvestter hardly felt the *Lung Tow* blow because complete lunacy not only reinforces hate, but makes one immune to pain. With a wild, inhuman scream, Silvestter again came at the Death Merchant, who was watching both the billionaire and Steele.

When Camellion had twisted Steele's leg and flipped the man to the floor, he had shaken up more than the big man's 240 pounds; he had also shattered the foundation of his confidence. Cowardice is a queer strain that can split a man two ways, leaving him half-worm and half-lion. There was just one thing that brought out the lion in Steele— Death! Death did to him what catnip does to a cat. Naturally not his own death, but the death of anybody or anything else. And here in the Hall of Conjuration Death was all around him! Roaring, hating Camellion with the kind of burning fury that the starving feel toward the well-fed, he charged, only a moment, only a few feet, behind Silvestter.

Only a fool refuses to acknowledge his limitations. Knowing he could not withstand another frontal assault by the two men—one of whom was so demented he could hardly feel pain—Camellion threw himself sideways to the top of the marble altar. He rolled to the other side, jumped down and stepped back, his hand going to the Marine knife at his belt.

Still drunk on the wine of illusion, on the myth of Satanism, C.W. Silvestter jumped on top of the altar and leaped after Camellion. And so did Steele.

The Death Merchant could easily have killed them both

with his Magnums. But why do it the easy way? It had now become a matter of pride: He had to kill Silvestter with his bare hands!

Richard let fly with the Marine trench knife, throwing it from his right palm, sharp blade upward. Straight as an arrow shot by Hiawatha's second cousin, the knife whizzed into Steele's throat, with such force that the point protruded from the back of his neck, the Guard snuggled up to his quivering Adam's apple. Instantly the blood flowed, spurting as thick as a pencil from around the Guard, two streams upward and out, two streams downward and out!

Jerry Joseph Steele was having the worst day of his life! His eyes rolled back in his head! He gurgled, his mouth opening and closing like a trap door. He moved his arms in a kind of flapping motion!

I think the dummy is going to try to fly off the altar! Camellion joked to himself as he prepared to meet Silvestter's charge.

Steele didn't fly. He only thought of what a fool he had been—dropped and died!

The Death Merchant sidestepped Silvestter's charge and, before the "Chosen One" could turn, Richard gave him a ferocious *Hiraken* knuckle blow to the back of the neck, then—as the madman spun—a fiendish *Shuto* side chop to the base of the neck. Although Silvestter was crazy and almost immune to pain, his bones were as normal as any man's. The *Hiraken* cracked his top vertebrae, and the savage shock of the *Shuto* chop numbed his brain to the point of unconsciousness. The Death Merchant now bored in. A devastating *Seiken* fist blow to Silvestter's solar plexus! A straight in *Nukite* bunched-finger stab to his throat.

The Chosen One wilted!

Time to send the Devil back to Hell! Camellion picked up Silvestter in a *Kataguruma* shoulder-wheel hold, held him high over his head for a moment, and then slammed him down on the altar, in such a way that the small of the madman's back hit one corner of the marble stone.

A sharp crack! A barely audible *"Satan help me!"* and Silvestter rolled from the altar to the bloody floor, falling next to a dead Jerry Steele.

Dying, but still conscious, Silvestter imagined himself to be on a vast plateau split in two by an abyss; on the farther side writhed his ambition to perform one last act before he died—*kill Richard Camellion!* Moments ago that desire had been his only ambition, but from magnificence it had shriveled into tumbleweed, lost in a terrible roaring that grew louder and louder. A great red eye stared at him! The eye grew larger and the roaring increased. Then absolute nothing, a total vacuum of nonexistence! Cleveland Winston Silvestter had been banished from the society of Life. Human events had spewed him beyond their orbit! Babies would cry, and nations would crash and go down to dust, and he would never know it . . . never hear the echo.

Cleveland Winston Silvestter, the "Chosen One," was dead.

Breathing rather heavily, the Death Merchant jerked out his Magnums and looked around through the clearing fog of smoke, the heavy silence a terrible weight on his mind.

To his right, Philippe de Gasquet walked slowly toward him, holding his arm. Scott McKillip had inflicted a deep slash before the Frenchman had taken the knife away from him and cut his throat.

Heck Geffling, J. Warren Kimber, and three weary commandos approached from the rear.

Bbbaaaaaaaaaaaaaaaaa!

Lucifer II had finally found the courage needed to flee the Hall of Death. Bleating loudly, the black billygoat ran through the blasted doorway of the operations room.

"I think we have won, monsieur," Philippe said in a pained voice. Drops of blood dripped from his fingers, splattering on the red marble floor. "All we have to do is pick up the radios, Wiseloggle, and the other man, and have Brisbane send in helicopters to take us away from this cursed place—is that not so?"

The Death Merchant nodded slowly. Yes, it was so . . .

The battle of New Eden was over.

The "devils" had been "exorcised"!

EPILOGUE

Station Iceberg in Rome was air-conditioned, although artificial cooling was unnecessary; the complex of rooms underneath Count Giolitti's wine cellar were too far down in the earth to be annoyed by the hot summer sun.

Richard Camellion didn't mind the almost-cold air of the station; neither did Nathaniel Wiseloggle. After suffering the purgatory that had been Queensland, both men wouldn't have minded a naked stroll at the North Pole! Laverne Meezoe, the other CIA agent in the Planning Room, welcomed the coolness as blessed relief from the scorching Italian sun.

Meezoe (who looked like Richard Nixon's twin brother) was the assistant agent in charge of Station Iceberg, the real boss being the chief of the CIA cell in Rome, a man who was—ostensibly—the Cultural Attaché at the US Embassy in the Italian capital.

"How do you feel, Wiseloggle?" Meezoe asked. Relaxed in a lounge chair, Meezoe looked at Nat, seated across from him on the other side of the room. His gaze then turned to Camellion, who was at the refrigerator, pouring a glass of cold apple juice.

"I can eat anything, even spicy Italian food," Wiseloggle answered, "and since it's been almost a week that I had the bout with food poisoning, I suppose I can say I'm back to normal and fully recovered."

He glanced briefly toward the door, and so did Meezoe, when the radio operator walked into the room and handed

Camellion a folded sheet of paper. Richard closed the door of the refrigerator, put down his glass of apple juice, and looked at the paper, on which were typed two words:

LASER WAR.

"I have to admit that back in the Australian bush, I was worried," Wiseloggle went on. "I thought I was going to die. The only thing that still bothers me is why I was the only one to get salmonella poisoning! We all ate the same food! Frankly, I'm puzzled."

"The answer is very simple, Nat," Camellion said, half in earnest, half mischievously. He wasn't at all surprised when Wiseloggle and Meezoe turned and searched him out with more than mildly startled glances.

"I know you were, Nat!" Richard said. He deliberately paused and took a sip of apple juice. "You see, I'm the one who poisoned you. I used a pinch of 'Destroying Angel,' a mushroom poison. I slipped it into your food the day before we flew to the Chalk ranch."

Meezoe sat stunned. The Death Merchant had spoken with assurance, and his words had aroused such wonder in Meezoe that the man didn't know what to say. He remained silent, his eyes darting from Camellion to Wiseloggle, then back to Camellion.

Was it the reflection of the overhead lights, or had Wiseloggle's face turned green? Strangely enough, he didn't seem to be emotionally staggered by Camellion's bombshell . . . only somewhat startled and cautious.

He regarded Camellion with expectation, his pipe poised in one hand. He suddenly grew impatient.

"Well, Camellion, we're waiting!" he finally said, treating it all as a joke. "What's the punch line?"

"There isn't any," Camellion said. "I poisoned you because you're the double-A we were looking for, the double agent who was working for Silvestter. I couldn't risk taking you to New Eden! You might have shot us all in the back! I didn't want to kill you—not then—so I did the next best thing. I put you out of action with my own brand of food poisoning."

Wiseloggle's eyes grew wider, and he drew back, his lips moving back over his teeth. Carefully he returned the pipe to his mouth and spoke around the stem.

"You don't know what you're talking about, Camellion," he said, his voice low and grave. "I don't think you're serious. But if you are, you're making a very big mistake, one I don't intend to stand still for. If I'm a double-A, where's your proof. Until I became ill—you say it was because you poisoned me!—I took the same chances you and the others took. I was also being shot at on the *Lonely Lady,* or have you forgotten that?"

"You were on the *Lonely Lady* because you didn't have a choice!" the Death Merchant said with a laugh. "None of us was supposed to be there—and we wouldn't have been if I had been smoked away in the marble orchard back in Brooklyn. But Steele sent boys to do a man's job. That is where you made your first mistake, Nat."

Camellion's easy manner abruptly changed, and his voice became serious, deadly and determined. "You were at the cemetary, Nat! It was you who fingered me and Brothers! You set us up for the hit!"

Wiseloggle jumped to his feet, his eyes blazing with the fierce flame of the trapped. He pointed the pipe at Camellion, poking at the air with the stem.

"You're a goddamn liar and as crazy as Silvestter was!" he shouted, losing all control. *"Where's your proof?"*

"If you weren't at the cemetery, how did you know about the funeral being conducted close to where the gun battle took place?"

Wiseloggle jumped again, as if slapped. "Who said I did?" he mocked.

"You did! That night at Station Yc/2B. You mentioned the funeral!"

"Then you must have said something about it to me and the others, or else I read about the funeral in the New York papers, in their accounts of the shooting!"

"I didn't tell you," Camellion said, a smile in his voice, "and not one New York paper mentioned the funeral. Yet you knew. You knew because you were there. And when the hit failed, you set me up to be wasted in Rome!"

209

Snickering nervously, Wiseloggle ran a hand through his blond hair and sat back down. He licked his lips, trying to think of something to say. He moved to the edge of his seat, then turned and stared angrily at the Death Merchant.

"You're out in deep space!" he said scornfully, and wiped sweat from his upper lip with the back of his hand. "How in hell could I have fingered you in Rome when I didn't even know what hotel you'd be staying at or the disguises you'd be using?"

The Death Merchant merely smiled and took another sip of apple juice.

Wiseloggle smirked, leaned back in his chair and pointed his pipe at Meezoe, whose suspicious eyes were scrutinizing his every motion and movement.

"Hell, why not accuse Meezoe or the dozen other agents here at Iceberg?" he snapped. "If you're going off the deep end, you might as well do a good job and make a complete fool of yourself. I myself didn't know what happened in the Colosseum until you told me—right here in Station Iceberg! Yet you accuse me of being responsible!"

"Welllll," Camellion drawled, hanging onto the word until it petered out like a dying sigh, "I didn't say you set me up for the hit after you came to Rome. You did it back in the States, the last time we met, when you came to my apartment at the Edison Hotel in Brooklyn. You had a couple of suitcases with you. One of those suitcases contained the device that picked up and printed my individual aura pattern. The New Dawn agents then used that 'printed' pattern to keep track of me in Rome. You didn't know what hotel I would use, but you did know I'd have to arrive at da Vinci Airport. All the New Dawn had to do was wait and listen in on the passengers coming through the terminal. When the vibratory pattern on the disk matched one of the passengers, they knew they had found their man —me! All they had to do was trail me in relays to keep track of me—right to the hotel. No matter what disguise I might use, there was no way I could disguise my aura. That's how they managed to trail me to the Colosseum! By picking up my aura with the gismo in the attaché case that Paval and I found on one of the jokers! But again Steele sent little boys to go the job of a giant. Pavel and I blew 'em away!"

Wiseloggle's scowl deepened as he abandoned hope of his own salvation. He felt he had teetered to the very edge of a vast pit and was about to fall off.

"You—you don't know what you're talking about, Camellion!" he said defensively. But his tone lacked conviction. He sounded more like a condemned man who was asking a priest how many more minutes it was to midnight! "Huh! I think you're cracking up! Your years of killing have finally unhinged your mind!"

"I think you're a treacherous, trapped son of a bitch!" Camellion said with startling sharpness. Watching Wiseloggle, he took another drink of apple juice, his lips thinning to a faint smile as he shot a look of pure scorn at the nervous man.

Color rushed up Wiseloggle's neck and rimmed the faint freckles on his cheeks. Bravely he forced a laugh, a laugh as short as the cluck of a hen. He wished his heart would quit its furious pounding.

"It was Pavel who figured it all out," Camellion said. "I don't have to tell you that the Russians are way ahead of us in research involving the paranormal, and you know how curious Pavel was about everything. While fooling around with the machine in the attaché case, he noticed it didn't emit any sound when the disk wasn't in place. He also noticed that even when the tiny disk was in place there were no beeps when I wasn't around. But the closer I got, the louder the beeps became! That got Pavel to thinking. After everyone else went to the airport to meet the British plane, he and I made some tests with the device, just to prove his theory."

"You're out of your mind!" Wiseloggle said weakly. He hunched down in his chair, put away his pipe, and glared sideways at Camellion. "Whoever heard of such a crazy device! A machine that can 'record' the 'human aura'! You don't actually think 'The Hub" will believe that bullshit, do you?"

Laverne Meezoe cleared his throat uneasily. "You have to admit, Camellion, that what you've said is pretty fantastic! After all, a machine that can—how would you say it? —'tune in the soul'? That's far far out!"

"The aura doesn't have anything to do with the silly concept of a 'soul,' " Richard said with a chuckle. He finished his apple juice, got up and placed the glass in the stainless-steel sink. He put both hands in the pockets of his slacks, but did not sit down.

"The aura is not the 'soul,' " he explained. "It is simply the magnetic field of the human body. 'Radiesthesia' is another name for it. All Silvestter's research boys did was find a modern scientific method to detect and record these waves. But that doesn't have anything to do with you, Nat. You're finished! Very shortly, you'll be joining Steele and Silvestter!"

Join Steele and Silvestter? Not if Wiseloggle could help it! Aware that his chances of escaping Station Iceberg were so slim as to be almost nonexistent, he also realized that if he allowed himself to be dragged back to the United States, his chances of survival would be even less—right down to zero, none at all! A CIA death squad would derail him for sure! Here, right now, he did have some chance, small as it was. Meezoe wasn't armed, and Camellion wasn't wearing his deadly Magnums.

He had better take that one chance!

Wiseloggle reached down as if to scratch his left leg, and then reached for the Beretta .380 in the ankle holster. He was pulling the pistol from the leather when the Death Merchant's first slug hit him in the side of the neck!

The thought in Nat's mind was more painful than the slug—*I should have known! I should have guessed! The clever bastard tricked me into making a move. I never actually had a chance!*

The Death Merchant's second slug caught him behind the ear, deafening him, lifting him, suddenly stabbing him with a pain so sharp it seemed to sever life from body. That's what the slug did! Every conquest Nat had ever known vanished like a spray of broken bubbles under the impact of death. Here was the endless road! Here was the leap beyond perfection. Here was oblivion.

Nat Wiseloggle fell sideways and crashed to the floor, his eyes open, his mouth shut, his brain dead.

The Death Merchant returned the .25-Bauer pistol to his right pocket and shrugged at Meezoe who had gotten to his feet and was staring at him. The radio operator and two other CIA agents had raced to the room, weapons in their hands.

"You knew, didn't you?" Meezoe said, somewhat awed. "You knew he'd convict himself by going for some iron—didn't you!"

"I gave him a chance," Richard said, looking down at the corpse of Wiseloggle. "He had to die! Here or in the States! What's the diff? I had intended to say nothing until we had returned to the US and then confront him with the evidence once we were at 'The Hub,' but the message I got changed my plans."

The two words flashed sinisterly in his mind: *Laser War!*

"I've got to go waste some sandcrabs!" he said.

The other four men looked puzzled.

"Sandcrabs?" echoed Meezoe.

"Arabs in North Africa," the Death Merchant said.

PINNACLE BOOKS

THE INCREDIBLE ACTION-PACKED SERIES

DEATH MERCHANT

by Joseph Rosenberger

His name is Richard Camellion; he's a master of disguise, deception and destruction. He does what the CIA and FBI cannot do. They call him THE DEATH MERCHANT!

Order		Title	BookNo.	Price
_____	#1	The Death Merchant	P021	95¢
_____	#2	Operation Overkill	P245	95¢
_____	#3	The Psychotron Plot	P117	95¢
_____	#4	Chinese Conspiracy	P168	95¢
_____	#5	Satan Strike	P182	95¢
_____	#6	Albanian Connection	P218	95¢
_____	#7	The Castro File	P264	95¢
			and more to come . . .	

TO ORDER

Please check the space next to the book/s you want, send this order form together with your check or money order, include the price of the book/s and 25¢ for handling and mailing, to:

PINNACLE BOOKS, INC. / P.O. Box 4347
Grand Central Station / New York, N. Y. 10017

☐ Check here if you want a free catalog.

I have enclosed $_____check_____or money order_____
as payment in full. No C.O.D.'s.

Name_____

Address_____

City_____State_____Zip_____
(Please allow time for delivery.)

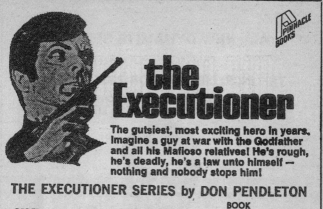

the Executioner

**The gutsiest, most exciting hero in years.
Imagine a guy at war with the Godfather
and all his Mafioso relatives! He's rough,
he's deadly, he's a law unto himself —
nothing and nobody stops him!**

THE EXECUTIONER SERIES by DON PENDLETON

ORDER		TITLE	BOOK NO.	PRICE
_____	# 1	WAR AGAINST THE MAFIA	P401	$1.25
_____	# 2	DEATH SQUAD	P402	$1.25
_____	# 3	BATTLE MASK	P403	$1.25
_____	# 4	MIAMI MASSACRE	P404	$1.25
_____	# 5	CONTINENTAL CONTRACT	P405	$1.25
_____	# 6	ASSAULT ON SOHO	P406	$1.25
_____	# 7	NIGHTMARE IN NEW YORK	P407	$1.25
_____	# 8	CHICAGO WIPEOUT	P408	$1.25
_____	# 9	VEGAS VENDETTA	P409	$1.25
_____	#10	CARIBBEAN KILL	P410	$1.25
_____	#11	CALIFORNIA HIT	P411	$1.25
_____	#12	BOSTON BLITZ	P412	$1.25
_____	#13	WASHINGTON I.O.U.	P413	$1.25
_____	#14	SAN DIEGO SIEGE	P414	$1.25
_____	#15	PANIC IN PHILLY	P415	$1.25
_____	#16	SICILIAN SLAUGHTER	P416	$1.25
_____	#17	JERSEY GUNS	P417	$1.25
_____	#18	TEXAS STORM	P418	$1.25

AND MORE TO COME . . .

TO ORDER
Please check the space next to the book/s you want, send this order
form together with your check or money order, include the price of
the book/s and 25¢ for handling and mailing, to:

**PINNACLE BOOKS, INC. / P.O. Box 4347
Grand Central Station / New York, N. Y. 10017**

☐ Check here if you want a free catalog.

I have enclosed $_____check_____or money order_____
as payment in full. No C.O.D.'s.

Name_____

Address_____

City_____State_____Zip_____
(Please allow time for delivery.)

PINNACLE
BOOKS

ALL NEW DYNAMITE SERIES

THE DESTROYER

by Richard Sapir & Warren Murphy

CURE, the world's most secret crime-fighting organization
created the perfect weapon — Remo Williams — man programmed to become a cold, calculating death machine.
The super man of the 70's!

Order		Title	Book No.	Price
_____	# 1	Created, The Destroyer	P361	$1.25
_____	# 2	Death Check	P362	$1.25
_____	# 3	Chinese Puzzle	P363	$1.25
_____	# 4	Mafia Fix	P364	$1.25
_____	# 5	Dr. Quake	P365	$1.25
_____	# 6	Death Therapy	P366	$1.25
_____	# 7	Union Bust	P367	$1.25
_____	# 8	Summit Chase	P368	$1.25
_____	# 9	Murder's Shield	P369	$1.25
_____	#10	Terror Squad	P370	$1.25
_____	#11	Kill or Cure	P371	$1.25
_____	#12	Slave Safari	P372	$1.25
_____	#13	Acid Rock	P373	$1.25
_____	#14	Judgment Day	P303	$1.25
_____	#15	Murder Ward	P331	$1.25

and more to come . . .

TO ORDER
Please check the space next to the book/s you want, send this order
form together with your check or money order, include the price of
the book/s and 25¢ for handling and mailing, to:
PINNACLE BOOKS, INC. / P.O. Box 4347
Grand Central Station / New York, N.Y. 10017
☐ Check here if you want a free catalog.

I have enclosed $_____check_____or money order_____
as payment in full. No C.O.D.'s.

Name_____

Address_____

City_____State_____Zip_____
(Please allow time for delivery.)

EXCITING NEW ADVENTURE SERIES!
crackling tension, slick and explosive

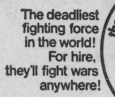

The deadliest
fighting force
in the world!
For hire,
they'll fight wars
anywhere!

the private army of colonel tobin

By Alan Caillou

Order		Title	Book No.	Price
_____	#1	Dead Sea Submarine	P015	95¢
_____	#2	Terror in Rio	P035	95¢
_____	#3	Congo War Cry	P071	95¢
_____	#4	Afghan Assault	P097	95¢
_____	#5	Swamp War	P164	95¢
_____	#6	Death Charge	P268	95¢

and more to come . . .

TO ORDER
Please check the space next to the book/s you want, send this order
form together with your check or money order, include the price
of the book/s and 25¢ for handling and mailing, to:

PINNACLE BOOKS, INC. / P.O. Box 4347
Grand Central Station / New York, N.Y. 10017

☐ CHECK HERE IF YOU WANT A FREE CATALOG.

I have enclosed $_____check_____or money order_____
as payment in full. No C.O.D.'s.

Name_____

Address_____

City_____State_____Zip_____

(Please allow time for delivery.)

THE PENETRATOR

by Lionel Derrick

Mark Hardin. Discharged from the army, after service in Vietnam. His military career was over. But *his* war was just beginning. His reason for living and reason for dying become the same—to stamp out crime and corruption wherever he finds it. He is deadly; he is unpredictable; and he is dedicated. He is The Penetrator!

Read all of him in:

_____	P236	THE TARGET IS H, No. 1	.95
_____	P237	BLOOD ON THE STRIP, No. 2	.95
_____	P318	CAPITOL HELL, No. 3	.95
_____	P338	HIJACKING MANHATTAN, No. 4	.95

TO ORDER
Please check the space next to the book/s you want, send this order form together with your check or money order, include the price of the book/s and 25¢ for handling and mailing, to:

PINNACLE BOOKS, INC. / P.O. Box 4347
Grand Central Station / New York, N. Y. 10017

☐ Check here if you want a free catalog.

I have enclosed $_____check_____or money order_____
as payment in full. No C.O.D.'s.

Name_____

Address_____

City_____State_____Zip_____
(Please allow time for delivery.)